THE ROUGH YEARS

By the same author

THE
ROUGH YEARS

by

CHAD WALSH

MOREHOUSE-BARLOW CO.
New York

268
W16 R

© 1960 by Morehouse-Barlow Co.

Library of Congress Catalog Card No. 60-12312

Seventh Printing, November, 1965

April '66

PRINTED IN THE UNITED STATES OF AMERICA

FOR THE JACKSONS

Bob
Jackie
Demi Lee
Megan
Jill

FOREWORD

THIS book has a double personality. It is, in the first place, a story about high school students and a few of the adults who weave in and out of their lives. As such, it can be read like any other novel. But I had an additional purpose in mind when I wrote *The Rough Years*. The plot and the various episodes are meant to present and dramatize the problems, challenges, dilemmas, and possibilities of the 'teens. I've tried to work it out so that each chapter can be used as a springboard for group discussion.

None of the characters in *The Rough Years* is intended as a model of the Christian life, nor is Trinity Episcopal Church presented as an ideal parish. The church in my mythical city of Blanton is inclined to be timorous and blundering. Much of the plot centers around its gradual and sometimes painful awakening to new life.

I got the idea of writing *The Rough Years* because, a few years ago, I published a novel called *Knock and Enter* which has been widely used in Church Schools and Confirmation classes. The present book is an attempt to provide food for thought and discussion at a higher age level. The same characters appear here as in *Knock and Enter,* but they are five years older. There are a few additional characters. I hasten to add that the plot of *The Rough Years* is entirely separate, and that no familiarity with the earlier book is needed.

A great many people—teenagers as well as adults—helped me write this book. Some gave me ideas for it; others read the manuscript and suggested changes. I am indebted first of all to my wife, Eva, and our children—Damaris McGuire, Madeline, Sarah-Lindsay, and Alison—all of whom avidly followed the progress of *The Rough Years*. In addition, to mention the persons whose names I can readily recall, I should like to thank Robert Anderson, Ted Benson, Patty Boyle, John H. Brennecke, Mary Day, Carol Dell, Edward T. Dell, Jr., Todd W. Ewald, Douglas Fenning, Patricia Ford, Carol Fuller, Edmund Fuller, Graham E. Fuller, Katy Grandstaff, Robert S. Jackson, Judith Kullberg, Dick Langford, Helen Milton, James Patterson, Jim Rayburn, Katherine Scott, Mandy Teare, and Veronica Waggoner.

One name I must single out in special appreciation. My former student, Jacqueline Jackson, who has become an outstanding author of juvenile novels, was of invaluable assistance to me. If this book has some reasonable coherence of plot, it is due in large part to Jackie's generous and discerning help.

Chad Walsh

CONTENTS

THE ROUGH YEARS

1

A THURSDAY IN BLANTON

THE DOOR opened with a cold gust of October air. Steve Hadley and Betty Bowman came inside. Jerry turned around from the grill. "Hello, Betty. Hello, Steve," he said.

"Hello, Jerry," Steve answered. "How's business?"

"Lousy," Jerry replied. "What'll it be?"

"Coke," Betty said.

"Double chocolate malted for me," Steve said. "Why don't you try one, Betty? Jerry can really make 'em."

"A girl has to watch her figure."

"I can watch it for you."

Betty laughed with appreciation. Jerry dutifully joined in the laughter.

"But seriously, Steve, I'd be fat as a pig if I ate everything I'd like to. You wouldn't want me to be like that."

They sat down at the farthest table. Jerry made a mental note of this. When couples wanted a chance to talk privately, they always chose that table. By unwritten law, no one would join them without a specific invitation.

Right now the Shack was empty except for the three of them. The usual noisy, chattering, and laughing after-school throng had come and gone. The next crowd would not appear until early evening when various students would stop by for a quick doughnut or beverage before going on to Blanton Senior High for rehearsals in drama, music, and public speaking.

"Here you are," Jerry said, setting the Coke and malted down in front of Betty and Steve.

"Thanks," Steve said.

Jerry paused the suggestion of a brief moment, but Steve said nothing more.

"I wonder how long Jerry's been running this place," Steve remarked, as Jerry headed back to the grill.

"It's been here as long as I can remember," Betty said, wrinkling her nose in thought. "Tom and I were about three when Daddy came to the church here, and I guess I was in the fifth or sixth grade when I had my first date at the Shack. It wasn't with you, Steve."

"Better late than never," Steve said. "So Jerry was dishing out the Cokes and malteds back then? That was before Dad moved to Blanton. I'll bet Jerry has really knocked around," Steve added with a sideways glance toward the grill. Jerry was frying two hamburgers for himself and pouring a cup of coffee.

It was true that Jerry had knocked around. About twenty or twenty-five years ago, when truant officers were still genial and understanding, Jerry had decided that the tenth grade was not for him and had left without a formal good-bye. He traveled for a time with a circus. Some said he was an acrobat, others that he was the barker outside the fat-lady side show. Then there was an interval with migratory fruit pickers out in California. A returned sailor spoke of meeting him in Singapore, years ago. An elaborate tattoo on his right arm showed a bathing beauty in a fashion associated with pictures of one's mother as a young woman.

"Really knocked around," Steve repeated, after the two of them had been sipping in silence.

"He certainly has," Betty agreed. They fell silent again.

Jerry sat down on one of his counter stools and took a good bite of hamburger. He caught a glimpse of Steve and Betty out of the corner of his eye. They were unusually quiet. Steve seemed to be nervously fidgeting. Nice-looking pair, Jerry thought. Betty was as blond as her father, tall, and reasonably slender. Steve was only a couple of inches taller than Betty, but thickset and very strong, looking like the football quarterback that he was. There was something about his crew cut, his round face, large gray eyes, and slow-spoken way that Jerry liked.

How long had they been going together? Jerry searched his memory. It was at least two years, he was pretty sure. Before that one of them used to appear occasionally with someone else, but no longer.

Well, whatever was troubling the couple in the farthest booth, they obviously wanted to keep it to themselves. That was all right with Jerry. He served as father confessor frequently, but only upon invitation.

"They've asked me again," Steve broke the silence.

"The Omega Alphas?" Betty countered.

"Who else?"

"What did you tell them?"

"Nothing."

"Why?"

"Wanted to think."

Another silence. "They gave you a bid last year, too, didn't they?" Betty asked, sipping her Coke.

"Yeah," Steve said. "About this time of year. When I first made the squad. They hadn't looked at me before."

"Something holding you back?" Betty asked at length.

"Guess so," Steve answered. "Wish I knew what it was." He stirred the remains of his malted with a long spoon. "I don't like to do things I have to hide. When I do something, I want to be able to say, 'Look here, see what I've done.' "

Betty smiled with a touch of mockery. "Is that another way of saying you're afraid you'll get into trouble if you join and the school finds out?"

Steve laughed contemptuously. "The school knows all about the Omegas, but they don't do anything. They can't. You can't kick out five per cent of all the boys in school, not when they come from the best families. Can you see the school expelling Bill Pendleton, the president? You can't expel the son of William Pendleton, Sr. I'll tell you what I think. It's a gentlemen's agreement. The school says 'nothing doing' to secret societies, so its conscience is lily white. Then it just looks the other way. Simple."

"Why do the Omegas matter so much either way?" Betty asked with a return of her little frown. "What's so wrong about them? Aren't they just about like a college fraternity? I've wondered sometimes if it wouldn't be better if the school changed its policy and let them come out in the open. Then their dances and things wouldn't have to be undercover, and there could be some supervision."

"I don't know. The line the school takes is that the Omegas are antidemocratic and all that bull. They want us to be one big, happy family—I guess that's the line."

"That's making it so complicated," Betty said. "If a group of people find they enjoy being together, what's wrong about their starting a club? I can't see that the future of democracy and western civilization hangs in the balance, one way or the other."

"Maybe you're right," Steve admitted. "Wish I knew."

Silence fell. Betty began to tap with the big toe of her right foot. Steve was twisting his fingers. "Look here," he finally blurted out. "You want a pin?"

"What an awful way of putting it!" Betty flared back. "You

talk as though I were a little girl with her tongue hanging out for a lollipop."

"Keep your shirt on and forget it," Steve said. Betty sucked up the remaining drops of Coke. "Another one? Or a doughnut?"

"I shouldn't have it, but just this time . . . a doughnut."

"Two doughnuts," Steve called.

Jerry put down his coffee cup and came over. "Two doughnuts," he said, and placed them on the table.

Betty smiled. "Thanks," she said.

She and Steve said nothing more. Jerry went back to his supper at the counter.

Steve was halfway through his doughnut before he spoke again. He sounded tired. "Didn't mean it the way you took it," he said. "I meant that we've been going steady for a couple of years now. I'd like to give you something, a pin or something you could wear, to show . . ."

"Wear it where it wouldn't show—"

"What does that matter? You and I'd know you were wearing it."

Betty impulsively reached over and laid her hand on Steve's. "You aren't thinking of joining the Omega Alphas just so you can give me a pin that nobody will ever see?"

"It isn't that."

"Forget about the pin," Betty interrupted. "Forget about it!" Her voice began to rise a little. Jerry glanced their way. Betty spoke more softly. "You can't always decide things by asking what I want. Decide for yourself. If you think you'd enjoy the Omegas, join them. But don't join them just to pick up a bit of gold-plated jewelry to please me."

"That isn't it!" Steve burst out.

"Then what is it?" Betty asked.

"It's—it's—why do we always have to talk and talk and get

everything all mixed up? Look here, all I was getting at—here we've been going together for two years now . . ."

"That's what you just said."

"I want to get it straight. Isn't it time I gave you something to show I mean it?"

"Will it mean any more if you do give me something?"

"Betty," Steve said slowly, "you are the strangest girl I ever . . ."

"Are you just getting to know me?" Betty smiled with an effort.

Steve savagely finished his doughnut. He looked up. "You were all set to have me join the Omegas."

"Join them. I won't stop you."

"But do you want me to?"

"Do what *you* want to."

"Lot of help you are." Steve looked down. Betty was fiddling with her doughnut.

"Here," she said as she shoved it across to him. "You finish it. I've got to watch the avoirdupois."

Steve ate the rest of the doughnut. "Better push along," he said.

They rose and walked to the counter where Steve counted out the nickels and dimes. "Night, Jerry," he said.

"Night," Jerry replied.

They went outside. As they walked along, they talked of football and the last church picnic and the possibility of a picnic for two if the weather held good. When a silence threatened to intervene, they even discussed Senior English and their course in American Problems.

They were almost out of anything to talk about when they reached the old rectory and saw it massively outlined against the deepening dusk. "Well, see you tomorrow," Steve said. He paused clumsily, then turned and walked rapidly toward his house next door.

Betty started to open the front door. Suddenly a sob escaped her. He hadn't even kissed her good night. She fumbled for a handkerchief and dabbed at her eyes as she tiptoed into the hall.

There was no one in sight, but the place was not deserted. From somewhere in the back part of the house came the repeated tones of a clarinet. On Thursday afternoons, Sue, who was in the last year of junior high, had orchestra practice, and always when she came home, she was steamed up and ready to go on with the clarinet.

Thursday afternoon . . . Betty glanced at her watch. There were only two minutes to spare. *"Cross Your Heart,"* Betty said to herself, repeating the name of the TV program about to begin.

Her sobs ceased. She strode into the living room and on through the dining room to the den where the TV set was exiled. Sue, slight, straight as a ramrod, and still wearing two pigtails which reached almost to her waist, was standing in front of her music stand. She was practicing tone quality on the clarinet, repeating the same E flat endlessly.

"Hi, nuisance," Betty said, and she sat down in front of the TV. She twirled the knobs. The image was born, grew brighter and clearer. Betty moved her chair a little farther back. Her ears skillfully separated the repeated tones of Sue's clarinet from the words of the young man on the screen who gazed straight at her with lustrously dark eyes and said, in a slow southern voice, "Cross your heart you'll tell the truth." With a flourish of trumpet music, he faded to smaller size, and a young couple, looking as though they were standing at the bar of judgment, loomed on the screen. "Let me present Mr. and Mrs. Robert Densmore, Bob and Karen. Married five months, is that right? Glad to have you here, Bob and Karen. Cross your heart, Karen, was it love at first sight?"

"No," said Karen in a cool voice. "He took some getting used to."

"How about you, Bob? Cross your heart."

"She looked all right in that sweater," Bob said. "But what a line she was handing me."

Betty listened eagerly. This promised to have its drama. Suddenly an arm reached over her shoulder, and fingers twirled the knob. The image faded into a little star and then blackness.

"Hey!" Betty commanded. "Let go of that." She reached to turn the knob, but Sue's hand stopped her. "What's the idea—who do you think you are, half pint?"

"Got to practice," Sue said.

"You can practice after supper."

"I've got to practice *now*."

A shrewd suspicion flashed across Betty's mind. "Did little Reggie challenge you?"

"Yes," snapped Sue.

Betty knew Reggie—Reginald Debord—by reputation. In the ninth grade with Sue, small for his age and wearing goggle-like glasses, he was none the less a very gifted clarinetist, perhaps a shade more so than Sue, though it was nip-and-tuck between them. The Blanton Junior High orchestra had a system whereby the first musician in any section could be challenged at the beginning of every Thursday rehearsal. Sue had held the chair of honor for two weeks, her longest stretch.

"Did Reggie challenge you and win today?" Betty asked.

Sue did not answer. She returned to the music stand. The clarinet once more dominated the airwaves. Betty quickly reached for the TV and adjusted the volume to maximum capacity. The interviewer roared from the screen like a voice over the P.A. system at a railroad station: "Cross your heart, Bob. When you bring home an unexpected guest to dinner, what does Karen say?"

Sue took the clarinet from her mouth. "Turn that thing off!" she shouted.

"Go upstairs and practice."

"I can't! The light's no good. The acoustics are *awful*."

"Then wait till the program's over."

"I can't!" Sue reached once more for the knob, but Betty's hand was firmly over it. Slowly, very deliberately, Sue laid the clarinet down on a chair, returned, bent over, and bit Betty's knuckles.

"Ouch!" Betty screamed and jumped up. Sue moved in swiftly to turn off the TV. That done, she picked up her clarinet and did a series of trills in the fourth octave. Betty leaped toward her and grabbed the bell-like end of the instrument.

At this moment a voice spoke from the hall door. "Stop it," Dr. Bowman commanded. "If you aren't breakable, that bit of ebony is—$180 worth." He walked over and deftly took possession of the clarinet. "Now sit down, both of you," he ordered.

"She knew it was my favorite program," Betty said.

"She knew I had to practice!" Sue flared back.

"Sit down." They sat. "There's been enough noise in here. You were acting like a pair of three-year-olds. We'll give the TV and the clarinet both a rest."

"That isn't fair!" Betty protested, leaping up. "Sue can practice later, but I can't see *Cross Your Heart* later."

"It won't warp your life if you don't see it," her father said quietly.

"You always take her side!" Betty screamed. "I think this whole family stinks!"

"Upstairs with you," Dr. Bowman said.

"I'm going upstairs. I don't want to be down here," Betty said, heading toward the hall.

"Stay up till you're called," her father added.

The clumping of Betty's feet grew fainter as she swiftly

mounted to the second floor. Sue picked up her clarinet. Her father put out his hand. "After supper," he said.

Upstairs, Betty lay face down on her bed and sobbed. "Acting like a ten-year-old again," she moaned. "Betty, won't you *ever* grow up? No wonder Steve doesn't know what to make of a crazy, mixed-up kid like you!"

The door slowly opened, and eight-year-old Nancy stood there uncertainly. She was as blond as Betty, but not very pretty at this stage of life. A tooth on one side was missing, and her thick-rimmed glasses were not alluring. Nancy had come from her room next door when she heard Betty storming up the stairs.

"Nancy!" Betty implored and held out her arms.

With a leap, Nancy was on the bed with her. Betty hugged her, and Nancy dreamily stroked Betty's hair. By the time their father came to summon them for dinner, Betty was able to speak without the hint of a sob or screech in her voice.

2

A FRIDAY IN BLANTON

FRANK BUELL was upstairs in his room, writing in a diary which had a lock and key. Like Steve, Betty, and her twin brother, Tom, he was in the twelfth grade. They lived far apart, however. Frank's home was in Oak Hill, the suburb to the west of the city. It had been started about twenty years earlier when the advancing factories and slums moved into the old and fashionable North Side. It was then that those who could afford to flee fled. Oak Hill had sprung up, as though at the touch of a magician's wand. Already it looked mellow and traditional, thanks in large part to the landscape architects who had planted half-grown trees on any lawns which did not already have native oaks, elms, or maples.

Frank glanced at his watch. Seven o'clock. He continued writing. Five minutes later he heard steps outside his door, and a quietly taut voice spoke, "Frank, time for dinner." Frank slowly put down his fountain pen, locked the diary, and stepped into the hall.

His mother—his stepmother, rather—looked at him in a troubled way. "Frank," she asked, "why can't you ever be on time?"

"Sorry, Sally," he replied and followed a few paces behind her.

He sensed the slight twinge of irritation in her. The question of names had always been a tense one, ever since John Hampden Buell, Frank's father, had remarried. Frank's parents had been divorced when he was eight. For about three years after that, Frank frequently saw his mother. Her second husband was friendly and pleasant. When she divorced him and chose for her third husband an engineer named Roger Lindquist, the visits ceased. Mr. and Mrs. Lindquist were first in Peru, then in Pakistan, then in Finland—countries not to be too quickly visited. Letters from his mother did not cease altogether, but they became less frequent. Finally, a few months before this Friday evening of Frank's life, Mr. and Mrs. Lindquist had moved to Los Angeles. There had been one letter, but so far no suggestion that Frank fly out for a visit.

As for Frank's father, John Buell, he had remarried about two years after his divorce. Frank was ten at the time. From the first, there had been the problem of names. "Here's your new mother," Mr. Buell had said hopefully, and Frank had run from the room and hidden himself. Sarah Buell had come to his room late that night and tried to take him in her arms. He had pushed her away and hated himself for doing it. She had talked a long time of how she wanted to be a mother to him and of the good times they would all have together.

"But you *aren't* my mother!" ten-year-old Frank had said, pounding his fists against the pillow as though he were much younger.

His stepmother had looked at him gravely, then laughed. "All right," she had said. "I'm *not* your mother. Then I'll just be Sarah."

She was almost ten years younger than his own mother and might indeed have passed for an older sister. Some devil in his heart drove Frank to say Sally more often than Sarah, and sometimes he shortened it to Sal. His stepmother was more patient about this than his father. There had been long, heart-to-heart talks and short, sharp talks. Frank's answer to any kind of talk was silence and a quick retreat to his room and his diary.

"A handsome boy," Sarah Buell was thinking to herself. If only she could break through, but it had been seven years now. An icy correctness and courtesy was the best she could expect. He was a handsome boy of medium height, slender and straight, with curly blond hair and blue eyes that should have been open and gay, not withdrawn and tormented. "A father's son," thought Sarah, except that Mr. Buell, hostile to exercise but increasingly friendly to social drink, had lost the erect carriage and trim figure he had when they first met.

Sarah caught herself walking more slowly as they came to the dining room. She had come to dread dinner time. It was the silences, or the occasional words which were worse than silence. Where was the John Buell she had married? His idealistic dreams of a new start, his gaiety, his sudden tenderness? Gone, all gone, replaced by a sluggish and dull obstinacy. Day by day nothing would change in him. He would become only more completely what he already was.

When she had married John, she had believed what he told her: that he and his first wife had not truly loved each other; that he now knew love for the first time; that love was all, and love was enough. She looked across at him and saw him, middle-aged, with sagging and florid cheeks, hurt and sullen eyes. "Love is not enough," she said sadly to herself.

The three of them ate dinner. It was not as bad as it was sometimes. No one said much. When they finished, Frank asked, "Can I take the knockabout?"

His father's face flushed. "Don't they ever give you any homework?"

"Did it all in school. I had two free periods today. Besides, tomorrow's Saturday."

"All right, all right," Mr. Buell said resignedly. "Be in by twelve."

Mrs. Buell turned to Frank as he walked by and spoke in a low voice. "Take it easy, Frank. Remember last time."

Frank said nothing. Patting his pocket to make sure his wallet was there, he put on a light topcoat, walked out of the house, and stood on the large lawn. In the deepening night he could see the scattered lights of Oak Hill houses. He lived in one of the most strictly zoned areas—no building lot permitted of less than two acres. A good deal of woodland wildness had been preserved all around. Behind the Buell house was a small brook which cut across one corner of the lot in a tangle of willows and alders. It was the geometrical lines of lights from the houses of Oak Hill, however, that caught and held Frank's attention. Like the lights of a prison, Frank thought. He hurried to the small, foreign-make car, started it smoothly, and drove toward the city.

Darkness deepened as he drove along. The lights of the houses came closer together. It did not take long to leave the two-acre section of Oak Hill. Oak Hill itself was only a small appendage to Blanton, a bright and beautiful but diseased parasite, drawing its life from the teeming city, or so it seemed to Frank.

He was soon downtown. Here and there he glanced at the announcements in big capital letters above the entrances to movie theaters. Nothing interested him. Several times he almost stopped at a tavern, but he continued driving.

Without quite planning it, he soon found himself in the middle of the North Side. The shop signs began to change. There were more names that ended in syllables like -ski and -ino and -ez. The look of the people altered, too. It was as though he had moved a thousand or two thousand miles south to a sun-drenched land where faces were darker and eyes more piercing. He noticed especially the Puerto Ricans, ranging from pure Spanish types to some as dark as American Negroes. A handful of them had moved from New York a few years ago. Now there was a colony.

That door to the right. Where had he seen it before? It led into what had once been a mansion, but was now obviously a rabbit warren of small, crowded flats. He had been there once. Slowing down, he remembered. It had been last spring when he was in debate. He had driven some of the other debaters home. One of them—what was her name?—lived here and asked to be let off. Rosa, that was it, Rosa something-or-other. She was about a year younger than himself, a grade behind him. "Thank you," she had said, carefully pronouncing the difficult *th;* and then she had said with a sudden smile, "*Gracias.*" Afterwards he had wished he had thought in time to say, "*De nada,*" but his classroom Spanish had never been put to a quick test before.

Rosa. He hadn't consciously thought about her since that night, but here he was at her place. What was her last name? He laughed. Suppose he went from flat to flat, asking for Rosa. It was a common name. There might be half a dozen Rosas in the building. He had more than three hours left.

Frank opened the shabby outer door and went inside. On the first floor there were two doors to the right and two to the left. With a laugh, he knocked at the first one to the right. A gray-haired man opened it and looked at him gravely. "Excuse me, is Rosa here?" he asked.

The man had a troubled expression. "I—am—sorry," he said slowly. "My—English—"

This time Frank remembered his Spanish. "*Está Rosa aquí?*" he asked.

The man's face brightened. "*No hay ninguna Rosa aquí,*" he answered. A little boy of five or six, the man's grandson, Frank surmised, spoke up eagerly. "Rosa? You mean Rosa

Arrondo, mister? Upstairs, on the third floor. The door with the knob broken—you'll see it, mister, right upstairs."

"Thanks," said Frank to the boy, with a *gracias* and slight bow to the grave grandfather.

Third floor up, the door with the broken knob.

Frank walked up to the second floor. The banister rail was broken in one place. A clutter of cardboard cartons lay at one end of the corridor. A broom leaned crazily in an empty bucket. From one door came the smell of cooking, rich with some kind of savory flavoring.

Up to the third floor. It was neater here. The boards were swept and scrubbed. There were three doors to the right, three to the left. He looked to the right—that was it. The knob on the farthest door had cracked in two, and only half of it was left.

Somehow gay and content with the world, Frank knocked. Rosa herself opened the door and smiled at him with vague recognition. She was short for her age, and slender, but already more definitely a woman than most of the girls Frank knew. Her hair was almost jet black, and the natural wave had been only slightly assisted. Her complexion was a deep olive. Her black eyes looked at him without surprise.

"Hello, Frank," she said. "Come in."

"Thanks," said Frank as he entered the flat. His eye traveled around the room. Wallpaper was carefully pasted back where it had come off, but it was missing entirely from large sections of the faded plaster. Furniture of the kind that was fashionable twenty years ago, before it became available in cheap stores on time payments, filled the room. The sofa against one wall obviously opened into a day bed. Did Rosa sleep there? There was a faint smell of scrubbing powder and a shabby, desperate cleanness to it all.

Rosa's father rose and came forward. On the sofa was a roly-poly little woman, Rosa's mother, smiling uncertainly.

Rosa turned to her parents and said something in rapid Spanish. All Frank could catch was his own name, strangely alien in sound when embedded in a Spanish sentence. Mr. Arrondo extended his hand and slowly said, "How do you do, Mr. Buell?"

"*Tanto gusto en conocerle,*" Frank said. The man's eyes lit up with astonishment and pleasure, and he turned quickly to his wife, "*El joven caballero habla español.*"

Frank walked over to Mrs. Arrondo and bowed. "*Tanto gusto en conocerle,*" he said, hoping it would work as well as it had the first time. Mrs. Arrondo replied in a brief torrent of syllables too fast for his ears.

"I'm afraid I've used about all the Spanish I know," he apologized.

"Mother stays home most of the time, so she doesn't understand English well," Rosa said, "but Daddy works at the shop and speaks it all day long—don't you, Daddy?"

"O.K., yes," he answered.

"I wish I really knew Spanish," said Frank. "It's a beautiful language. But you know how it is in school—the class is too big for any real practice in speaking it."

"Yes, a beautiful language," Mr. Arrondo agreed. "But here in the United States, you want to get along, see? You learn English. Spanish no good. Please, sit down."

"Thank you," said Frank, uncertain where he should sit.

"Frank's a senior," Rosa said. "We were on the debating team together last spring, and he drove me home one night."

Mr. Arrondo said something in Spanish to his wife, and she beamed as she replied to him. "Mama says 'Thank you,'" Rosa interpreted.

"It was a pleasure," Frank said, and he smiled to himself. At that time, last spring, it had been neither a pleasure nor a pain, but pure routine, dictated by school custom. Whoever had a car automatically offered a ride to anyone who didn't.

"Want to watch TV?" Rosa asked him. Her parents had it on and were gazing intently at it.

"Not unless you do. Let's sit over there and talk."

"Let's." They walked to a small table at the other end of the room and sat down by it. "What shall we talk about?"

Frank laughed. Except in debate club they had never said more than hello to each other.

"What is there for anybody to talk about?" he asked in sudden bitterness.

The tone of his voice seemed to have no effect on Rosa. "What is there for anybody to talk about?" she repeated. "Everything, I guess . . . if they want to."

I'd better watch myself, Frank thought. This girl isn't an analyst; this chair isn't a psychiatrist's couch. "Tell me about yourself," he said finally.

"There isn't much to tell—that would be interesting, I mean. We came from Puerto Rico when I was five years old—I still remember the big plane—and moved from New York when I was eleven or twelve."

"Do you like school?" Frank asked.

Rosa's face puckered in thought. "I never thought of it that way. You just go, don't you?"

You just go, don't you? Frank repeated to himself. There were many things like that, things you couldn't do anything about: divorces and remarriages and the words that sometimes burst forth from your mouth, though a minute later you would bite your tongue off if you could call them back, but you never could. A word spoken sets up sound waves that spread out and out like ripples on a pond. The words he spoke seven years ago to Sarah were now somewhere in interstellar space, faint and immortal, all their bitterness and cruelty traveling toward the most distant galaxies, beyond all calling back and cancellation.

Frank did not realize how long his silence had lasted. Rosa jumped up lightly. "I'll make some popcorn," she said.

"Let me help," he volunteered.

They set a hot plate up on the table and were soon taking turns shaking the frying pan. The grains of corn heated rapidly and exploded like little sputniks.

"Butter and salt," Rosa said. Frank transferred the popcorn to a bowl. Rosa swiftly melted some butter in a pan, then poured it over the popcorn while Frank stirred and sprinkled salt. "Here are some little bowls," Rosa said. They filled four of them.

Frank took one in each hand and walked over to Rosa's parents. He placed the bowls on the table by the TV, and Mrs. Arrondo said a careful "Thank you."

Returning to their own table, Frank sat down beside Rosa. For a time they munched their popcorn. What could he talk about? Remember, he told himself, this girl isn't mother, priest, or analyst. Don't spill over.

"You planning on going to college?" he finally asked.

"I don't know," Rosa said. "There are lots of things to take into account, aren't there?"

Mr. Arrondo had now risen and was coming toward them with two small glasses. "*Vino?*" he asked.

"*Gracias,*" said Frank as he took the proffered glass. Rosa took the other. As her father returned to the TV, Rosa smiled suddenly and spoke in a low voice. "To tell the truth, I like milk shakes better, but Daddy's so proud of this wine. He makes it himself every fall."

"Here's to Blanton High," said Frank, and he lifted his glass, "and to all parents, monogamous or polygamous, and to all stepparents and any other specimens of humanity I forgot to name. And to you, Rosa, and your popcorn."

He took a substantial sip and Rosa a small one. "You ought to be back in debate this year," Rosa said. "You can make the words roll out."

"They roll out whether I want them to or not. That doesn't mean they make sense. But nothing much else does, so what does it matter?"

Rosa looked at him intently as he lapsed into silence. There at the little table, in their quietude, she suddenly felt as though she were the older one. "You're very bitter, aren't you?" she asked gently.

"Yes, I guess I am. Aren't you?"

"Why should I be?"

"Look around you."

Rosa flushed. Very becoming, Frank thought, was the quick reddening of the dark olive cheeks. "Mother and Daddy—" she began.

In genuine horror, Frank exclaimed, "I didn't mean *them!* Count your blessings. You've got the pair you started out with."

"Then what do you mean?" Rosa asked angrily.

"This room, this place, this house, this neighborhood."

"It's not Oak Hill," Rosa admitted with a strained smile.

"There isn't any fairness to it!" Frank was getting excited. "Why should I live in Oak Hill, and you . . . here? What have you got to look forward to?" he asked savagely. "Marriage soon after high school, babies, a place like this to live in, the same smells when you climb the stairs . . ."

"And all that's so terrible?"

"All that is what Oak Hill permits you. That is what my father in the kindness of his heart permits you. That is what I shall permit you when I take my father's place."

"You must have a lot to look forward to," Rosa said quietly.

Mr. Arrondo came over and refilled Frank's glass. "*Bueno?*" he asked with a big smile.

"*Muy bueno*," Frank replied, and he took a hearty sip.

"More popcorn?" Rosa asked. "Let's make some more."

"Let's go to a movie," Frank suggested. "Let the screen do the talking. It always says the right things." He emptied his glass and put it down on the table.

Rosa hesitated. "It's late," she murmured.

Frank glanced at his watch. "Second show will start in ten minutes. Ask your folks. Tell them I'll get you in by midnight. The magic carriage turns back into a pumpkin then, and the mice start squealing for their accustomed holes."

Rosa moved over to her parents and spoke in a low voice. There was a rapid exchange of murmured Spanish. Rosa came back smiling. "It's all right," she said.

Frank walked back to her father and mother. "*Muchas gracias*," he said, "*y gracias por el buen vino*. I'll have her back by a quarter of twelve, I promise."

Mr. Arrondo rose and gravely shook hands.

Frank and Rosa walked downstairs, past the floor with the empty cartons and the pail, and stepped outside. It was deep night now, broken only by neon signs and the headlights of roving cars. "Here it is," Frank said. He held the car door open.

"Where's the movie?" Rosa asked as she sat down.

Frank walked around and took his place at the wheel. "Let's explore and see."

They were soon out of the North Side. As they drove along, Frank vaguely noticed the Episcopal church to his right. He was baptized an Episcopalian, he thought fleetingly, but when his mother left, somehow churchgoing had left with her.

Beyond the residential area in which Trinity Episcopal Church stood, one came to the main business district. Frank slowed down a little. "You read me the names," he told Rosa.

"*The Broken Reed,*" Rosa began. "Here's another one—*The Bride of Death.*"

"Let's keep going. How about that theater over there?"

"I can't see it yet. Oh yes, *Singing in the Snow.* I think it's a musical."

"It is," Frank assured her. "I read the review in *Time.* One of those hearty athletic spectacles with tenors warbling to sopranos on skis and the wholesome outdoor life. Let's stop and see it."

"Let's do," Rosa agreed.

They entered as the newsreel was ending with a scene of rioting somewhere. There was a large building in the background with smoke pouring from it. The crowd in front carried banners written in some unfamiliar alphabet. The events of the day were quickly followed by an animated cartoon about a lovelorn mouse whose courtship was always being interrupted by his obsessive fondness for cheese, but all ended well. There was a tender fade-out of the two mice, their tails entwined, disposing of a round cheese as big as an angel food cake.

Singing in the Snow was just about as Frank had predicted. After an hour and five minutes of it, he whispered, "Let's get going."

Rosa studied his face sharply for a moment in the dim light, but merely said, "O.K."

They walked into a night where fewer headlights competed now with neon signs. Nearby was one of the smaller neon signs, OAKLEAF TAVERN.

"Oakleaf Tavern," Frank read aloud. "Sacred no doubt to the memory of Oak Hill from whence all blessings flow. How about a quick one?"

They went inside and sat down at a corner table. A waiter came over and looked piercingly at Frank, but he asked no questions about age. "What'll you have?" he demanded.

"Make mine a Coke," Rosa said.

"Coke for the lady," Frank said. "Bourbon on the rocks for me."

"O.K., coming up." The waiter departed with a scarcely perceptible backward look.

"Aren't you afraid they'll catch up on your age?" Rosa whispered.

"No," said Frank. "My father is John Hampden Buell."

"But—"

"No buts. I told you the truth, Rosa. There are two kinds of people—those from the North Side and those from Oak Hill. Jails aren't made for my kind. I can order a drink, and if anybody finds out—well, my father is John Hampden Buell."

Rosa flushed with dawning anger.

The waiter returned. "There you are," he said darkly, and he quickly withdrew.

"Cheerio!" Frank said as he took a good swallow of his drink. Rosa sipped her Coca-Cola through a straw.

"You talk as though people in Oak Hill and those on the North Side are as different as cats and dogs," she burst out.

"They are," Frank agreed, and he took another sip.

"Then why are you out slumming with me?"

"Slumming?" Frank put his drink down and looked at her incredulously. "Slumming?"

"Yes, I do live in a house where the stairs are broken and the hallways smell. My father speaks poor English and my mother almost none. My ancestors didn't come over on the *Mayflower;* they didn't even make it by the time of the Irish Potato Famine. I'm not a certified, native, white, Protestant, one hundred percent American. What do you want with me?"

Frank smiled at her and slowly, gently remarked, "So you're bitter, too."

"Are you surprised? I try not to be. But—"

"I'm glad," Frank added. "You seemed too serene to be real. Now I know you're human. You're bitter, and I'm bitter. What stronger bond can we ask?"

Neither of them spoke for a while. The angry flush had died out of Rosa's cheeks. Her earlier feeling of pity returned. After a time she asked with a slight arching of her eyebrows, "Why did you really come to the North Side tonight?"

Frank thought a while. "I don't know. It was just one of those things that happen."

"And I was one of those things?"

"Yes. A cosmic accident. A cosmic accident with a long history. Once upon a time two chemicals rubbed shoulders together and a one-celled form of life came into being. That's our distant ancestor. Then schools sprang up, and you and I both happened to take debate, and I happened to have a car, and I happened to drive you home one night, and six months later I happened to be driving, and I happened to notice your house. From our great-grandfather the amoeba to you and me in this bar, that's the long and the short of it."

"I'm not sorry for the accident," Rosa said.

"Thanks. It's all right with me, too." Frank looked her full in the face. "You still haven't told me what you're going to do when you finish school."

"That's a year and a half away. Maybe business school. I'm taking shorthand and typing now."

"Business school—and learn to say 'Yes, sir,' 'yes, sir,' to somebody from Oak Hill, somebody who owns you because he pays you, somebody who can pay you because he happened to be born on Oak Hill . . ."

"Do you have a guilt complex?" Rosa asked. "You talk as though your family's money were some kind of nasty disease."

"It is. And it's contagious. I'm doomed to be rich."

"Not doomed. You can give it all away, put on a robe and a pair of sandals, and beg your bread from door to door."

"A saintly panhandler? Theoretically, yes, I could do it when I get my hands on Dad's share of the corporation. I could do it, assuming that my loving relatives didn't succeed in having me committed to some institution for my own good. Hey, waiter—" he suddenly called across the room. "Another round."

The waiter returned with a Coca-cola and a bourbon on the rocks. "Anything to eat?" Frank asked. "Pizza?"

"That would be nice," Rosa said.

"Two pizzas."

"O.K." The waiter turned away with a vague aura of disapproval.

"My dear girl," Frank began.

"Rosa is my name."

"Rosa . . . Spanish for rose. A rose is well protected from the dangers of life. I hope you have sharp thorns . . . Rosa, my mind reverts to the theoretical possibility you stated—the life of voluntary poverty and renunciation, a consummation in the blessedness of heaven, a name in the calendar of the saints, a movie in full color and wide screen. Very alluring. I have my ascetic moods. But I can't do it."

"Why not?"

"Here you are," the waiter said gruffly, putting the pizzas on the table. He quickly withdrew.

"I remember now what I wanted to say," Frank exclaimed, picking up his glass. "*Skål!*"

"*Skål!*" said Rosa, and each drank.

"Back to my sainthood," Frank said, "I'll tell you why it isn't possible. Pavlov. Conditioned reflexes. I'm a hound dog. My salivary glands have been trained to slobber at the appropriate stimuli. Oak Hill. Great laboratory. Training ground for the glands. Money, good clothes, tasteful interior decorations, the

right make of foreign cars, liquor from the right cellars. I'll live
and die for them. Conditioned reflexes."

"Aren't you just talking about habits?" Rosa asked, watching
him as he neared the end of his glass.

"Another round?" Frank asked.

"Don't you think—" she began.

Frank signaled the waiter. "Another round."

The waiter approached, his air of disapproval deeper and
more somber. "This is what you wanted," he said in a low voice
of doom as he brought the new round.

"Cheers," Frank said. He took a deep swallow and coughed.
Putting his napkin to his mouth, he continued, "What is a man
but a dollar's worth of chemicals and a complex set of habits?
Habits make the man. Free will—a theoretical possibility. But
how often does it work? Talk to anybody who's smoked for
fifteen years. He's free to decide to give it up. But how
many do?"

The waiter walked in their direction and muttered as he went
past. "Closing in ten minutes."

"See?" Frank asked. "Pavlov. Conditioned to close at a certain hour. What time is it?"

"Ten of twelve," Rosa said, looking at her watch.

"Time to go. 'Promises to keep and miles to go before I
sleep'!" He drained the rest of his glass and left some money on
the table. "The carriage will be a pumpkin and the mice will go
whinnying—mice don't whinny—they'll go scurrying, that's it,
they'll scurry back to their lairs, their holes. I'll get you home in
time. I promised."

"I—I can walk back," Rosa said uneasily.

"Can't let you. Conditioned reflexes. Pavlov. I'm a gentleman,
you know, and fatally doomed to be a Princeton under-
graduate."

They were outside now and could see the suspicious waiter

turning chairs on end. "Conditioned reflexes," Frank murmured. "Let's step."

Rosa slid uneasily into the car. Frank bowed as she entered, lost his balance, and caught the door clumsily. Straightening himself, he slammed the door and raced around to the other side. "Six of twelve. We'll get you in on time."

"We don't need to hurry," Rosa said. "If I'm a few minutes late . . ."

"Promises to keep," Frank said. "Here goes!"

In Blanton the traffic lights cease to function after 11:30 except for some blinking yellows. Frank counted on this to speed his way to the North Side and Rosa's home. For several blocks they said nothing, though Rosa kept glancing sidelong at the speedometer as it rose from 30 to 40 to 60. They were at the edge of the main business district when it happened.

From the right a stripped-down jalopy, hardly more than a skeleton of a car, was coming with a speed of at least 70 miles an hour as Frank approached the intersection. Mechanically, seeing the car bearing straight down upon him, Frank stepped on the gas. Rosa glanced at the needle of the speedometer—75 now and rising fast.

It was never absolutely certain what happened next. Possibly the front bumper of the car from the right grazed against the rear of Frank's car. In any event, the driver never showed up to say. It might simply have been a case of Frank's car getting out of control in the effort to avoid the collision. He and Rosa felt the car hitting something; both of them vaguely knew it was rolling over and over. Then there was the darkness and silence.

When Frank regained consciousness, he dimly remembered that there had been a girl, a girl he had taken somewhere. What was her name? He had been driving her somewhere, maybe home, so why was he lying here on the grass? His face felt strange. He touched it with his hand. It was moist. He held his hand up. In the faint light from the street lamp, it looked red. Memory returned. He tried to rise but fell back weakly to the ground. "Rosa!" he called. There was no answer.

"Rosa!" he called again. Again there was no answer. With an effort that took all his strength, he slowly rose first to his knees, then to his feet. He looked around. There was the car, at the edge of a lawn. He made his way to it, each step being a separate task. The car was on its left side. The right side was badly crumpled. The telephone pole. He knew they had hit something. "Rosa!" he called. He peered through the door on the right side. Faintly he could see her in a twisted position on the far side of the steering wheel. She was not moving. He tugged at the door handle. It was locked from the inside. He ran around to the left side of the car and tried to push it upright, but that was an obvious impossibility. He felt himself growing faint; things were taking on a blurred, gray edge. He leaned a little while against the car.

Summoning up all his strength again, Frank started for the front door of the house on whose lawn he had landed. Before he got there, the door opened suddenly in a flood of light, and a man stood there in his dressing gown. It was Dr. Bowman. He looked at Frank. "Was there anybody else in the car?"

"A girl," Frank managed to say. "I can't get the door open."

Dr. Bowman turned aside and called into the house. "Ellen, telephone for an ambulance. Tell Tom to come running here. There's a girl trapped in a wrecked car."

A voice that seemed to come from inside said something. Lights began to go on upstairs. Suddenly there was a glare of lights from the house across the street.

"O.K., Dad," a boy about Frank's age said, as he bounded through the front door in his pajamas. Frank vaguely recognized him. Tom Bowman.

"Here," Dr. Bowman said, "give me a hand. Let's see if we can push this car upright."

Dr. Bowman and Tom leaned with all their might against the light car. Frank joined them. His weakness seemed to have disappeared. He forgot that he had been bleeding.

They pushed. The car rocked a little but heavily settled back on its side. Dr. Bowman looked across the street. "Hey, give us a hand!" he called out, as a man suddenly emerged from the brightly-lighted house across the way. The man ran over. A passer-by joined them. The five pushed. For a moment it was uncertain. Then—"Look out!" Dr. Bowman called. They jumped back. The car settled with a thud into its upright position.

"Now I'll open the door. Give me a hand to get her out," Dr. Bowman said.

Frank started forward to help, but the blue and white pattern of Dr. Bowman's dressing gown was turning to dull, confusing blotches of gray. Everything was becoming vague and gray. He seemed to have no control over his feet or hands. It was getting dark.

Dr. Bowman caught him just as he fell, and laid him on the grass. "Quick, help me get the girl out," he said to Tom and the two other men. He had the door opened now. From up the street could be heard the comforting wail of the ambulance siren.

3

A SATURDAY IN BLANTON

Tom," called his father. "Run up to the attic, won't you, and bring down the slide projector."

Five years ago Tom would have pointed out that his twin sister, Betty, was able-bodied, and why did she never do any of the going and fetching? Now he simply said, "O.K., Dad," put down his magazine, and started upstairs.

The old rectory had been built nearly eighty years ago when it seemed to be assumed that every rector would procreate at least six children, each of whom required a separate room. A rambling and spacious second floor ("Dust Trap, Incorporated," Tom's mother called it) led to a partially finished attic, which was large enough to enclose a compact, modern house. Dr. Bowman was the sixth rector to serve at Trinity Episcopal Church—it and the rectory were built the same year—and all of his predecessors had left traces of themselves in the attic. "A geologist could sort it out into strata," Tom said in fascinated disgust. "Just look at this." In one corner was a faded poster announcing a church bazaar to be held July 21, 1898, during the time of the second rector. Not far away was the heavy old lectern which had been removed from the church during the remodeling that the fourth rector sponsored. There it was, dusty and unused for forty years.

The slide projector belonged with the more recent strata. It stayed right at the top of the stairs. Tom started to pick it up. At the same moment, something caught his eye—a kite in the far corner. He went over and looked at it. There it was, with a large ball of string and a dusty tail of rags, ready for flight. Memories flooded back. He hadn't once thought about it in the five years, almost, that lay in between, but now it was vivid in memory—that day in late spring when he and Steve Hadley had made the kite and flown it. It was a few weeks after they were confirmed at Trinity Church. It had been a day of apple trees just outside the city in full flower, and birds everywhere, and trees in their first delicate trace of green.

He and Steve had made the kite as much for lack of anything else to do as for any other reason. At the time there'd seemed nothing memorable about the day. They had flown the kite at the edge of the country. They had lost interest. They had slowly walked home. On the way they had stopped at the Greasy Spoon on the North Side for a candy bar. Strange how golden and magic the memory had become in less than five years.

"Tom, hey, Tom," his father's voice rose faintly from two floors below. "How about that slide projector?"

"Coming," Tom called back. He picked up the projector and took it down to his father.

"Thanks," Dr. Bowman said, looking up from a sermon manuscript he was correcting.

"Anything else?" Tom asked.

"No, thanks. Run along and enjoy yourself."

"Thanks, Dad."

Dismissed for the morning and with nothing he had to do, he thought he might drop by Steve's. Then he remembered that Steve had gone with his parents to visit some relative or other about seventy miles away, where they used to live.

Tom started for the back door. "Oh, Tom," his father called. "Yes, Dad."

"Could you step here just a second, please?"

Tom walked back to the study. His father looked up. "These two teenagers that smashed up in front of here last night—how well do you know them?"

"I've seen Rosa around, and we know each other by name. Frank I know a little better; we have two classes together. I can't say I *really* know him."

Dr. Bowman tapped his pencil on a writing board and thought a while. "They'll both recover. Rosa's concussion was slight. Frank was all cut up on the cheek, but it's nothing serious. I worry about them, though, after they get out of the hospital—Frank in particular. Does he strike you as somehow desperate?"

"He keeps at a distance, at least it seems that way to me," Tom said. "He could be the biggest politician in school, but he deliberately bows out."

"There's no reason why everybody should be a back-slapping extrovert," Dr. Bowman said thoughtfully, "but I have a feeling Frank's solitary ways aren't exactly good for him. I don't know —it's just a hunch—but I seem to smell something unwholesome in the family situation. I'd like a chance to get to know him better. Do you think you could talk with him after he gets back to school and see if you can interest him in the Young People's Fellowship?"

"I'll try," Tom agreed doubtfully, "but I'm afraid I'm a poor salesman."

"I may have a chance to talk with him sooner. He and Rosa will probably be well enough by early next week for me to talk with them on my hospital call. Well, run along, Tom. And thanks."

Tom stepped outside. It was an Indian summer day with its clear, winy brightness of thin sunlight. A moderate wind, with just the right touch of approaching November in it, blew steadily and stirred the remaining leaves on the old oak tree in the back yard.

"Hi, Sis," Tom said, as he noticed that Betty had joined him.

"I'm bewildered, frustrated, and bored," she said. "Any good advice?"

"Yes," said Tom. "Let's go fly a kite."

"A kite?"

"There's one upstairs in the attic with five years' dust on it."

"That's what I need!" Betty exclaimed with shrill enthusiasm. "A kite, a kite, my kingdom for a kite. Sir brother, lead me to it."

"Stay put," Tom said. He disappeared into the house and soon returned with the kite. "O.K., Betty," he said, "let's march."

They threaded their way through the North Side, through the maze of factories beyond, through the tangle of railroad tracks, and out to where the countryside abruptly began.

As they went along, Betty suddenly turned to Tom and asked, "What would you do if you loved somebody but bit his head off every time you saw him?"

Tom slowed down. "You mean Steve?"

"If we've got to make it personal, of course I mean Steve."

"Sometimes a good biting wouldn't do Steve any harm," Tom muttered. "It might give him something interesting to talk about."

"But seriously—"

"I know, I know, Sis. As this lovelorn editor sees it, you're suffering from a first-class textbook case of frustration, as a result of going steady for two years. This condition is complicated by atavism, otherwise known as acting like a puling infant, as when you pull Sue's hair and go shrieking up to your room."

"The analysis is all too correct," Betty agreed. "I'm a slob, a juvenile, half-baked, atavistic slob. I'm mean to Steve, and I'm jittery as a Mexican jumping bean with everybody at home. What's the cure, Mr. Expert?"

"Oh, get married, I guess. That's what all the textbooks say."

"Phooey on you!" Betty exclaimed and lightly slapped him. "I mean here and now. What can I do to be a reasonably sensible and livable-with seventeen-year-old?"

"You've got me," Tom said. "Want to try flying it first?"

They were now at the top of a high hill. The wind was blowing steadily. Betty took the kite and slowly let out the string, a few feet at a time. The kite rose swiftly in a series of jerks. "You'd better take it," Betty said.

Tom took the string and smoothly played it out while the kite rapidly climbed. Soon it was several hundred yards away and high over a little barn which marked the first farm outside the city limits. Immeasurably above the kite was a white cloud, like an irregular ball of cotton, which moved with the same steady wind.

"Better pull it in till the wind lets up a little," Tom said. He cautiously drew at the string, but the pressure sharply increased. "Let's follow the kite," he said. He and Betty slowly walked down the far side of the hill. Tom carefully wound up the string a turn at a time. The kite twisted and bucked like a living thing.

"Oh, look," Betty exclaimed.

The string in Tom's hands had gone limp. Far away, over the barn, the kite was fluttering downward like a newspaper in the breeze. As they watched, it zigzagged beyond the silo toward the tall trees of a woodland.

Tom started running, but by now the broken end of the string was a hundred feet ahead of him and was moving through the grass like a swift snake. Tom stopped. "That's the way things end," he said matter-of-factly, and he smiled at Betty.

"Some things," she said as she smiled in return. "Twelve-year-old things, perhaps."

"Let's explore some," Tom said. "Look, you see the old grave-yard down at the bottom?"

At the bottom of a hill was a little cemetery which had once been used by the surrounding farm families. The church that went with it had long since burned down and been replaced several miles away by a new one. The stone foundations, Tom and Betty discovered, could still be traced among a tangle of bushes and briars, but it was the old graveyard that interested them most.

"Look how even the ground is," Tom said. "These graves are very old."

"Let's read some of the stones," Betty suggested. She bent over a tall, thin stone which leaned at a crazy angle and slowly read aloud its worn inscription:

> "ELIJAH WILKINS
> 1776-1848
> *A farmer lies beneath this soil,*
> *Taking his ease after his toil.*
> *Two hundred acres and a wife,*
> *Four sons, two daughters in his life*
> *He tended. Stranger, pause and say*
> *Are your crops as good today?"*

A long life, Tom thought, from the Declaration of Independence to the Mexican War. Around Elijah Wilkins' stone was a circle of others, as though some Oriental monarch had surrounded himself with his court. ABIGAIL ANN, HIS WIFE, Tom made out on an adjoining stone. Then his eye came to rest on another small stone: ELIJAH, JUNIOR, HIS SON, 1803-1821. "One year older than I am," he thought.

"Look," said Betty, "this must be the last of the Wilkinses."

She was standing by one of the most recent stones. It read, SARAH WILKINS, 1824-1902.

"The end of the Wilkinses," Tom murmured. "Whoever they are or were." His attention strayed to a very old stone in one corner of the cemetery. "Let's have a look there." They walked over. Near the top of the stone was carved a sun with streaming rays. Below was a name and date they could not make out for sure. Next came a short verse. "Listen to this," Tom said.

"You are standing where I stood
On eternity's dire brink.
Stranger, say a prayer and know
It is later than you think."

"Let's start back," Tom said abruptly. A cold chill passed through him. He started walking in silence, his hands in his pockets. Betty followed.

As they approached the section of big factories, Tom burst out. "I'm as mixed up as you. You've got boy trouble. I've got career trouble." He laughed ruefully. "Five years ago I had it all mapped out. I was going to be the new Einstein—invent the first space ship to Mars, and pilot it."

Betty smiled understandingly. "Physics and math have lost their lure?"

"To judge by the grades I got on the first tests, the answer is 'Yes, indeed.'" Tom sighed. "I wish I were crazily excited about something, anything. Anything would do. I'm interested in so many things, but not crazy about anything." He laughed. "Aren't we a couple of sad sacks, Sis?"

By now they were on the North Side. "How about a candy bar, if they still sell 'em for a nickel? I've got a dime wearing a hole in my pocket."

They went into the Greasy Spoon and bought their candy bars. As Betty was unwrapping hers, she looked toward a booth at one end of the room. "That boy in the jacket," she said. "I'm sure I've seen him."

"At school," Tom answered. "He's Sid Pruitt. You know, the head of the Stalwarts, that North Side gang."

"So he's the one Daddy was speaking about the other day." Betty took a second look at Sid Pruitt, from whose lips a mingled stream of tobacco smoke and rapid conversation was emerging. Five companions shared the booth with him.

"Let's amble along," Tom suggested.

They stepped outside and continued through the North Side, headed home.

Betty suddenly reached out to give Tom's hand a little squeeze. He smiled down at her protectingly, but with a questioning look.

"It is later than you think," Betty said with an involuntary shiver. She seized his hand again. "Tom, I'm afraid."

"Of what?"

"Of everything. Of the end—it comes so soon. Afraid of death. Afraid of life. Afraid I'll die before I really live. Afraid I'll mess up my life. Just afraid, I guess."

They walked on in silence for a while. Tom made no attempt to comfort her. He was sunk in his own thoughts.

At last he spoke. "It was the end of something or other," he said. "Something ended today."

But he wasn't quite sure what.

4

A SUNDAY IN BLANTON

OUR SPEAKER this evening is the Reverend Doctor Bowman, whom I have the honor to present," Peter Randall said, and sat down.

A round of applause and appreciative titters rewarded his words. Dr. Bowman stood up at the head table in the dining hall and looked about. Attendance fair, he noted. Attendance at the Young People's Fellowship had a way of fluctuating in inverse ratio to the number of high school weekend events. His eye expertly traveled around. The old faithfuls were there. Betty was near the front with Steve. Tom sat at the back by Helen Greenwood, but that was probably coincidence. Bill Pendleton was in the middle, bending over with a confident laugh to whisper something to the girl beside him.

He would put it on the line straight, Dr. Bowman quickly decided, with no attempt at the urbane lightness of touch which sometimes seemed to be the trademark of the Episcopal Church. "I asked your president for a chance to speak to you this evening," he began, "for several reasons. The first is that this ought to be a good evening for us to think hard and explore a little more deeply than we sometimes do. This morning we had our monthly corporate Communion. We've just now experienced the fellowship of the table and we have worshipped God in Evening Prayer. If all this hasn't made our minds and hearts a little more open to Him, we're pretty hopeless cases."

Dr. Bowman paused and looked around. Everyone, even Bill Pendleton, was listening intently. Some were frowning with a touch of apprehension, as though the serious tone of his beginning had aroused vague, nameless fears.

"Let's begin with a sociological fact," Dr. Bowman continued. "Trinity Church is in a changing neighborhood. It used to be in the most fashionable part of town. Fashion has now departed and makes its home in places like Oak Hill. The area around here has become very mixed in every way. Beautiful old houses are divided up into rooms and flats, little factories have sprung up here and there. And of course you know what's happened to the population. I daresay that if you took a census, you'd find that less than five per cent of the people in a radius of a quarter of a mile are Episcopalians. The majority are nothing or are nominal Roman Catholics, sometimes very nominal."

Dr. Bowman looked around again. The same intent gazes were fixed upon him. A wary look had come into Bill's eyes. He was on guard.

"The most recent wave of immigrants is the Puerto Ricans," Dr. Bowman went on. "They have particular problems. They're at the tail end of everything, such as housing opportunities. Because of language difficulties, they don't feel at home in the Roman Catholic churches. Many of these people are religiously adrift; their ties were weak to begin with, and often the ties have been altogether cut in America.

"Trinity is a very pleasant church. I love its quiet serenity. I love the easy friendship and understanding that exist among its parishioners, but time is catching up with us. Trinity Church has three choices. One is to concentrate on holding the loyalty of its present members, so that even if they move to the suburbs they will continue to worship here. We might be able to do this for one generation, even two. We couldn't do it forever. So there's a second alternative."

Dr. Bowman stopped and stared off in the distance. The

pause lengthened. Here and there someone scraped impatient shoes against the floor.

"The second choice is to shut up shop here and build a new church out in the suburbs, probably in Oak Hill. In that way we would be following our people in order to minister to them. Certainly, in one way or another, churches will have to be built in the new suburbs, regardless of what Trinity does or does not do."

Another pause. The look of apprehension and wariness in Bill Pendleton's face had deepened into a set expression.

"The third possibility," Dr. Bowman continued, "is to stay right here and do everything possible to attract and serve the people who actually live near the church." He paused again, then slowly continued. "For that to work, it means that all of us who are communicants of the Church are going to need some stretching of imagination, heart, and mind. It means inviting into fellowship a mixture of people with all sorts of national backgrounds, accents, and complexions."

Dr. Bowman's voice trailed away, and he stared off into invisible space. When he spoke again, his voice was lower. "I wonder if it would work. It's asking a lot of human nature." His voice grew stronger. "I've been having a series of talks with the vestry. We don't want to plunge in half-cocked on anything as difficult and challenging as this. If it's going to succeed, it'll have to have pretty solid support from the vestry, the congregation—and the YPF. You've a key role in my daydreams."

There was a stir of excitement in the faces before him. Some relaxed with pleasure. Others took on an added tenseness.

"Part of the over-all plan," Dr. Bowman continued, "would be to set up a special Spanish Eucharist, probably at nine o'clock. This would be mainly for the benefit of the older Puerto Ricans who don't know English well. I guess I can manage the language well enough to read the service, as long as no one asks me questions in Spanish. If we do go ahead and broaden the base of the church, and it begins to catch on among the Puerto Ricans, we'll try to bring in a Spanish-speaking curate."

The faces in front of him were perceptibly livelier now, with a mounting excitement. "Mind you," Dr. Bowman went on, "none of this is even in the blueprint stage yet. Nothing has been definitely decided. I've got a hardheaded vestry, and maybe it's a good thing. They keep my feet on the ground. But what I want to find out—and then I'll report it back to the vestry—is how you here feel about all this. Let's make it specific. In the first place, if we go ahead, are you willing to welcome into the YPF any high-school-age boys and girls who want to join, regardless of their background? And I mean really welcome them, accept them as part of the group, and take them into your activities. That's the first question. I'd like you to be thinking about it.

"The second question is the special thing I had in mind. All of you know about the Stalwarts, the group of North Side boys. As far as I know, it isn't exactly a criminal gang, but they could easily slip over into delinquency. They're certainly not doing themselves any good by running around together and holding meetings in places like the back room of the Greasy Spoon. Now what I want to suggest is this: What would you think of inviting the Stalwarts to hold their meetings in the parish house? We could also encourage any of them who were interested to join the YPF. As I see it, there would be two advantages in bringing the Stalwarts under this roof. It might give them a new orientation and keep them out of trouble, and it would give us some small-scale experience to see how broadening the base of Trinity Church would work out in practice. If the experiment went well, I think the vestry and congregation would take notice. But it's up to you. I can't force anything down your throats, and I wouldn't if I could."

Dr. Bowman suddenly smiled and turned to Pete Randall. "I guess this senator has ended his filibuster," he said. "No, he hasn't—one more thing. I don't know whether I can put this into words. I am haunted by a dream, an ideal. I have a picture in my mind and heart of what the Church is in essence and what Trinity Episcopal Church might become in practice. The Church is a place where all are welcome because all are equally precious in the sight of God. It is a place where differences of class and income and background don't vanish but simply become unimportant because there is one Christ, and He is all in all. We could be that kind of church. That's all. I hadn't meant to preach."

Dr. Bowman sat down and looked off once more into space. Pete Randall rose and swallowed hard. "You've all heard what our rector had to say. He wants an expression of opinion about taking these new people from the North Side into the YPF. All those in favor say 'Aye.'"

"Just a minute," Dr. Bowman said, leaping up. "Excuse me for interrupting. I think the YPF ought to discuss all this very carefully and prayerfully, and I doubt that you're going to be ready for any vote tonight. Wouldn't it be better to devote this evening to an initial discussion and then think about it a few weeks before trying to crystallize the opinion of the group? At least that seems the best way to me. And one other thing. I'm going to excuse myself now, so I won't be tempted to dominate the discussion."

"You don't need to leave," Pete assured him. "We're glad to have you here."

"Thanks," said Dr. Bowman with a wide smile, "but I've got a half-read copy of *The New Yorker* back home. If you'll excuse me . . ." He left to the sound of scattered handclaps.

"Well," said Peter, "we've got something solid to think about. Any comments?"

Everybody looked at everybody else and then at Pete. Little whispered conversations began to break out. "Would it mean we'd have to invite them to all our dances?" "Would they want to come, anyway?" "Would they really mix?"

"Can't hear them!" Mr. Steinbrecher, the lay counselor, shouted.

"Speak up!" Pete pleaded. "Talk loud enough for everybody to hear."

There was a hush, but no one spoke up.

"All right," Bill Pendleton said, rising. "If nobody else will say anything. I think it's a noble idea but completely impractical, and I'm against it." He sank down.

"Any other comments?" Pete asked and looked hopefully around. Another silence. "Has Bill voiced the sentiments of everybody?" He looked around desperately. "Anybody with any ideas? Come on, guys. Helen, what do you think?"

Helen Greenwood seemed to become smaller and less conspicuous in her seat. "I think . . ." she said in a low voice and stopped.

"Louder, please," Pete pleaded.

Helen spoke a little louder. "I think they wouldn't mix very well."

"Thank you, Helen," the president said. "Anybody else?" An uneasy pause. "Am I to take it that everybody agrees with the two who have spoken? Then let's go on to our next item of business."

"All right, all right," said Tom, leaping up. "If nobody else will do it, I will. I'm for the idea. Even if my Dad did dream it up, it's a good idea, and I'm for it. Trinity Church can continue as it is and be a very pleasant little club for the right people and wither away as it deserves to, or it can take a deep breath and go Christian."

"Well, that's giving us a lot to think about," Pete said. "Does anybody else feel the way Tom does?"

"I do!" several voices from different parts of the room said eagerly.

Steve Hadley slowly rose from his seat and looked around. He cleared his throat. "Seems to me—I mean—if we can get along with those guys in school, why can't we get along with them here? I think Dr. Bowman's got a point when he says that this church ought to serve the people who live all around here. I guess I'm for it."

Steve sat down. For a second he frowned as he remembered the Omega Alphas which he was still thinking of joining. Their membership was limited to "Christians of Caucasian stock." Nevertheless, he pushed the vague uneasiness aside for the moment.

"Any more comments?" the president asked.

Bill Pendleton arose, stuck his hands in his pockets, and slowly looked from face to face. He paused with a public speaker's sense of timing. One of his two older brothers was a member of the House of Representatives, and the other was a rising TV star; a sense of the magic and power of language seemed to run in the family. Bill's mother had died of cancer a few years after he was born, and his brothers, before they went away, had been as much like solicitous uncles as ordinary brothers. Bill dragged the delay out to the last possible second. With sure instinct he knew when to end it. He spoke at last, "Mr. Chairman, we have heard the eloquent pleas of the rectory crowd. I do not hope to match either their eloquence or their influence. I have no inside track in these matters, but perhaps I can at least say how this problem seems to a run-of-the-mill garden-variety Christian."

Bill looked around again and slowly resumed. "In theory, the idealists are right, completely right. If we make it to heaven, we certainly aren't going to worry about the language, education, race, or background of anybody there. And they won't worry about us. But we aren't living in heaven. We're living in Blanton. We have to take social realities into account. Look at us here in the YPF. To the sociologist, we're a pretty homogeneous group—from middle-middle to upper-upper, mostly. It ought to be easy for us to get along together, to understand one another, to practice Christian love. But we're always tangling, always antagonizing one another, always getting upset. If we do such a lame job of being Christians among ourselves, what are the chances of our doing even as good a job when we bring in a lot of people with completely different backgrounds? Let's be realistic."

Bill looked around for so long that the president was almost ready to speak. Then Bill added quietly, "Ideally, yes. Practically, no. Remember back in Confirmation class when we were told that humility was one of the great Christian virtues? Let's practice it. Let's not overestimate our degree of Christian commitment. We're beginners and have a long way to go. With all due respect to the rectory crowd, I say let's see if we can make a real go of acting like Christians among ourselves for a few months. If we succeed, it'll be time to talk about bringing in every Tom, Dick, and Harry."

A slight sharpness came into Bill's voice as he finished. He looked around, laughed good-naturedly, and sat down.

"Well," said Peter. "Any more discussion?"

Several voices rose in a confused clamor. "I move we turn on the jukebox," somebody said at the back. There was a wave of relaxed laughter throughout the room.

"Let's all agree to think about everything that's been said tonight," Peter suggested. "Then we can take it up again at a meeting a few weeks from now. O.K., who's got a nickel for the jukebox?"

Someone put in five nickels and the music started blaring out. Volunteers quickly pushed the tables and chairs to the far end of the room. Couples began to dance.

Tom watched them a while, then became aware of Helen Greenwood beside him. "Dance?" he asked.

Helen smiled shyly and rose. They walked over and started toward the middle of the floor. "Let's go over that way," Helen suggested, and they walked to the other end of the room where fewer couples were dancing.

Tom, though not an impassioned dancer, was a moderately good one. For a time they danced in silence. Then he looked down and caught Helen's eyes. She was watching his face intently, a tentative smile on her own. Rather pretty girl, he thought without excitement, but timid and uncertain of herself. He had seen her often, of course; she was a workhorse in the YPF and very faithful at choir.

"What grade are you?" Tom asked in order to make conversation, though he had a pretty definite idea.

"Junior," she said.

They danced some more. By this time, a number of the students were drifting away, though a hard core of devoted dancers stayed on. "Can I see you home?" Tom asked.

"Thanks so much," Helen said. "That's nice of you."

Cold gusts of air slapped them as they stepped outside into the darkness. "Sorry I don't have a car," Tom said.

"That's all right. I like to walk," Helen replied, as they moved briskly along.

Helen's home was five blocks away—a house built in the functional style of the "international" movement—simple and beautiful in a severe, unornamental way. Her father, Tom recalled, was one of Blanton's most prominent attorneys.

"Well, good night," Tom said as they stopped in front of her house.

"Good night and thanks," Helen said, and she paused uncertainly. "Well, good night," she said again.

Was she expecting him to kiss her good night? He wasn't sure, and the desire to do it was not overpowering.

"So long, be seeing you," Tom said, and he started back home.

5

A PICNIC FOR TWO

ON A SATURDAY afternoon several weeks later, Betty stood by her window, looking at the cold, scudding clouds and watching the bare trees dance in the rough wind. "Better dress warmly," she told herself, for once anticipating the advice of her mother. She put on a warmer sweater and came down to the deserted living room. She looked out the window again. It was silly to let her mood be so influenced by the weather. What right did she have to think that Indian summer ought to last forever?

As Steve walked over to the rectory, he was puzzled at his own mixture of feelings. There was still the delight he had felt when he called up that morning and asked Betty whether she could go for a picnic, and she had said Yes. At the same time, he felt nervous. Betty had been so jumpy lately. She was always snapping at him when he least expected it, and the more earnestly he talked with her and tried to find out what the matter was, the more her smile and manner took on an edged mockery. Did she think he was dull or weak? He had begun to wonder.

Mingled with these already contradictory emotions was something else. As though he were projecting a series of Kodachrome slides, Steve saw himself walking hand in hand with Betty through a verdant countryside that bore little resem-

blance to anything near Blanton in November. He saw himself
and Betty building a fire, cooking and eating hot dogs. In his
imagination, the gift of language suddenly became his. He
could say things, he could speak from the heart. They would
draw closer together. Betty's sharp manner and mocking smile
would be gone. Gradually the need for words would vanish.
They would be alone in an enchanted world that belonged to
them only. At this point, the brightly colored daydream faded
into sweet chaotic vagueness, but the sense of mystery and
magic lingered with him as he rang the rectory bell.

Betty came to the door. "Hello, Steve," she said.

"Hello, Betty." He paused an awkward moment, then aimed
a kiss which went slightly awry and landed on her upper lip.

"Try again," she said, and she kissed him. "All set?"

"Yeah," he answered, pointing to the large sack he was
carrying.

As they started down the street a gust of wind blew a little
whirlpool of brown and withered leaves against their feet.
"Colder today, isn't it?" Steve said.

"We'll be all right," Betty answered. "I like it. Look—look
at those clouds."

Steve glanced to where a particularly low and dark cloud
was moving fast across the overcast sky.

"Guess the Indian summer's over," he said.

"Skating season soon," Betty remarked. "Think we'll have
enough snow for skiing?"

"Can't ever tell," Steve said.

"I hope so. I'm an awful skier but I like to try."

They were soon beyond the North Side and among the big
factories. All at once they were in the open country.

"How about this road?" Steve asked. It was one that turned
off the main highway, beyond the farmhouse over which Tom
and Betty had sailed the kite.

"O.K.," said Betty. "Doesn't look like it's traveled much," she added, as they started up the side road.

It was little more than a pair of tracks. In many places there were thick clumps of withered grass. To the left and right stood high wire fences now grown up with bushes and small trees so that they looked like English hedges.

"You can't feel the wind as much here," Steve said.

You can't see much light, either, Betty added to herself. It was almost like a tunnel they were going through—a tunnel of faded green and crinkled brown.

After a few hundred yards, the road suddenly ended in front of a small farmhouse. "Look how run-down it is," Steve said. The house had only a few flecks of white paint still clinging to it. Some of the clapboards had fallen off. In front were the remains of a flower garden and some old lilac bushes mixed with young saplings. The grass all around was thick and uncut.

"How's this for a picnic spot?" Steve asked.

"Fine," said Betty. "Show me how a Boy Scout builds a fire in this wind."

"Let's see—I'll find some stones to make a little fireplace." Steve looked around. He found two long, flat stones at the edge of what had once been a little flower bed and put them about a foot apart. Next he placed balls of crumpled newspaper between the stones and added some kindling from the large paper sack. "Let's look around for some bigger stuff."

"Here are some fallen limbs," said Betty, and she dragged them to the fireplace.

"O.K."

"Where's your Indian fire stick?"

"Here." Steve took a box of kitchen matches from the big sack. "Here are the hot dogs. You want to take them?" He struck a match and held his hand cupped over it, but the flame flickered out before it had a chance to ignite the paper. "Try

again," he said. This time he succeeded in lighting the newspaper, and the flame raced at a sharp angle up into the kindling. Soon the bigger wood was blazing fiercely.

Steve broke off two slender switches from a nearby bush and
began toasting hot dogs. Betty rummaged around in the sack
and came up with a bottle of catsup, some rolls, and a box of
marshmallows. Reaching deeper she discovered two bottles of
pop and decapped them.

"Have a bite," Steve invited. Betty opened her mouth, and he
popped the end of a hot dog into it.

"It's good," she said. He handed her the hot dog on the stick.

They were soon on their second round of hot dogs, sipping
pop from time to time. The half-charred, half-raw meat that
would have provoked a mutiny at home seemed a gourmet's
delight in the open wind together.

"You warm enough?" Steve suddenly asked.

"I'm all right," Betty said, edging as close to the fire as she
dared.

"You sure?" Steve asked doubtfully. "That wind is really
cold."

Steve fixed himself a third hot dog. Betty turned to the
marshmallows and began toasting one. "Open your mouth!"
she commanded, and she poked the brown marshmallow between his teeth. "Uh," he said, tasting the marshmallow in
combination with a portion of half-raw hot dog. He put a
marshmallow on his stick and quickly toasted it. "Jump, Fido!"
he ordered, and Betty jumped, catching the marshmallow
neatly between her teeth. She giggled.

They fed each other marshmallows for a few minutes more
as the fire sank to a bed of coals which only occasionally
flared up.

"Want to explore around a bit?" Steve asked at last.

Beyond the little farmhouse, a wood lot began. It looked

very dark. Indeed, the whole landscape was darkening fast. The sun must still be above the horizon but there was no trace of it. The dark gray sky pushed steadily downward. "What's that?" Betty asked, holding her hand out.

"First snow of the season," Steve said, noticing a few scudding flakes. "Are you sure you're warm enough?"

"I'm all right," Betty said.

Steve looked at her hard. Her teeth were chattering a little. "Want to start back home?"

"Mother said if I was home by seven-thirty—"

"O.K." Steve looked around. "We've got plenty of time. What do you say we go up on the porch here and have a look in the house?"

From the porch they could look through a window into the dimness of a living room. Vaguely they made out a few chairs, a big sofa, and a potbellied iron stove by the far wall. "They must have left all the furniture," Steve said. He walked to the front door. "Look, it's open. Want to have a look inside?"

"Let's do," Betty said.

The door creaked as they went in. Steve closed it and led Betty from the hall into the living room. "Feels warmer here, doesn't it?" he said. He paced around the room and stopped by the big stove. "Look, they left some wood and kindling here. What do you say to a fire to thaw us out before we start back?"

"That would be nice," Betty said. As she said it, she felt a little uneasy, but she didn't quite know why.

With no wind to interfere, Steve soon had a crackling fire going in the stove. The warmth spread farther and farther into the room. He moved the sofa closer to the stove. "Let's sit here," he said. Betty sat down beside him. The bright fire shone through the grillwork on the stove; it was reflected on Steve's face and gave him a ruddy glow. They took their sweaters off.

Betty glanced toward the window. Early darkness was deepening. The wind was whistling in gusts through bushes and trees. Sometimes a cold gust forced its way through the cracks in the dilapidated old house, but the stove grew hotter and hotter. It created a charmed circle of warmth and flickering light.

Steve's arm was around her waist. She leaned closer to him and put her head on his shoulder. For a long time, it seemed, they sat there, saying nothing. At last he lifted her onto his lap and kissed her.

The warmth of the stove enveloped them. It was hard to believe there were other people existing in the world and that a network of responsibilities—home and school and church and past and future—existed only two miles away, in the city of Blanton. It was as though the rest of the human race and all history had been swept into the discard. There they were, as new and untried and free as the first man and first woman.

They did not hurry. It was a sweet eternity, an unhurried leisure of love, before Steve's hand gently closed over her breast and drew her tighter to him. Their kisses lengthened. Neither of them had spoken for a long time.

Betty was drifting, and she wanted to drift. She did not put it into words, but she was weary of responsibility. She wanted a decision to be made between Steve and herself without the interminable back-and-forth of talking it out.

Steve, too, was glad to be free of the lash and net of words. He, too, vaguely and half-consciously wanted to drift to the point where words would not be needed again. Dimly, at the back of his mind, was a thought that he tried not to examine. Was Betty really looking for some way to break things off? Did she actually love him? Had he disappointed her in some way? Did he look weak in her eyes? Was there a touch of contempt (or perhaps call it pity) in her feeling toward him? What could he do to prove himself in her eyes? (And that was the only way to prove himself in his own eyes.) Such were the vaguest of thoughts half-formed in Steve's mind. They were all the more powerful for their vagueness.

As he gently stretched her out on the long sofa and lay down beside her, an unmistakable sense of guilt flashed through his mind, but he quickly banished it. After all, it takes two.

At that moment, Betty seemed to hear a bell ringing sharply in her mind. She knew what was happening, but by a deliberate effort of will she silenced the inner peal of warning. What was about to happen was not her doing, she dreamily assured herself. She had made no decisions. Things were simply happening. That was all. Her mind drowsed into deep peace. The warmth from the stove felt good. She idly entwined her fingers in Steve's hair. One bare breast felt the touch of Steve's lips. His hands stroked her other breast, and slowly, tenderly, explored further. The warmth of the fire and the warmth she felt in her heart and her body merged into one. She twisted her fingers more tightly in his hair and kissed his throat as he leaned over her. . . .

"Don't!" she screamed and listened with amazement to her scream. She rolled off the sofa, stood up, hastily grabbed her clothes and started buttoning them with shaking fingers.

"Did I do something wrong?" Steve asked. He stood up, clumsily working on his own clothes.

Betty was still busy taking care of herself. What could she answer? It wasn't the moralist in her that had made her scream "Don't." At least she didn't think it was. It was the panic-stricken little girl that had called a halt. Things had gone too fast. Plain fear and panic had overwhelmed her. That was all there was to it. At least it seemed that way.

Betty looked at Steve and smiled uncertainly. "Come on, let's see if we can race this storm home."

It was dark when they stepped outside. The little picnic fire had gone out. A driving snow was sweeping across the yard.

"Race you down to the highway!" Betty called. She was off down the lane before Steve could collect his wits.

With a last look back at the little old farmhouse, he started after her.

6

INCIDENT AT THE SHACK

NEXT MONDAY Steve hunted out Bill Pendleton at school and told him he was ready to join the Omega Alphas. Bill shook his hand heartily and said that the initiation would be set for Saturday night.

As the week wore on, Steve found himself asking *why* he had made the decision. The more he thought about the Omegas and their rumored activities, the less interesting they seemed. After the recent meeting of the YPF and Bill's speech . . . if Bill was a typical Omega . . . Steve wasn't very much one for worrying about abstract principles, but he did sense that if Trinity Church moved toward broadening its base, it would be evolving in an opposite direction from the ideals of the Omegas.

Yet he went grimly and glumly ahead to become a member, as though in some irrational but deep way he hoped that life's snarls would become unsnarled. At least it was something definite. He could say Yes and set wheels in motion. It also kept him from thinking about Betty quite as constantly. The initiation Saturday evening would mean no date with Betty. There wouldn't be a long evening with each one careful not to say anything that would lead their memories back to the deserted farmhouse, or set in train similar events. After he had his Omega pin, he'd give it to Betty to wear on her bra, the way the girls did, and that would make things definite between them—not a formal engagement, but more definite than just dating.

Around six o'clock that Saturday evening the Omegas arrived in five cars which they parked with their front bumpers almost touching the Shack. They poured into the building, Steve looking somehow accidental and out of place in their midst.

The Shack was empty except for Jerry behind the counter and Frank Buell who had a livid scar like a jagged streak of lightning down his right cheek. Seeing the throng, Frank rose a little unsteadily from the front booth, bowed to Bill Pendleton, and murmured, "Make way for the sacrificial victim." While several Omegas stared at him, he paused at the counter, paid up, and departed with a quick "Good night" to Jerry.

As he walked over to the table where Bill Pendleton was sitting, Jerry said in a low voice, "Be on the lookout. The Stalwarts are mad."

"Hey, guys, wait here a minute," Bill said, and got up. He and Jerry walked to the counter. "What's the trouble?"

"I don't know everything," Jerry said, "but from what I picked up, their president and vice-president found their tires all slashed to slivers after their last meeting, and for some funny reason they think you or one of the brothers had a hand in it."

"I can't imagine how they got that idea," Bill said.

"You can't?" Jerry asked in an absolutely dead voice and looked him long in the eye. "All right, if you can't, you can't. But I've warned you."

"Thanks," said Bill, and he returned to his booth.

They ordered and were soon served. The twenty or so Omegas, members of an organization which theoretically didn't exist, ate with a curious lack of noise and conversation. There was something cathedral-like about the atmosphere. Steve found himself comparing it to the hush during a Communion service; the next moment he quickly banished the thought as somehow blasphemous although he wasn't quite sure why.

Finally the meal was at an end. "Let's get going," Bill said. They all rose. Steve, exercising the traditional privilege of Omega initiates, paid for them all as they filed out past the thoughtful gaze of Jerry. They passed through the door and walked around to the parking lot. "Hey! What's doing here?" somebody yelled. The rest ran to join him.

"Look there!" Bill called.

The five cars were still exactly where they had been parked, but in the middle lane, between the two rows of parking stalls, were four other cars. These were parked with exquisite precision so that only inches separated their sides from the rear ends of the Omega cars.

"No room to back out here," Steve said in a blurred mixture of emotions.

The Omegas stood a little while studying the alien cars. Several were familiar enough. One was the jalopy that belonged to Sid Pruitt, the Stalwart president. It could be seen every day in the parking lot at Blanton Senior High, except on those days when Sid had more important business than school.

"Come on, you guys, cut it out!" Bill Pendleton roared in fury. "Move this junk away, or we'll move it for you."

There was no reply. Several of the Omegas ran to the alley behind the Shack, but came back to report that no one was there.

Bill looked around. "Last warning," he yelled. "Take these wrecks away or don't blame us."

There was still no reply.

"Come on," Bill said in a businesslike tone. "We'll start with this one." Half a dozen Omegas joined him at the two ends of Sid Pruitt's jalopy. "That's it—one, two, three, go."

The old car rocked crazily. "Again, push!" Bill grunted. They pushed harder. Suddenly, with a lurch, the jalopy fell over on its left side. The sound of shattering glass was all around them as they jumped back.

"Next," Bill called. "Come on, guys."

Bill and his team went to work on the second car. Another group of Omegas gathered at the third car and prepared to give it the same treatment. Just as both groups were counting "One, two—" a voice yelled so loudly that they let go.

"Cut it out!"

They looked around. Jerry was standing at the edge of the little parking lot. "Act your age," he said tersely, "or I'm calling the cops."

Bill let go of the second car and looked at Jerry. "Hello," he said. "We're helping the Stalwarts move their cars."

"Cut the bull," Jerry said curtly. "This place has got a decent reputation, and I'm going to keep it."

"Call the cops if you want to," Bill said coolly. "O.K., fellows, back to your stations. One, two, three . . ."

Jerry watched a moment, then he shrugged his shoulders as the second car rolled over with a loud tinkle of shattering glass. "Crazy kids," he said to himself. "O.K., the cops." He walked back into the Shack.

The spirit of the thing had now stilled Steve's uncertainties. He joined a team, and they started to work on the third car. "Heave ho!" one of the Omegas said. The car began rocking crazily. "One more shove!" the self-appointed leader shouted. Steve pushed harder. The car trembled.

"Up and at 'em!" a voice called from the alley. Steve looked up and hastily let go of the car. It looked as though the alley were sprouting people, all on the run, all galloping toward the parking lot. There must have been fifty figures rushing forward from their hiding places.

"Hey, look out—get ready—" Bill shouted, but before he

could finish his sentence, the parking lot was overrun. "Let go!" Bill yelled in a fury, but it was no use. The Omegas were outnumbered more than two to one. Each was quickly pinned to the ground by two or more Stalwarts. The few who wriggled loose fled ingloriously and disappeared up the side streets.

"O.K., O.K.," Bill managed to say, gasping. "You win. Now let's call it off."

His suggestion was greeted with a chorus of mocking laughter from all over the parking lot. A moment later half a dozen additional figures erupted from the alley and came onto the lot. They slowed down as they approached the cars. Each had something bright and gleaming in his right hand.

"Fix 'em all," Sid Pruitt, who was standing over Bill, commanded.

With exaggerated slowness the new arrivals fanned out, one to each Omega car. The bright things flashed; there was the sound of hissing air from slit tires.

"You'll—you'll pay for this!" Bill began, but Sid Pruitt casually stepped on his chest and ended his remarks. A raucous chorus of laughter drowned out his next attempt to speak.

The multiple hisses of air died down. Sid Pruitt looked around. "O.K., fellows, let 'em up now."

The badly bruised Omegas, some bleeding from cuts made by shattered glass, rose and rubbed themselves.

"Run along, little boys," Sid said as he gave Bill Pendleton a resounding spank in the rear.

With a lunge and a roar of anger, Bill leaped at Sid. The latter calmly stepped aside and watched his adversary stumble and fall to the ground. Very quietly, it seemed, and very slowly, Sid took a knife from his pocket, touched it carefully, and the long straight blade shot out. He pointed it downward. "You see this?" he said. A sudden fury passed across his face, and he kicked Bill savagely. "Get goin'!" he screamed.

Bill arose. He looked at the knife. He looked around. The tire-slashers were scattered among the other Stalwarts, with knives in their hands.

"You win—this time," he said. "O.K., brothers." He turned to the Omegas. "Meeting called off for tonight."

The mocking laughter of the Stalwarts dinned in Omega ears. At this moment the unmistakable wail of a police siren sounded from downtown, not more than a few blocks away. The Stalwarts disappeared into the alley as quickly as they had come.

The Omegas were still looking at their cars. "Quick," Bill said. "We'll worry about the cars tomorrow. Run up that side street."

They disappeared up the side street. By the time the police car screeched to a halt, the officers saw assorted cars in various stages of wreckage, but not a Stalwart nor an Omega.

7

DOORS THAT OPEN AND SHUT

IT WAS the following Monday that Frank, still a little weak
in the legs, returned to school. Once during the day he saw
Rosa far off down the corridor, but when he waved and started
toward her she gave no sign that she had noticed him. By the
time he fought his way through the crowd she was there no
longer.

After school, Frank caught a ride downtown with Bill
Pendleton. Bill let him out in the heart of the business district.
"Thanks," Frank said. Then he looked around for the florist
shop. It was strange to think that life had gone on as usual
during the couple of weeks he had been in the hospital. Not a
single new thing met his eyes as he glanced at the familiar
stores.

He crossed the street and stood outside the florist shop. He
caught his reflection in the window. He stood there a long
moment, soberly studying the angry, raw new flesh of the gash
on his cheek. Blanton hadn't changed, but he had. He patted
the scar. Too bad it hadn't come from a German duelling episode. Too much drink and contact with a knob on a dashboard
—not much glamor there. "Serves you right," he said to his
ghostly reflection. "Won't you ever grow up, you lousy
bastard?"

"Probably not," he added under his breath and walked into the florist shop. "Five dollars worth," he said.

"What kind?" the clerk asked. "We have some fine chrysanthemums, just in, and these roses are very special—"

"What you think best," Frank said. "Make it ten dollars worth. It's for a girl."

"I get the idea," said the clerk. He bustled around, carefully choosing. When he had wrapped the bulky bouquet in paper, he turned to Frank. "A card, sir?"

"No, thanks."

Frank paid and left with the huge bouquet tucked under his arm.

Kitty-cornered across the street was a candy shop, crisply hygienic and high-priced. Frank went into it. "A five-pound box of chocolates, mixed," he said.

"For a girl?" the pretty woman at the counter asked sympathetically.

"That's right."

"Is she reducing?"

"What?"

"If she's reducing, and most of them are, we have a special mixture I'd recommend. It isn't *quite* as fattening."

Frank laughed. "She looks all right to me."

"Men are poor judges," the woman said severely. "They never notice the difference ten pounds either way."

"I'm sure you're right," Frank agreed. "But this time, don't worry about dieting. Just give me your tastiest mixture."

"Then this is just the thing for you," the woman said, relieved of all responsibility. "Shall I wrap it up for you?"

"Please."

"Beautiful day, isn't it?" the woman remarked. "For so late in the year."

"Like Indian summer," Frank added. He paid, put the box

of candy under his other arm, and left. His legs were beginning to feel shaky. Nearby was a drugstore. He stopped there and ordered a cup of coffee.

As he sipped the black coffee and rested, he felt his strength coming back a little. The stronger he felt, however, the more he dreaded what lay ahead. Several times, after he came home from the hospital, he had tried to call Rosa. Usually her mother answered, said a slow "I do not understand English," and hung up. Once her father had answered and said "She is not at home" and slammed the receiver down. Though he had called around supper time several different days, Rosa never answered. "The old run-around," he told himself. "Serves me right." Somehow, when he saw her at all in school, it was always at a distance, and she slipped out of sight if he came near.

Frank stood up and resumed his walk. It was only a few blocks to Rosa's home on the North Side, but the walk seemed endless. He could have taken a taxi, but he didn't. The weariness and ache in his legs seemed a kind of penance and expiation.

At last he saw the house. It looked even shabbier and more pitiful in its decayed splendor than he remembered it. Outside the front door, as he drew near, were the inevitable children, playing and quarreling noisily. They stared at him with probing curiosity as he opened the front door.

Up the stairs to the second floor and on up to the third he walked, slowing down as he neared his goal. He was shaking. He paused to catch his breath. Finally he knocked. There was a low scurrying about inside and quick voices. The door opened a crack, a little more. Mr. Arrondo was standing there. Behind him, and a little to one side, was Rosa. She had no expression on her face.

"Excuse me," said Frank. "May I come in and talk with you?"

Mr. Arrondo looked Frank up and down, slowly. Then suddenly his face twisted in anger, and he clenched his fists. "Go away!" he screamed.

Frank stood there, trying to think of what to say. He caught Rosa's glance. She was very pale. While he was still struggling for words, Mr. Arrondo slammed the door. There was the sound of a key turning.

Perhaps he should have left the two presents outside the door, left them with a note and not have knocked at all. Wearily he felt in his pocket for a pen or pencil. He had forgotten both. With a sense of deepening exhaustion, he left the gifts by the locked door and started down the stairs, holding onto the rail for support.

Outside, he hailed a passing taxi and gave his address. The driver, watching him weave uncertainly into the cab, asked, "You all right, mister? Have one too many?"

"One too many," Frank admitted, "but not the kind you mean."

"Wise guy," the driver muttered, but he was used to wise guys.

Soon Frank was home. He stumbled upstairs to bed and lay there in a misery of self-reproach and frustration that kept him from falling asleep. After an endless time, Sarah called him to dinner. When the meal was over he felt stronger and, as he put it to himself, a shade less "neurotic."

"You're sure you're all right?" Sarah asked anxiously as she put on her coat.

"Oh, sure," Frank said absently.

She looked at him hard and questioningly, but he seemed comfortably settled in an easy chair in the living room where he was thumbing through the *Blanton Daily Times*.

"I'm ready now, Jack," she called. Mr. Buell, straightening his tie, came downstairs, and the two of them left for the PTA meeting at which he had agreed to speak on "Business and the Public Schools."

Frank fidgeted with the paper and finally laid it down on the coffee table. He *had* to reach Rosa. He didn't know what he would say or whether anything he could say would make any difference, but he had to reach her.

He gave a quick laugh. A wild idea had occurred to him, one so crazy it might work. He went to the telephone and dialed the Arrondos' number. A man's voice answered "Hello."

Disguising his own voice as much as possible and striving for his best possible pronunciation, Frank asked *"Está Rosa allí?"*

"Momentito," Mr. Arrondo answered. It had worked! Frank waited. A few seconds later he heard Rosa's voice say, "Hello."

Frank spoke low. "Don't say anything. This is Frank." He caught a slight gasp at the other end. Speaking more rapidly, he continued, "I'm sorry—I've got to tell you I'm sorry." He stumbled for words. "When can I—" There was some kind of noise at the other end, a confusion of sharp, quick voices. The phone went dead.

He listened, and then put the phone back and lay down on the sofa. He was so tired, more than tired. All at once, he found himself weeping. This was something he had not done for years. He dabbed at his eyes with a handkerchief, but he made no effort to stop.

"Damn it!" he exclaimed. The doorbell was ringing. Hastily drying his eyes, he smoothed his hair and walked to the door and opened it. "Good evening, Dr. Bowman," he said in slight surprise. "Won't you come in?"

"Thank you, I will," Dr. Bowman said.

"Have a seat."

"Thanks." Dr. Bowman sat down on the sofa, and Frank

sank into a deep chair facing it. "I hadn't seen you since you left the hospital. I wanted to make sure everything is all right. How are you feeling?"

"As well as I can expect," Frank replied. "I still get tired easily, but except for this little souvenir"—he touched the scar on his cheek—"I'm all right."

"How about Rosa?"

"I wish I knew." Frank fell silent. Should he spill over? Dr. Bowman had been kind the night of the accident; he had come to the hospital several times. Why not? "I've tried to reach her," Frank said at last, "but her family runs interference. I don't blame them."

"Neither do I," said Dr. Bowman with a half-smile. Frank looked startled, then smiled uncertainly. "But I'd like to help if I could. May I ask like a busybody—why are you so anxious to see her? If I'm not poking my nose . . ."

"There's no mystery," Frank said. "I want to tell her I'm sorry about that wreck."

"Will telling her change anything?" Dr. Bowman asked.

"No, but I want to tell her anyway. And I suppose I want to give her the chance to spit in my teeth or order me out of the room or do anything else I deserve. Then I'll have a cleansed feeling about it all and be at peace with the world. Oh, let's not get psychological and slip over into all that rot!"

"Agreed," Dr. Bowman said. "Let's not. But one thing—can I help? I'm planning to see Mr. Arrondo soon. I wanted to sound him out on some vague ideas I have about broadening the base of the church and, if you like, I could talk with him and see if I could arrange for you to see him. Then you could ask about seeing Rosa."

"Thank you," said Frank, with a touch of coldness. "I got in this fool mess by myself and I'll have to get myself out of it."

"I can't help?" Dr. Bowman asked. "I'd probably louse it up

if I tried to. Speaking of Mr. Arrondo, that reminds me. I suppose you know about the fracas between the Omegas and the Stalwarts Saturday night?"

"It's all over the school," Frank said. "And I saw the Omegas at the Shack a little while before it started."

"The immediate trouble seems to have blown over," Dr. Bowman continued. "The police called in the leaders of both groups and laid down the law to them. Neither side made any formal charges, so that's how it stands. But I'm thinking more of the long-range thing. The Stalwarts are pretty certain to drift into delinquency if someone doesn't do something."

"How about the Omegas?" Frank asked. "Rumor has it that they're doing some neat tire-slashing."

"That's true," Dr. Bowman agreed, "but in general the passion of the Omegas seems to be snobbery, and there's no law against that. It might land you in hell but not in jail. The Stalwarts, though, are likely to get involved in definite crimes. I'm not sure, but this round of petty housebreakings and robberies that Blanton's been having lately—well, I suspect that the Stalwarts may have a hand there."

Dr. Bowman paused and looked at Frank.

"What did you have in mind?" Frank asked.

"It's still in the daydreaming stage," Dr. Bowman said, "but I'd like to see Trinity Episcopal Church invite the Stalwarts to meet in the parish house."

Frank sat up a little straighter. "How would that set with the members of the church?"

"Well, very poorly with a lot of them."

"Poorly with most of them, I'd think," Frank said. "I can imagine the idea would spread consternation throughout Oak Hill. They'd think you were inviting in the inmates of a reform school to deflower their daughters."

"I know," Dr. Bowman said, smiling quizzically, "but I'd like to see Trinity make a definite effort to attract the people who actually live in the neighborhood. The first and experimental stage, however, would be to get the Stalwarts to meet at the parish house and to encourage them to join the YPF and be active in it. I'm not going to go ahead on this until I get a green light from the YPF itself. Their attitude toward 'outsiders' is the crucial thing." Dr. Bowman stopped a moment, then smiled again. "Frank, how about helping me do it?"

"Church politics?" Frank asked.

"Yes," Dr. Bowman agreed. "I want you to join the YPF and use your influence—you have a lot of it, you know—to win them over to this idea of broadening the base."

Frank seemed to be thinking hard. When he spoke at last, there was no edge of flippancy. "I don't know what to do. I think your attitude toward the Stalwarts is wonderful, but how can I get mixed up in the YPF? I'm not a Christian."

"Are you sure?" Dr. Bowman asked.

"I was baptized, if that's what you mean—but it didn't take. I'll tell you what I believe. I believe in the Golden Rule even if I do nothing about it. I believe that God is theoretically possible, but I've had no dealings with Him if He does exist. I think the story about Christ is very beautiful, and I wish everything people said about Him were true, but I don't see any strong evidence that it is. So if you call me a Christian, you're stretching the word so far that it doesn't mean anything."

Dr. Bowman's forehead wrinkled. "If you have intellectual problems about the existence of God and the significance of Christ, perhaps I could lend you some books I have," he said.

"Thank you," Frank said. "It isn't that. I've never doubted that it's intellectually respectable to be a Christian, just as it is to be a scientific humanist or a Marxist. My trouble is a different kind. If what people say about Christ is true, it ought to make a difference. Christians should be different from other people.

There ought to be a different quality to their lives. If I could see that difference, I would think that the weight of evidence was on the side of Christianity. But—if you'll excuse my dogmatic way of putting things—I can't see any difference. On the street, in the classroom, everywhere, the Christian and the agnostic seem to behave pretty much the same. *That's* why I'm a skeptic. Show me some church with a ten per cent production rate of saints, and I'll look up and pay attention."

"Maybe saints aren't as visible as you seem to think," Dr. Bowman said. "*Life* and *Look* seldom write them up while they're alive. But you're right, of course. There's an old platitude, 'Christianity isn't taught; it's caught.' Of course, that's an oversimplification; but, by and large, it's true. Christianity is something that's communicated from people who are on fire with Christ. I'm convinced that the Church is quite literally the Body of Christ. That means that it isn't at all like a country club or a PTA or Rotary. It's a unique thing. The power and possibilities potential in each parish are unlimited, since God is the source of strength. For those potentialities to become real, though, each parish has got to pull as far away as possible from the 'club for nice people on Sunday morning' concept and move toward making the Church all-inclusive. Then I think you'll begin to see your saints, in the actual laboratory of rubbing shoulders with all sorts of people under the church roof. Then you'd begin to get the kind of proof you want . . . I'm sorry, Frank, I find as I get older I have more of a tendency to sermonize."

"I'm rather glad you did," Frank said slowly. "I suppose that as a conscientious agnostic I take this religion thing more seriously, say, than such potential saints as Bill Pendleton, the president of the Omegas. He's one of your faithful, isn't he? I'm afraid I'm an all-or-nothinger. Christianity is either moonshine or it's true. If it's true, it's more important than everything else in the world put together. But," he smiled again, "I'm waiting to see some proof—of the kind I want."

"While waiting, how about helping to furnish some of the proof?" Dr. Bowman asked.

"You mean, by joining the YPF?" Frank laughed. "Are all the Episcopal clergy as Machiavellian as you are?" He paused. "Well, let me think about it."

And so they left it. After a bit more desultory conversation, Dr. Bowman departed. By now weariness was flooding through Frank. He went upstairs and lay down and fell asleep while still in his clothes.

Next morning between breakfast and school he found time to write a short letter and mail it:

DEAR MR. AND MRS. ARRONDO:

I was a selfish fool. I don't deserve to see you or Rosa again, but will you at least let me come and tell the three of you this? Then you can decide whether you ever want to see me again.

Sincerely yours,
FRANK BUELL

Three days went by with no answer. A couple of times he saw Rosa at school. She was always at some distance, and from her manner it was clear that she was trying to avoid him.

When Frank came home Thursday afternoon, a letter was waiting for him. He opened it and read:

DEAR MR. BUELL:

Rosa is the only child we have. I ask you to keep away from her.

CARLOS ARRONDO

A surge of anger went through Frank. It was true that he had been at fault, but he had manfully admitted this. He had crawled on his belly, so to speak, and eaten dirt. Who did Carlos Arrondo think he was?

"Watch yourself," Frank said to himself, becoming aware of his reaction. "Oak Hill is taking over."

He brooded all evening on the impasse and in the morning made a last desperate move. He went to the office of Miss Scoggins, the principal's secretary. "Yes?" she said sharply. She of course knew all about Frank.

Frank smiled with a touch of helplessness. "Can you help me?" he asked. "I've been trying to get in touch with Rosa Arrondo to ask her pardon, her forgiveness—"

"I should think you would!" Miss Scoggins interrupted. "That poor girl."

"You are right," Frank said earnestly. "I don't deserve to see her again. But I want to see her again, just once. That's where I need your help. Do you think there's any way you could get this to her?" With a trusting smile he handed a sealed envelope to her.

Miss Scoggins studied the envelope and then studied Frank's face. The spoiled young man had shown enough decency to acknowledge his fault, and (this was not in her conscious mind) his wavy hair and blue eyes were very appealing.

"It's quite irregular," she said at last, "but this once . . ."

"Thank you so much," said Frank, smiling gratefully at her.

"Remember, it's just this one time," Miss Scoggins warned.

"I'll remember," Frank promised. "Thank you again."

The remainder of the day passed very slowly. When the closing bell rang, Frank hastened to the Shack to see whether his note had achieved results. He sat in the farthest booth.

"Anybody coming to meet you?" Jerry asked.

"Hope so," Frank said. "Meanwhile, a Coke and hamburger, medium rare, no onion."

Frank was almost through his hamburger before Rosa came.

"Hello," she said as she sat down beside him.

"Hamburger and Coke?" he asked.

"Yes—if we can have them quick."

"I'll tell Jerry to hurry." Frank went to the front to give the order and came back to the booth. "They'll be ready right away. How many minutes can I have with you?"

"I'm late already," Rosa said. "I'll have to leave in ten minutes, or Mama and Daddy . . ."

"Fair enough," Frank said, taking his wrist watch off and putting it in front of Rosa. "Ten minutes maximum."

Jerry came over with the hamburger and Coke. "Hello, Rosa," he said. "Anything else?"

"No, thanks," Frank answered. Jerry left them.

"Do you know why I wanted to see you?" Frank asked.

"I think so," Rosa said.

"I want to ask you whether you can forgive a fool who almost killed you."

"I'm not the one to forgive you," Rosa said. "But I've prayed to Him to help you."

"Let's leave *Him* out of the picture. Have *you* forgiven me?"

"There's nothing to forgive. You were very upset, and you drank too much. You risked your life as much as mine, and I came out of it a lot easier than you did." She glanced at his jagged scar, and a troubled look passed over her face.

"Then it's all right?"

"It's all right with me."

"But not with your father and mother?"

"Not with them."

"They told you not to see me?"

"And I mustn't after today. I thought I ought to see you just this once—I wanted to, I had to—so you'd understand."

"Do you always do what your parents tell you to?" Frank asked in honest surprise.

"No, I don't," Rosa said gravely. "But I try to. Shouldn't I?"

Frank fell silent. A vast longing filled his heart, longing for a home like Rosa's in which there were parents who deserved respect and took respect for granted, parents one could obey without hypocrisy. How great a chasm was fixed between him and Rosa. Not so much of social class, though that was there, but the greater and well-nigh unbridgeable chasm between those who have a real family and those who merely live with people who happen to be relatives by blood or marriage.

"I've got to go now," Rosa said. She started to rise.

Frank picked up his watch and put it back on. "Ten seconds to go," he said. "Will they ever let me see you again?"

Rosa thought a while, then spoke seriously. "I don't know. Leave them alone now. We'll have to wait and see."

She was standing by the table. Frank rose. "Thank you for the ten minutes and twenty seconds," he said.

"Thanks for the hamburger," Rosa replied. As she brushed past him she added, so low he hardly caught it, "Let's hope."

8

CAUSES AND EFFECTS

THE FLURRY of public excitement over the incident at the Shack soon died down. After all, it was tame and unbloody compared to the movies which constantly showed teen-age life as it really is. Nothing very tangible resulted except that the high school PTA held a panel discussion on "The Sources of Juvenile Delinquency," and Mr. Crews, the senior counsellor, composed an eighteen-page memorandum urging the legalization and regulation of the Stalwarts and Omegas and left it on the desk of the principal, Mr. Johnston. Finally, the *Blanton Daily Times* ran an editorial on the responsibility of parents, church, and school, and four letters-to-the-editor advocated the old-fashioned woodshed.

Even though public impact of the incident was trivial and fleeting, it had a more powerful effect on the relations of Steve Hadley and Tom Bowman. This happened a few days after the Omegas had made a second and successful attempt to initiate Steve into their brotherhood. Tom was morally sure that Betty was secretly wearing Steve's pin. This was all right with Tom, but at the same time some devil nagged him on to sow a few harmless nettles along the path of true love.

Tom had long since discovered in the course of their many quarrels that the surest way to drive Steve into a heavy and helpless fury was to turn Socratic and ask innocent questions.

This time the two of them were in Tom's room, ostensibly to review for a test in American Problems. After half an hour of desultorily quizzing each other, Tom closed the book and asked in an offhand way, "I'm interested in the Omegas. Why did you join?"

Steve fell into the trap. "Would you like to join?" he asked eagerly. "I'll speak to the president—"

"So you admit you belong," Tom said with a touch of sternness. "You don't even plead the Fifth Amendment. You admit you belong to an outlawed organization, in plain disregard of the rules and regulations of Blanton Senior High School."

"Oh, that bull," Steve said. "Mr. Johnston and everybody else know about the Omegas. They just keep their consciences pure by passing rules and then looking the other way. Mr. Johnston's nephew is the secretary."

"An interesting item of information," Tom said. "The corruption spreads deeper and farther than I knew." Steve seemed on the point of speaking, but Tom went gravely on. "Let us consider this matter systematically. If you've joined an illegal and banned organization, it must be for weighty reasons which you can rationally defend. What are these reasons?"

"Aw, there's nothing to it," Steve said uneasily. "They're just a bunch of guys you can have fun with. That's all they are."

"I see. That makes it clearer," Tom said judiciously. He paused. "A bunch of guys who possess a bit of Greek jewelry to demonstrate they're a bunch of guys, and who prove they're a bunch of guys by turning cars over and scampering away from the police. I see."

The familiar red flush was mounting up from Steve's neck to his ears. "Look here, Tom," he said angrily, "I don't buy that line. The Stalwarts asked for what they got."

"The first step toward a lifetime of antisocial behavior," Tom said earnestly, "is to pay criminals the compliment of imitating their practices."

"Cut it out, cut it out," Steve said in exasperation.

"Let's continue to look at this matter rationally," Tom said in a soothing voice. "If you didn't join the Omega Alphas in order to participate in their antisocial activities, there must be some other and compelling reason. Is that not logical?"

"O.K., have it your own way."

"Splendid. Let us now consider other possible motives. I have been told that membership in the Omegas is equivalent to being listed in the social directory; that it proves you've really made it; that you can rub shoulders with the rich, the ancient families of Blanton, the certified all-American one-hundred-percent thoroughbred livestock—"

"That American Problems stuff! Look here, Tom, they're just a bunch of guys like anybody else, guys that have fun together—"

"Until death do them part. Brothers to the dying gasp."

Something from the initiation ritual stirred in Steve's memory, and he became more earnest. "That isn't anything to joke about. With most guys it's friends today and to hell with you tomorrow. Not the Omegas! You can joke about the brotherhood, but it's the real thing. You find out after you join. Why, after we finish high school, if one of us gets in trouble and needs a helping friend—"

"I see, I see. This is very interesting," Tom agreed. "A vast network of Omegas, reaching in due time into the higher echelons of business and government. I see you, Steve, a prosperous businessman at the age of forty, experiencing a little difficulty with Uncle Sam over income tax matters. The scene is very vivid. You appear with apprehension before the tax examiner. Then comes the moment of recognition. Omega meets Omega. Pins are secretly displayed. Case dismissed."

"You're in one of your moods. Let's hit this book again," Steve pleaded.

"As you say," Tom amicably agreed. He thumbed through

the chapter on which they were going to be examined. "What was the American divorce rate when this book was written?"

"Do you think we have to remember all those figures?" Steve asked anxiously.

"It's very important. Marriage is the foundation of society. Anyway, I suppose the rate's gone up since the book was published . . . Steve, did you join the Omegas so you could pin Betty?"

"What business is that of yours?"

"Just an impersonal curiosity. Did you think she'd flap her angelic wings and soar away if you didn't pin her down?"

Steve didn't answer. After a moment he picked up his copy of the American Problems text and arose. "I'll take my chances on this test. So long, Tom."

"Good-bye for the nonce," Tom said. Steve walked from the room.

As quarrels went, it was a mild one, and Tom knew that next day things would be all right again. Their friendship had survived much more intense verbal exchanges, not to speak of a considerable number of fist fights in their earlier days. The only thing different this time was that Tom could not summon up any joy by gloating over Steve's discomfiture. Some devil had made him try to confuse and irritate Steve, and he had merely hurt him. In one way, Tom heartily envied his victim. At least Steve knew what he was going to do with his life. Steve was clearly and happily following in his father's footsteps. After high school, he would go to a college with a good department of business education, and then he would decide what kind of business he would go into. Steve's life could be predictably charted. Tom's could not. Once he had known, had known with a romantic certainty engendered by a vast familiarity with science fiction magazines. Courses in science had modified his ideas. Memorizing the Latin names of microscopic creatures and the bones of vertebrates had not endeared biology to him, and the mathematical abstractions of physics seemed impossibly remote from the old boyish dreams of space-ships bound for Mars. Tom was beginning to suspect that he wasn't a born scientist, but he hadn't found anything he liked better. A spotty and fluctuating academic record reflected his indecision.

Meanwhile he was always rummaging through the family's bookshelves and reading almost anything he found there—even science books—in preference to studying any textbook. Very often he preferred to be in his room or wandering the labyrinthine byways of Blanton, not consciously thinking of anything. When serious thoughts did come into his mind, it was curious how often they related to the day that he and Betty went kite-flying. More than once, as he sat restlessly in his room or aimlessly roamed the streets, he found himself reciting loud enough for his own ears:

> Stranger, say a prayer and know
> It is later than you think.

Stranger . . . say a prayer. Stranger on the face of the earth, going you know not where, say a prayer. It is later than you think.

9

THE MICROCOSM

As MR. JOHNSTON pushed aside his morning mail and looked at the stack of teachers' memoranda on his desk, he had to admit that he was feeling discouraged. Eighteen years ago, when he took on the dire burdens of the principalship, he had been sure that Blanton Senior High could be molded into a harmonious little commonwealth of co-operation and democracy and that it would then become the model for the community of Blanton. He saw now that in reality the antagonisms and prejudices and blindnesses of the community, as well as its occasional virtues, were faithfully reflected in the students of Blanton Senior High. The school had not remade the city.

Had he been naïve when he began with such glowing hopes? Had he asked the impossible? Or had he merely expected things to change sooner than was possible? Perhaps there was no reason for discouragement. He must be more patient. Rome was not built in a day.

Mr. Johnston picked up a neatly typed document which was bound in a gray folder. "The Omega Alphas, the Stalwarts, and Related Problems," the cover read. The memo that John Crews had promised to prepare. Mr. Johnston sighed. Excellent man, John Crews, doing a good job as counsellor. Mr. Johnston sighed again. He preferred not to think about the Omega Alphas and the Stalwarts. He knew without reading the memo that Mr. Crews would urge that both organizations be brought above ground and legalized ("with the elimination of any anti-democratic restrictive membership clauses") and that each be integrated as far as possible within the life of the school. Fine in theory, Mr. Johnston was willing to concede, but could one imagine the *Blanton Daily Times* taking a similarly benign view after its recent thunderings on the subject of juvenile delinquency and the dangers of coddling? Even the PTA was a dubious ally.

Mr. Johnston put down the memo and resolved he would read it when he was feeling better. He picked up the next document, a much thicker one, labeled "Interim Curricular Recommendations." This report, the fruit of more than a year's work by a special committee of teachers, administrators, and community leaders, promised further anxieties. He could almost have written the first paragraph without reading it. He glanced at the beginning. Yes, it began as he was sure it would: "In an age increasingly dependent on scientific and technological advances for sheer survival, the function of the public schools. . . ." He read quickly on.

There was discreet tapping at the door. "Come in," he called. Miss Scoggins, as pinch-faced as ever, came inside and hastily closed the door. "It's about the Greenwood girl," she said in a disapproving voice.

Mr. Johnston nodded. "Is Mr. Greenwood on the way over?" he asked.

"And Mrs. Greenwood."

Mr. Johnston's spirits sank lower. "Show them in when they come," he said.

"Yes, Mr. Johnston." Miss Scoggins turned to leave, but as she opened the door she wheeled around and said savagely, "Some girls need to be whipped! That's what's wrong with this school. You never whip anybody." With these words she made her exit and closed the door noisily.

Mr. Johnston sat back in astonishment. Ordinarily Miss Scoggins was his alter ego. She thought his thoughts. He could give her a two-sentence summary of a letter, and she would turn it into two pages, faultless even to the most minute turn of a phrase. In the fourteen years she had served him, she had seemed completely in sympathy with the school policy, which was to assume that anything a student did wrong was probably the fault of the home, or else of the community, or conceivably (though rarely) of the school, but never of the child. The child, in the official philosophy of Blanton Senior High, was infinitely plastic. Like modeling clay, he could be molded into any shape desired.

What now astonished Mr. Johnston was that he was so little shocked by Miss Scoggins' outburst. It seemed to express something he had not dared admit to himself. For a few instants his mind created a series of vivid pictures, and he found them charming. He saw himself armed with a stout birch rod. A succession of students filed into his office, one at a time. Not the Greenwood girl—he felt genuinely sorry for her—but the bright loafers and the budding rapists and the perpetual troublemakers—he saw them appearing one at a time. In his mental ear he heard the emphatic swish of the birch rod and could feel it quiver in his hand as it made resounding contact with the solid and sensitive flesh. He remembered the remark of a visiting English schoolmaster who had been badgered into appearing before the PTA. During the question-and-answer period some teacher had asked, "If a pupil asked you *why* he should do an assignment, what would you say?" The Englishman had smiled mockingly and answered in a clipped Oxford voice, "I'd whip that child."

"I'm turning into a black reactionary," Mr. Johnston said, and he laughed to himself. His brief play of imagination had refreshed him. Almost light-hearted, he picked up the curriculum report once more and started reading it. His attention soon wandered. The report sounded so familiar. After all, he had attended most of the committee meetings.

Once the matter of curriculum had seemed very simple—"real life experiences," meeting the "felt needs" of the child, etc. Translated into terms of courses, this meant cutting down four years of Latin to two and advising as few students as possible to take it; steering students into Spanish instead of French, and social studies instead of Spanish; the multiplication of shop and vocational and home economics classes, the institution of a required course in driver training, and an elective in "the Art of Living" (dating, marriage, shopping, child rearing). Mathematics of the more austere kind continued to be offered "for the exceptional students" (at this time "exceptional" still meant exceptional), but business arithmetic was recommended for the common student. The pure sciences, such as physics and chemistry, were praised and admired at Blanton Senior High, but less often elected. The college admission boards had muttered and threatened, but there were always enough colleges to accept the Blanton High product, and Blanton High had stuck to its principles.

That was all in what Mr. Johnston called the "first period," when the emphasis was on a combination of social adjustment, self-expression, and the practicalities of daily life. A number of courses in painting and music also dated from that period. But hot and cold wars had brought a change. People discovered that America's various enemies and rivals, benighted though they were, knew what they were fighting for, and many young Americans didn't. From this discovery came another required course at Blanton High, "American Problems." It was designed to teach patriotism and enlightened social attitudes simultaneously.

Now the third period was in full swing. It could be called

the space-age era. The pressure was for mathematics and not of the business arithmetic kind; for physics and more physics; for English composition; even for foreign languages wherewith to make contact with other portions of the human race. The report which Mr. Johnston was now twisting in his fingers reflected all the anxieties of the new era. Mr. Johnston found himself a house divided. He had lost his old certainties about the purposes of education; he was willing to admit to himself that "self-expression" and "life-adjustment" are not enough, but he was not by any means completely converted to the growing demand everywhere that the emphasis be on straight subject matter.

There was a crisp knock at the door. "Come in," he called.

Miss Scoggins slipped in and quickly closed the door. "They're here," she said in a hollow voice. "And the girl's with them."

"Show them in," Mr. Johnston said, trying to make it sound quiet and self-assured. Miss Scoggins departed.

Helen Greenwood, Mr. Johnston thought to himself. One of the quieter girls in Blanton Senior High. Her name seldom came up at faculty and counsellors' meetings, for she was not sufficiently outstanding in either a good or bad way to attract attention. Her work stayed pretty much on a steady "B" level with an occasional "A," and she was no discipline problem. Not a bad looking girl. Actually, she would be rather attractive if she had more confidence, but she seemed shy and uncertain by temperament. She was never the center of anything. Mr. Johnston always thought of her in connection with more popular and colorful students. At parties, or when students gathered in informal clusters, Helen would be on the fringes, eagerly but uncertainly joining in the laughter, hoping to be noticed. In short, she was as far removed as one could imagine from the bold adventuress or female libertine.

A superficial observer might have asserted she would be the last to get into trouble, but Mr. Johnston was not superficial.

He had been through all this before—it happened every year with one or two and sometimes with considerably more. He knew that it was the Helens of this world, uncertain of themselves and perpetually seeking reassurance, who have the weakest defenses.

"Come in, won't you?" Mr. Johnston invited as the door opened.

The Greenwoods entered his office and looked around at its tidy order of desk, bookcases, and filing cabinets. "Have a seat, please." Mr. Johnston pulled up a chair beside the leather sofa and sat down. The Greenwoods, with Helen in the middle, took the sofa.

"I suppose we might as well get down to business," Mr. Greenwood said. He was a man in his early fifties, his dark brown hair still hardly touched with gray. A strikingly handsome man with a severe, driving strength in his face, he was one of the city's most respected lawyers and, like his wife, a staunch friend of the public schools.

"You know the story," he said. "There's no use repeating it. It's the same story you must hear all the time. The question is— what should we do?"

There was a silence which Mr. Johnston finally broke. "Marriage is out of the question?" he asked gently.

"The boy flatly denies that he's the one."

"Then you've talked to him?"

"Yes. He's one of the pious songbirds down at the Episcopal church. Helen met him in the choir. I talked with him last night. He denied everything. I know he was lying, but I couldn't give him a lie-detector test."

Helen had been sitting with her face frozen and expressionless. A flash of anger now passed across it, and she burst out vehemently, "I wouldn't marry *him!*"

"Not even if he asked you to?" Mr. Johnston asked, still in his gentle voice.

"Never," Helen said. Her voice was rising. Mrs. Greenwood reached over and patted her hand uneasily.

"Why not? If he wanted you to?"

"He doesn't love me. I don't love him. I don't think I *ever* did—"

Mr. Johnston hastily interrupted. "We don't need to go into all that. It's water over the dam now. We're trying to decide what's best for your future."

"I don't care about my future," Helen said, then froze into the same dumb silence.

"Mrs. Greenwood and Helen and I have talked this all over," Mr. Greenwood said. "Marriage is out of the question—"

"Why did this have to happen to us?" Mrs. Greenwood interrupted bitterly. "We've done our best to avoid the usual mistakes that people make in bringing up children. We've really tried and done our best."

"Of course we have," Mr. Greenwood said in a low voice to his wife. "But we came here to see Mr. Johnston about the practical plans we'll have to make now."

Mrs. Greenwood took out a handkerchief and wiped her eyes with determination. Her mouth was twisting, but it was soon under control, and a rigid calm returned to her face.

"What we came to see you about," Mr. Greenwood explained, "are the practical things to be done. You must know how to handle these cases. Is there any way Helen can go away somewhere and have everything taken care of—the adoption, I mean—and what can she do so she won't lose out on her schooling?"

"I'll answer the last question first. I can arrange for her to take correspondence courses in her high school subjects from the state university. If she passes them, she'll get full credit for the year's work and can enter as a senior here in the fall."

"That's a relief," Mrs. Greenwood said. "But the other thing—"

"I can't arrange it myself, but I know the person you should
see." He scribbled on a piece of paper. "Here's the name and
address of the social worker who handles these cases. Tell him
the whole story. He'll arrange for Helen to go off to some city
—you can tell people she's had to leave for a change of climate
or something of that sort—and he'll fix it up so she has a place
to stay where she'll be looked after, and nobody from Blanton
will discover her."

"And the—adoption?"

"He'll help arrange that, too."

Mr. and Mrs. Greenwood glanced at each other. "Then that's
all there is to it?" Mr. Greenwood asked.

"Unless you think of something else," Mr. Johnston said.
"Just see this social worker. Helen can pick up her books when
the arrangements are all made for her to go away for a while.
I'll send a memo to her teachers then, saying she had to drop
out for reasons of health. There's one thing—I'm afraid it's
going to cost a great deal—room and board, hospital expenses . . ."

"I can take care of that," Mr. Greenwood said. "Well, thank
you. I don't know what we would have done if you hadn't
helped."

"Thank you so much," said Mrs. Greenwood.

"I'm glad I could help," the principal replied. On an impulse
he took Helen's hands in his. "Remember, dear," he said, "this
isn't the end of the world. Plenty of the girls you know have done
the same thing. You happened to be one of the unlucky ones.
If you learn from experience, it won't be the end of your life
but a new beginning. I'm counting on you. I hope to see you in
the senior class next fall."

He helped Helen to her feet. She smiled uncertainly but
gratefully. "I'll try. I'll try to do my best," she promised. "You're
all so good to me."

10

ENDS AND MEANS AND PEOPLE AND PARENTS

TOM HAD BEEN planning to hunt Frank out and talk with him as his father had suggested, but with Tom, intention was one thing and deed another. "Closer to Skid Row every day," he sometimes told himself sternly. Certainly this school year was the one in which he had revealed the least ability to make up his mind to do something and then do it. "A natural derelict and parasite on society," he added to himself, somehow enjoying the accumulation of abusive terms.

It was the last day of school before Christmas, and the students had just streamed out of the combined gymnasium and assembly hall where there had been a program of Christmas music and a Nativity pageant. Outside, the low sun was dull in a nest of vague, dark clouds. The snows of recent weeks had melted into mud, and the mud was half frozen into rough patches on lawns. A few fluttering flakes of snow descended here and there.

"Tom!" a voice called. Tom snapped out of his reverie. "Hello, Frank," he said.

Frank came over and fell into step beside him. "I want to talk with you. Are you busy now?"

Feeling a little guilty that he hadn't taken the initiative

himself, Tom hastened to say, "Not doing anything. How about
the Shack?"

When they got to the Shack and looked inside, they discovered the booths were jampacked, and a double line of students
was up by the soda fountain. They looked at each other and
continued down the street. In the downtown section, the sound
of Christmas carols assailed them from three or four directions
as the big department stores competed in musical piety, and in
the course of this short stroll they had their choice of five Santa
Clauses. "A flanking attack," Frank called it. "We're caught,
Tom. If Christ doesn't get us, Santa Claus will."

"Christ is supposed to have got me when I was baptized, and
again when I was confirmed. I sometimes wonder . . . Maybe
I'm like a mouse that's escaped a few feet from the cat, but the
cat is watching all the time. Oh, all this doesn't add up much.
I guess I don't have much sense of direction."

Frank looked far ahead. "I think I've got a sense of direction,
but it leads to an early grave or a cell in some correctional institution. I'm the prize exhibit of the death wish, and I want to be
a Samson and pull the columns of the temple down so I'll have
some company."

By now they were on the North Side. Frank looked around
with the fascination which he always felt here. A kind of desolation had come to the familiar streets. Fewer clotheslines were
strung outside. There weren't as many children playing in the
streets as he remembered.

"Let's go in here," Frank suggested.

Tom recognized the Greasy Spoon. "I've been here before,"
he said, stepping inside.

Sid Pruitt and four companions came in the front door and
brushed past them. "Hi, Frank," Sid said.

"Hi." The five newcomers moved on through a door into
what must have been a back room.

"Do you know him well?" Tom asked.

"I wish I knew him better," Frank said. "He comes of a tenant farmer background, I know—I mean, his father does—but I think the family came to Blanton before he was born. His father's on relief half the time—hits the bottle hard. It all sounds like one of these model cases from a sociology textbook. Sid's already been in juvenile court a couple of times. What fascinates me about him is his ability to lead that gang of his. He's not the biggest or strongest one in it, but he's got something the others haven't."

"You sound like a social scientist!" Tom exclaimed.

"Here, let's sit down here," Frank said, moving toward one of the booths. "What would you like?"

"Tell the truth, I don't seem to be hungry."

"Tell the truth, I'm not either."

"Let's not make it a compulsive ritual. Let's assert our individuality by not eating. Let's roam around the sidewalks of the North Side a bit."

"Agreed."

They went outside and began strolling down the street. "I'd been meaning to hunt you out," Tom said after a time, "but I don't do anything I plan nowadays. I wanted to see if you'd be interested in coming to YPF. Dad says he mentioned it to you. I could come for you in the car."

Frank laughed, almost boisterously. "Thanks for the delicate courtesy," he said. "Yes, I did lose my license after that smashup in front of your house, and the judge says it'll stay lost till I'm twenty-one."

"Then how about it? The next meeting is the second Sunday after Christmas."

"Maybe . . . I'll let you know." Frank's face was working. Finally he said, "I need to talk with somebody. I've tried this stiff upper lip stuff long enough."

Tom waited patiently. Frank's face was contorted with an inner intensity and suffering. At last it took on a forced smile. "I was about to spill over on you about families and that sort of stuff," he said. "Maybe I will yet. But Christmas is coming, so let's let it ride for now." Tom began to be a little uneasy. There was a stormy intensity behind Frank's light manner. You couldn't tell what was coming next. At the same time, Frank was interesting. You could predict Steve, but not Frank.

"Let's talk about the Church," Frank said, walking more briskly. "I told your father that as far as I'm concerned, Christianity is like one of the better Walt Disney full-length fairy-tale features—maybe I didn't put it quite that way. He invited me to come to YPF anyway. I've been thinking about it and have arrived at what is probably an untenable position. It won't hurt my agnostic conscience to rub against pious shoulders, so long as they don't object. If the YPF is doing things worth doing, and I'm interested in them, why should I let a little question of credal belief stand in the way?"

"Deeds, not creeds?" Tom asked. "Dad would probably say that's a half-truth."

"If it's a half-truth, it's enough to keep me going for the present," Frank said. "I'd settle for a quarter-truth or an eighth-truth."

"Then you'll come to the next YPF meeting?"

"Probably. But I'll phone you . . . I like your father's idea of broadening the church out to take in everybody who's willing to come. From what he says, he wants it to be a real cross section of the town like the schools. Of course, most of the chummy stuff and 'democratic spirit' in school is double talk to make the teachers feel good. Oh, why can't I give the school credit? They are at least trying to create a sense of community there."

"It isn't easy in the church," Tom said. "In school, people can have a casual, superficial relation, so it's easier to go through the motions of accepting everybody. But somehow in a church it's all or nothing. You've got to be prepared to accept people completely and be accepted completely, or the whole thing becomes a masquerade."

"I can see that," Frank said. "What I can't see, to tell the truth, is why your father's holding back. He wants to bring in the people who actually live in the neighborhood. Why doesn't he go to their homes and simply invite them to come? He wants the church to sponsor the Stalwarts. Why doesn't he see Sid Pruitt and talk it over with him? He wants to work the Stalwart members into YPF activities. That's simple—invite them to come."

"We're kindred spirits," Tom said. "Shake." They stopped walking and solemnly shook hands. "I'm great at telling other people they should move faster," Tom continued, as he resumed walking. "I can be as moral and absolute as they come when it's somebody else who has to do the doing. I've often talked to Dad just the way you've been talking."

"As one prig to another," Frank said, "let me ask some questions. Or one question. Seriously, why is your Dad moving so slowly? I'm not exactly infallible in faith or morals, but my understanding of Christianity is that it's a sort of life-and-death religion, and Christians aren't supposed to play it safe."

Tom grinned. "I said just about the same thing to Dad once. I can't remember what his answer was. I guess it didn't convince me. But to be fair to Dad, I think he looks at it this way. He wants to build solidly. He could move faster than the congregation and vestry are psychologically prepared to move, and pretty soon there'd be a big blowup that would leave things worse than they were. I think he believes that if he and the vestry and congregation can all move forward at about the same pace, any progress that's made is more likely to be permanent."

"I suppose so," said Frank doubtfully.

"Look at the senior and junior wardens," said Tom, warming to the subject. "Both the salt of the earth. But salt is better as a preservative than as a fertilizer. The senior warden, Mr. Jenkins, staged a walkout from the church a few years ago when a boy who'd been in reform school came back and attended the services. Mr. Jenkins is back in the fold now and has the highest lay post in the parish, but he isn't exactly a wild-eyed radical. Neither is the junior warden, Steve Hadley's father. He came into the church after fighting the idea of joining for a long time—he'd had too much 'church,' he said, when he was a boy—and now that he's in, he's thrown himself into church work. But he's cautious by nature and wants to think things over a few years before doing anything about them."

Frank looked thoughtful. "I think the trouble with me is that I want my Christians to be dressed in togas and sandals and go around all day with spiritual songs on their lips. The practical and psychological necessities of parish life—the political calculations, the manipulations—somehow they don't seem to belong."

"They don't," Tom agreed. "But as Dad sees it—his long-range strategy involves getting a Spanish-speaking curate. That requires two things: some Spanish-speakers in the congregation and the willingness of the vestry to move in that direction. So Dad has figured it out that what he needs is a demonstration of the good results that would come from broadening out. That's why he's so anxious to get the Stalwarts into the YPF and bring in other young people from the North Side. The church would be doing a useful job in trying to control juvenile delinquency; at the same time, the YPF would be a little laboratory, and if things went well, the vestry and congregation would be more willing to take chances. He's really counting on our age group to be a little more daring, maybe more idealistic, if you want to put it that way, so we can set the example for our elders. Quite an assignment."

"Agreed," said Frank. He sighed. "I wish I weren't such a rigid absolutist. That's the trouble with being an agnostic. You can't ever take your morals off and relax a while. All the time you have to be proving to yourself and other people that you're more Christian than the Christians. I'm sure your Dad's approach is more likely to get results than mine."

"What's yours?" Tom asked.

"If I could imagine myself in one of those round collars, and it takes a bit of imagining, I suppose I would barge ahead, invite every Tom, Dick, and Harry, and if the vestry and congregation didn't like it, I'd stand up at the high altar and pronounce a solemn curse on the whole crew, then shake the dust off the soles of my shoes and depart. I know it's impractical."

Tom laughed. "You may see Dad doing it yet. If he gets his dander up, he can be awfully stubborn and drastic. I ought to know."

Frank glanced at his watch. "Better head back now," he said.

"Let me drive you home," Tom offered. "The car's over at the rectory."

It was almost dark now, except for the light from neon signs and street lights. "Hey, Rosa!" Frank suddenly called. Tom looked around. Across the street was Rosa.

"Rosa!" Frank yelled again. Rosa heard him this time. She stopped short and looked uncertain. Then it seemed—though the uncertain light made it hard to be sure—that she smiled briefly. She waved and hurried up the street.

"Rosa!" Frank called again and started after her. He had run only a few feet when he came back. Tom looked at him questioningly. Frank laughed. "Out of bounds—by the rules of the game." Tom was still puzzled, but Frank dropped the subject. "Let's go," he said.

They were soon at the rectory, and Tom got the car and

drove Frank home. They parted with a vague understanding that Tom would phone to see whether Frank wanted a ride to the next YPF meeting.

That evening at dinner Tom noticed with a shock how tired his father looked. Later in the evening when he went upstairs, not to study but to be alone and away from the high pitch of girlish voices, he found himself thinking of his father with a new compassion and respect. Dr. Bowman, he saw, was like a sentry in a lonely post. Right now he was caught between the caution of people like his senior and junior warden and many of the congregation and the impatience of people like Frank and a fair number in the congregation. He was a dangerous radical or a benighted reactionary at one and the same time. No wonder that he looked tired, like a man who has been a long time in an exposed position and is constantly buffeted by opposing forces.

All at once, Tom knew how wonderful his father was. He wanted to run downstairs and tell him so, but something stopped him. As a second best, he sank to his knees and prayed God's blessing and strength and guidance for his father. "And for me, too," he whispered at the end. "I need it, too. And help me pass my math and physics. Help me get into college."

He stood up. "You lazy bum," he said to himself. "Can't you do anything for yourself?"

Downstairs, Dr. Bowman was yawning. "Nine-thirty," he said. "Think I'll turn in. Coming with me, Ellen?"

"I'll wait up," Mrs. Bowman replied, "till Betty gets in."

"Oh, she's all right with Steve," Dr. Bowman said. "I wouldn't worry."

"You go on up," Mrs. Bowman said jumpily. "I've got a book to read. I'll stay down here."

Her husband bent over and kissed the top of her head, then he started slowly up the stairs, yawning as he went. Advent was always an exhausting season for him, almost as much so as Lent. There were so many church problems. Everything seemed now to be stalled at dead center. He was soon in his bed, sound asleep.

Certain of the seniors had arranged for a small dance at a restaurant a few miles out in the country. The event was designed to celebrate the beginning of the Christmas holidays. Betty and Steve were going with another couple, Pete Randall and his girl friend, Janie Blavatsky. The dance was due to end at twelve sharp. Dr. and Mrs. Bowman had given Betty one o'clock permission, and she had seemed content—the extra hour was adequate for a last minute trip to some place for additional refreshments on the way back to Blanton.

Mrs. Bowman read a little while, then tiptoed upstairs and stood outside the master bedroom. The faint, regular rhythm of snoring came to her ears. She felt a touch of irritation as she walked back downstairs. She stretched out on the sofa and picked up her book. If the house were burning down, he'd sleep until the firemen arrived.

Not that there was really much to worry about. Steve was very reliable. The restaurant where the dance was being held did not serve anything alcoholic. Probably they'd get tired of dancing and be home early. Likely as not all four would tumble into the house, raring to make popcorn or dance to the phonograph. You could never tell with teenagers. Sometimes they didn't utilize all the rope you gave them.

Nothing really to worry about . . . if only Steve were driving. But it's Pete's car, and he's driving. He seems all right, but we don't know him the same way we do Steve.

With a sigh and a determined gesture of her hands, Mrs. Bowman shifted the book into good reading position and began at chapter seven.

Time passed, still more time. She was on chapter nineteen

now. She glanced at her watch. Twelve-five. The dance was over. They might stop somewhere on the way home for a sandwich and coffee, but in an hour . . .

Twelve-thirty, twelve-forty-five, at last one o'clock. Mrs. Bowman pressed her face to the window. There was no sign of a car about to stop. One-fifteen. No Betty. One-thirty.

Mrs. Bowman went upstairs and woke her husband. "What is it? Is it morning already?" he asked groggily. "Is breakfast ready?"

"Betty isn't back yet!" Mrs. Bowman hissed into his ear.

"Betty? What time is it?"

"After one-thirty. She promised to be in by one."

Dr. Bowman woke up a little more and hastily dressed. They went downstairs.

"Don't you think we ought to notify the police?" Mrs. Bowman asked. "Anything can have happened."

"What time is it now? One-forty. Let's give them till two."

"Some crazy driver may have run into them. Henry, do you think we should check at the hospital, just in case?"

"She had identification. They'd notify us. For all we know, those kids may just have a flat tire."

"They could at least phone us."

"I know, I know. But teenagers don't think of things like that."

Mrs. Bowman set her lips grimly. "I'll wait till two, but not a minute longer." She picked up her book. Dr. Bowman began skimming the newspaper he had been too tired to read.

All at once Mrs. Bowman put the book down and went to the phone. "Hey, what are you doing?" her husband asked.

She was dialing and paid no attention. "This is Ellen Bowman," she said into the phone. "Has Steve come back yet? . . . No, I haven't seen Betty either . . . You don't know what's delayed them? . . . Thanks, do call if you hear anything, and I'll call if I get any word . . . Good-bye." She hung up.

"The Hadleys are sitting up, too, both of them, and they're worried sick," Mrs. Bowman said with an accusing look straight at her husband. "And they say that Pete Randall had a near accident driving just last month."

"Why didn't they peep up? Lot of good it does to learn about it now."

"I'm going to go outside and look," Mrs. Bowman said. Dr. Bowman rose. "No, no, you stay here," she said. "I'll just have a look around. You stay here in case the phone rings."

She threw a coat around herself and strode outside. Something of her restlessness was beginning to touch Dr. Bowman. He remembered the night that Frank Buell had crashed in front of the rectory. That sort of thing happened all the time, particularly with teenagers. Maybe he really should call the hospital and the police, just in case . . .

His wife returned. "Not a trace," she said.

"I'm going to phone the police and the hospital," Dr. Bowman said.

"No, no, wait till two," Ellen Bowman said. "They may have just run into some kind of delay on the way home."

Her husband gazed at her with amazement and incomprehension, but he had long since given up the illusion that the female mind was an open book to him. "O.K.," he said. "I'll call at two."

The clock on the mantel ticked and ticked. It struck two. Dr. Bowman walked into the hall without a word and began dialing. "Is this the hospital?" he asked. "Do you have any record of anyone admitted this evening after an automobile accident? I'm checking up on my daughter, Elizabeth Bowman . . . Yes, I'll wait . . . Thank you."

Dr. Bowman cupped his hand over the mouthpiece and called to his wife, "They're checking."

At this moment the front door burst wide open. There stood Betty, her cheeks happily flushed and her eyes alive with excitement. "Good night, good night," she called, and a chorus of good nights came from the street. One voice was recognizably Steve's.

Dr. Bowman hung up the receiver abruptly. "Betty! It's a relief to see you!"

"Why?" she asked. "Oh, Daddy, we had the most luscious time!"

"Why? It's two o'clock."

Betty glanced at her wrist watch and said in an innocent voice, "Is it really that late?"

"Yes, it is," her mother stormed at her. They were all in the living room by now. "Your father and I have been sitting up waiting for you. He was just now calling the hospital and was about to call the police."

"Oh, Dad, you wouldn't be that silly!" Betty pleaded.

"Silly? We were scared stiff. Anything could have happened," her mother insisted. "You promised to be home at one. You agreed that one was a reasonable hour. No wonder we were worried."

"If we can't trust you to keep your word," Dr. Bowman said, "then it's no more late permission for you. When you finally grow up, we'll treat you accordingly."

"You won't let me grow up!" Betty screamed with the tears beginning to come. "You won't let me use any judgment at all. If I'm five minutes late—"

"An hour late," her father corrected.

"All right, an hour late," said Betty defiantly. "If I'm an hour late, you act as though it's a crime. You can't hover over me next year in college. Why don't you start trusting me a little, now?"

"What delayed you?" Mrs. Bowman asked.

"It wasn't anything," Betty wailed. "If you'd only trust my

judgment a little. Pete and Janie wanted to drive across the state line and stop at a place—"

"For a drink?" Mrs. Bowman asked. The neighboring state, which began about ten miles away, had lenient liquor laws.

"Yes, but Steve and I just had Cokes."

Mrs. Bowman continued, "So a boy who'd been drinking drove you home—an hour late."

"He'd just had a few beers. He drove perfectly all right. If he hadn't, Steve would have taken over." This was said with a touch of pride.

"One thing," Dr. Bowman interjected. "Why didn't you at least phone us so we wouldn't worry?"

"The phone there was always busy," Betty said sullenly.

"I'll bet you tried hard," her mother said in an acid voice. "Well, to bed with you."

"We'll talk about this more tomorrow," Dr. Bowman said.

"Let's get it over with now," Betty said desperately.

"All right," her father agreed. "You've got to learn that when you make a promise, it's a promise. No more dating in the evenings till after Christmas."

Betty burst into tears. Then her face blazed with anger. "The trouble with you and Mama is you're a pair of rigid old fogies. You treat me like a ten-year-old. You won't let me grow up. I—hate—you!" Her voice rose to a screech as she ran up the stairs, two and three steps at a time.

11

COMMON AND UNCOMMON SENSE

IT WAS TWO days before Christmas. Mrs. Greenwood sat on a severely functional sofa and chainsmoked. This was a rare thing for her. She was moderate in most things, from potatoes to cigarettes, and had a secret contempt for people who were too self-indulgent.

It was only a week since they had talked with Mr. Johnston, but all the necessary preparations had been made. The social worker was kind and efficient. Right after New Year's Helen would go to the distant city; her room and board were already arranged.

Beulah Greenwood chainsmoked, and the same questions kept going through her mind. Why, *why* had this happened to them of all parents and Helen of all girls? Beulah and Perry Greenwood came from similar backgrounds—one of the things that had first brought them together. Both had parents who were the last of the Victorians. Many things were simply not talked of, and since they weren't talked of, it was assumed that they didn't exist.

When they married, they resolved that their home would be freer, less choked with inhibitions, than the homes they had known. They were determined to "talk things out," which they did with each other, in every question from sexual adjustment to financial planning. When their daughter, Helen, came along, they vowed that she should grow up in an atmosphere where she would feel free to say anything she wanted to and ask all possible questions.

It hadn't worked out that way. In spite of the books on child psychology, Helen had failed to pepper them with questions about sex and birth. Sometimes they felt an awkward compulsion to steer her around to the subject, but she seemed bored by it. On the other hand, from the time at the age of three when Helen asked, "Where was God before He was?" she had steadily assailed them with metaphysical and religious questions until she sensed their uneasiness and ceased asking them.

"We've got to work out this question of religion," Beulah sometimes told Perry or Perry told Beulah, but somehow they never got around to working it out. They knew what they were against—the "Bible-from-cover-to-cover churches," the churches that regarded every innocent pastime as a sin. But they were less sure what they were for. Mr. Greenwood had leanings toward the Unitarian Church, with its emphasis on reason and social ethics and its lack of a formal creed. His wife hadn't gone so far as to have a definite preference. Meanwhile Helen, at the age of five, had asked why she didn't go to Sunday School like other children. Most of her closest friends were Episcopalians. After some anxious conferring, her parents had started sending her—"at least it isn't fundamentalist or puritanical," Beulah had admitted. Later Helen had been confirmed and had moved from junior to senior choir, but her parents had not followed her example.

Certainly Helen's mistake could not have been caused by an atmosphere of tabu in the household. If she were too shy to talk, there were plenty of books in the bookcases on all aspects of growing up, books by the most respected authorities in the field. Something had gone wrong.

Well, Beulah told herself, one thing was clear. She and Perry mustn't do anything to make Helen feel guilty. The poor child was already in a psychological hell. It would be cruel to add a moral burden on top of that. Helen had done a foolish and immature thing which would inescapably complicate her future, but the three of them must work it out so that the rest of her life would not be ruined.

Helen, upstairs, was going through some of her things, picking out those she would want in the distant city. She did this mechanically while two sets of savagely vivid pictures danced in her mind.

The first set was of a night not very long ago, a car ride into the country, the perfunctory and mechanical love-making, the exact moment that she knew she willed not to resist, the unsuccessful attempt to summon up emotions of either romantic or purely physical love, the ride back to town with oceans of silence pierced by small islands of nervous chatter.

The other set of pictures prefigured the future. She saw herself in a hospital, gleaming and hygienic, surrounded by skillful and infinitely tactful nurses and doctors. As in a vision, she beheld the doctor giving her something to put her out until after the baby was born. She could see her unconscious body in the miracle of giving birth, the baby in the nurse's arms, the quick efficiency of it all, the baby taken away before she woke, the whole thing, the whole miracle of the new life, as though she had had no part in it, the baby cared for and put out with the right family for adoption, herself returning to Blanton and enrolling in the twelfth grade, the baby that she had never seen, laughing and crying and growing up ... somewhere ... with somebody.

Mother and Daddy were very kind. Mr. Johnston was very kind. The social worker was kind. The nurses and doctors would be kind. Kindness was so thick in the air she could hardly breathe. She remembered the story of *The Scarlet*

Letter, about a woman who had been compelled to wear a red A as the confession of her guilt. Her thoughts traveled to certain Indian sects in the southwest who lash themselves until the blood runs, in an ecstasy of purification. Those things, however, belonged to the dark past. Such simple means of erasing the consequences of a silly deed were not available to her.

With every breath of air, she breathed in kindness. She went downstairs. "I'm going over to see Dr. Bowman," she told her mother.

Beulah Greenwood looked up apprehensively. "What do you want to see him about?"

"I ought to tell him I'm dropping out of choir after Christmas."

"Be back by supper," her mother said. Helen started for the door. Her mother called after her, "Be careful what you tell him. Just say the doctor thinks you'll have to go to a better climate for a while."

Helen murmured something not too audible and left. Her mother stared anxiously after her.

When Helen rang at the rectory door, Tom opened it. "Hello, Helen," he said. "Come in."

"Is Dr. Bowman home? Could I see him?" she asked as she entered.

"Something about choir or YPF?" Tom asked. "Wait a sec. I'll tell Dad you're here." He vanished and soon returned. "Dad's in his study. Come along, I'll take you there."

"Thanks," she said, as she followed him.

"There it is. Go on in."

As Tom left, Helen slowly opened the door. It seemed very heavy. Dr. Bowman rose from an easy chair and smiled at her. "Have a seat, Helen."

She sat down and tried to find words. The silence continued until Dr. Bowman broke it. "How's school going this year?"

"All right, I guess," Helen said.

"The choir? You like the new music?"

"It's fine—I love it—but what I came to tell you—I won't be in the choir any more."

Dr. Bowman's face dropped. It was never easy to assemble a good choir, and Helen's soprano, while far from professional, was pleasant and dependable. "Is anything wrong? In the choir, I mean?"

"The choir—it's fine. It's just that after Christmas—I've got to go away for a while." All at once it seemed she would strangle if she didn't talk. She began to cry.

Dr. Bowman watched her soberly a moment, then pulled his chair a little closer. "You have something you want to tell me?"

"Yes," she sobbed.

"Then tell me. That's what a priest is for. It won't go any further."

For a time she could not speak, but finally she told him the whole story. Dr. Bowman listened carefully, asking a few questions along the way.

After she had finished, he said, "Do you mind if I ask you some more questions?"

"It's all right," she said, feeling somehow a little better.

"Had you been drinking?"

"He had a little. I hadn't. I don't like it."

"Were you in love with him?"

"I thought he was nice then—but love—no."

"Then it was just a physical thing—you were swept off your feet—"

"No!" Helen said with a shudder. "I wasn't swept off my feet. You're trying to find excuses for me like everybody else!"

"Then why did you do it?" he asked very softly.

Helen didn't reply.

"Let me tell you why," Dr. Bowman finally said, "and you can say whether I'm right. You did it because you were lonely and you wanted to feel that you belonged somewhere and were important to somebody. You did it because you wanted to be somebody. Was that it?"

"I suppose so," Helen dully answered.

"You're not the first," he said. "I've talked with many young people, boys and girls who've done the same thing, and not one in twenty is the victim of irresistible passion. The Romeos and Juliets are a lot more common on the stage than in real life."

Both fell into silence. There was more Dr. Bowman could have said, but he must be careful. Though her parents never came to church, he knew them fairly well through civic committees on which he served with them. They were the kind of parents who are stronger on anxious concern for their children than on plain, outgoing love.

At last, he spoke. "Helen, I don't think this is entirely your fault—" then paused, wondering if he were about to slip into saying something about her parents.

Helen saved him from his dilemma. "I knew you'd say that!" she exclaimed shrilly. "Everybody says that! Nobody will blame me for anything! Everybody makes excuses for me!" She was sobbing with something close to hysteria.

"Helen!" he commanded. "Stop it. Stop it, I say." Her sobs continued for a moment, then abruptly ceased. "Look at me," he said sharply, and she turned dully to face him. "Listen carefully. The first thing is this: there are many worse things you could have done. The sins of the spirit are worse than those of the body. Being proud and self-righteous because you don't drink will send you to a lower circle of hell than being a drunkard. It's worse to spread vicious stories about people and murder their reputations than to do the thing you did. There are plenty of ways you could get to hell quicker and land deeper."

"Kindness, kindness again, never my fault—" Helen began.

Dr. Bowman cut her short. "I said you could have done worse things. I didn't say you hadn't done a bad thing. You have. The important thing is to understand why it's bad. Sex isn't bad. Wanting to be possessed by a man isn't bad. God made you so that you will have this desire. No, Helen, that's the trouble. Sex and desire are so good that God wants you to give your whole desire to one man and spend a lifetime exploring what it means to be in love."

"Yes, I know that, but—" Helen interrupted.

"What's wrong is that you've behaved like a child. You've taken this wonderful gift that God gave you and made a toy of it. It's as though you took a beautifully bound book down off the shelf and used its pages to write shopping lists. Your trouble wasn't that you took sex too seriously, but that you didn't take it seriously enough. You expected too little of it."

Helen was now calm enough to speak. "Mr. Johnston and Mother and Daddy keep saying that I must make a fresh start when I come back and not let my life be wrecked by something I can't undo. But how *do* you make a fresh start?"

"You can't," Dr. Bowman said.

"There's no way at all?"

"Not by yourself, there isn't. By yourself, you're like somebody who's dipped his hands in a kind of ink that won't come off. The stains will be with you till death and go with you to the grave."

"Then all I can do is simply learn to live with the stain? It serves me right, I know."

"Helen," Dr. Bowman said, "all of us have indelible stains—if not for your reason, then for another. And none of us can wash them off by ourselves. If we could see ourselves with God's eyes, we'd look pretty blotched and dirty."

"Then all we can do is learn to live with the dirt?" Helen asked.

"No," said Dr. Bowman.

"But you said—"

"I said you can't wash the dirt and stains off by yourself. You can't. But it can be done for you."

"You mean by Christ? I know that theoretically, but I can't really feel it—now. I've made the mistake, and it seems immoral for someone else to pay the price!"

"Look at it this way, Helen," Dr. Bowman pleaded. "Is any murderer good enough to bear the weight of murder? Is any liar good enough to bear the weight of lying? Is any fornicator good enough to bear the weight of fornication? Is any of us good enough, enough centered in God, to take upon himself the full consequences of his own sins?"

Helen was silent. Dr. Bowman continued. "Only Christ, who never lied, never murdered, never fornicated, can bear the full guilt of lying, murder, and fornication, and every other sin, and take it off your shoulders. So He's the only way to get rid of those stains. If I knew of another way, I'd tell you, but I only know of this one."

Helen spoke slowly. "Of course, I've known all this in an abstract way. From Confirmation class on, probably earlier. But I can't really believe it in my heart. I keep thinking it's some more of the same kindness, kindness, that I get everywhere." Her voice rose. "I'm drowning in kindness!"

"Drowning is sometimes a good thing," Dr. Bowman said quietly. "Baptism is a kind of drowning to make it possible for you to have a second birth and begin a new life . . . But that's off the track. This kindness of Christ's is a very tough kind of kindness."

"Tough? How?"

"Yes. For you to receive Christ's kindness, you have to admit you are helpless without it."

"I'm willing to pay the penalty!" Helen insisted. "I want to!"

"There's your starved ego speaking again," Dr. Bowman said firmly. "You'd like to set up a system of moral accounting and balance the books with something dramatic like a whipping post or public penance. Come now, isn't that it?"

"At least I'd feel I'd suffered for my own mistake," Helen said sullenly. "It was *my* mistake."

"So it was. And as long as you try to pay the price of it, the stain remains and gets darker with every attempt you make. I'm sorry, Helen. If there were an easier way, I'd tell you, but the only way I know is the one I've told you. Your choice is either Christ or your inverted ego, feeding on self-abasement and swelling with secret pride."

Helen was sunk in thought. When she spoke again, it was in a calm and almost lifeless voice. "Then what I must do is just passively say, 'Let Christ do it'?"

"Half true," Dr. Bowman said. "If God, through Christ, offers us forgiveness, we don't have to be stricter with ourselves than God is. Take what's offered you."

"I suppose so," Helen said. Then she added, "I still feel as dirty as ever."

"I said it was half true. The other half is just as important. You can't really accept this forgiveness unless you first admit to yourself and to God the full weight of what you've done. That means getting rid of the comfortable alibis in the back of your mind. It means giving up the neat psychological extenuations, even though they contain their fragments of truth. It means saying to God, 'I take responsibility for what I did. And I did what I did because I put my ego in place of You.' If you can say that and really mean it, you will go on and say, 'I know I'll do things like this again and again—if not the same thing, perhaps worse things, though they may not get me into trouble. I'll keep on putting my ego first, if I don't put You first. Help me, God, help me to open myself so fully to You that You will come first in everything, in every moment of my life.' That's what you need to say. Now tell me honestly, Helen. Which is easier? Is it easier to endure a sound whipping or to say the words I've just said?"

Helen smiled faintly and said, "I think I'm beginning to see myself for the first time. It isn't very pretty. Always looking for some way to feel important . . ." She began to sob, quietly this time. "God have mercy on me," she said, "God have mercy. I can't do anything more."

They sat there quietly a little longer. At last Dr. Bowman asked, "You really mean what you said?"

"I think I do. God help me, I hope I do."

"I think that's as far as we can go now. You're trying to put yourself in God's hands. It can't be done all at once—not usually." He seemed to be pondering. "Helen," he said intently, "I want you to come with me into the church and tell God your story and the decision you've made. I think He'll make His forgiveness clear to you there." He stood up.

Helen rose without speaking and the two of them went out of the house the back way. As they walked toward the entrance of the church, Dr. Bowman said in a more relaxed voice, "By the way, I hope you'll put me in touch with the social worker in the city where you're going. I think I could help in finding the right kind of foster parents. I know priests all over the country, and people are always coming to them asking about adoptions—fine people, the right sort for your baby."

"Thank you," Helen said in a low voice.

They were now at the church door. The two of them went in together. Dusk seemed to have come early here, except for a western window which glowed in red, blue, and green with a picture of Christ sitting at a table surrounded by His disciples, including the one who that night would betray Him.

They stood a moment there and something of the quietude flowed into Helen. Dr. Bowman was in no hurry. When he spoke, it was to say simply, "I'll be back in a few minutes in the sanctuary. You can go up and kneel at the altar rail. That's where Christ has come into your very body so many Sundays. Remember that. Kneel there and say a prayer to Him. Then when I come back into the sanctuary, you tell God the things you've done. You'll hear His answer."

Dr. Bowman slowly walked toward the sacristy. Helen hesitated a few seconds, but the deepening dusk of the church was assimilating her into its peace. As she walked up the central aisle, the red, green, and blue from the western window made brief patterns of clear colors on her.

12

AN INDECISIVE DECISION

SOMETHING'S wrong, Steve admitted to himself. Christmas had come and gone; school hadn't started yet. Steve had time to think and brood. Something's wrong, he mentally repeated. Something's wrong between Betty and me.

It's nothing that's easy to put your finger on. When we're together, first we talk about this and that, nothing important. Then all at once we blow up about something, and next day I can't remember what it was. I wish I could understand Betty. Wish I could understand myself.

Steve found his thoughts going in a weary circle. While he was thinking, his imagination danced between two extremes. At one moment his mind's eye dallied with the imagined sight of Betty. Item by item he undressed her as she looked up at him in adoring anticipation. Yet in the very midst of these mental pictures, Steve would suddenly find himself irritated. The alluring picture of Betty would fade. She would have her clothes back on; the look of fond surrender would be gone; she would be sitting up and saying something that would lead him to say something. In no time they would be at it again, one misunderstood word leading to another.

It doesn't all fit together, Steve told himself. Something's wrong. I wish I knew what. I can't talk to Mom or Dad. They'd tell me to buck up. They'd say such things are natural at my age, or else they'd get too worried. Then I'd have that to worry about. If Betty weren't Dr. Bowman's daughter, I'd go to him. I wish I knew some other priest well. I need to talk with somebody. How about Mr. Crews?

The more Steve thought about Mr. Crews, the better the idea seemed. The other students who had conferred with Mr. Crews seemed to have confidence in him. They were convinced at the very least that he was on their side and that he took them seriously. So the next Monday, the first day of school, Steve made an appointment to see him.

When Steve stepped into the office, his first impression was that it didn't look much like an office. The walls were hung with reproductions of moderately modern paintings. Ivy encircled the two windows and potted plants in full flower were placed at strategic spots. The desk was inconspicuously in one corner. In the middle of the room was a coffee table with a bowl full of mixed chocolates. Around it was a tumbled assortment of teenage, hot-rod, and charm magazines.

"Glad to see you, glad to see you," Mr. Crews said, heartily shaking Steve's hand. "Here, sit here." He motioned to a chair by the coffee table. Steve sat down, and Mr. Crews drew up a chair beside him. "Help yourself to some chocolates—no limit on the bag. They're my form of bribery to get people to come here. The ever-normal chocolate bowl."

Steve laughed and accepted the invitation. For a moment they were silent, and Steve was almost ready to get down to business when Mr. Crews seized the initiative by turning the conversation to football. He had a photographic memory. He analyzed every outstanding play Steve had made during the past two years and discussed with manly directness those that Steve had fumbled. Then he turned to the history of football, revealing an encyclopedic knowledge. Steve played the game, but he had never attempted to learn its connections with the village life of the Middle Ages. He listened with open-mouthed admiration.

Next, Mr. Crews began asking him a series of questions concerning life at Blanton High: how he felt about the tone of student-faculty relations; how well the student government system was working out; what his attitude would be toward incorporating such groups as the Stalwarts and the Omegas into the recognized life of the school. At this last question, Steve looked embarrassed. Mr. Crews seemed to make a mental note. Soon after, he changed the subject by remarking, "I've been talking too much. What's on your mind, Steve?"

"Betty and me."

"Nice girl," Mr. Crews said thoughtfully. "And pretty. Pretty and bright. Lots of fun?"

"Used to be."

"You having 'going-steady' trouble?"

"What do you mean?"

Mr. Crews laughed. "It's a phrase I made up. I mean that when you've been going steady a couple of years, and marriage is still pretty far off—it isn't easy, the waiting—the tensions build up, the frustrations. Each of you begins subconsciously to blame the other, but it isn't really anybody's fault. It's the situation itself."

"I guess you've said it."

"Do you mind if I talk like a sociology textbook for a little while longer?" Mr. Crews asked.

"Go ahead, please," said Steve, a little puzzled. He had the feeling that he and Betty were slowly fading away and being replaced by "teen-age boy" and "teen-age girl."

"Every social system," explained Mr. Crews, "has its built-in strains and tensions. That's especially true when it comes to dating and courtship. The only way the strains could be avoided would be for everybody to get married at the age of puberty, and this isn't very practical. So society experiments with different ways of handling the strains and tensions during the period between puberty and marriage."

Steve nodded. He understood this, but what help was it? He was interested not in the intentions of society but in how he and Betty could get things straightened out and not always be flying off the handle with each other.

"The tensions and strains of dating and courtship vary according to the pattern prevailing in a particular society," Mr. Crews continued. "Back in the 1920's or 1930's, you and Betty wouldn't have had the *same* anxieties and problems you have now."

Steve had heard his parents talking about that period of time, but to him Calvin Coolidge or Franklin Roosevelt seemed as remote as Abraham Lincoln. "Wasn't that when they used to date first one girl and then another, and there was a stag line at dances and lots of cutting in?"

"That's right," said Mr. Crews. "A boy or girl gained prestige by going with as many of the opposite sex as possible during high school and college. You would date girl A one weekend and girl B the next weekend and girl C the following Wednesday. Then you might decide to ask girl B for something again, and the next time it could be girl D. And all the while the girls were doing the same thing. If a girl went with just one fellow, everybody assumed it was because she couldn't land anyone else. At dances, you'd arrange in advance with the other fellows to cut in on your date, and you'd cut in on theirs, so all the girls would feel they'd been given a big rush. If you didn't do this, if you danced with your date all evening, you'd have a tearful girl on your hands when you took her home, and she'd secretly vow never to go out with you again."

"Sounds exciting in a way," Steve said. "But how did you ever get to know anybody well?"

"Sometimes you didn't," Mr. Crews conceded. "You'd know a lot of girls fairly well, but you might not get to know any of them very well until you were maybe in your early or mid-twenties and about ready to settle down. Then you'd start definitely courting one girl."

Steve thought a while. "Wasn't it a kind of selfish system?" he asked finally. "Nobody was really responsible for looking after anybody."

"That's true. That's where the stresses and strains came in. If a girl weren't a Venus, she might sit by the telephone night after night, wondering if it would ever ring. That Saturday dance might come around, and no date."

"It must have worked out better for the boys," Steve reflected.

"Maybe. I'm not sure. Each boy was competing against the pack. He might date an attractive girl one time. Next week if he called her up it was 'Sorry, but So-and-So has already asked me.' Then he'd have to go down his list, and he might end up with some sad specimen of girlhood from the bottom of the barrel. I suppose it was an exciting social system—most people were left guessing from week to week—but there was precious little psychological security. Maybe that's one reason that it's pretty well passed out of existence, as far as I can see."

The word "security" stirred something in Steve's mind. "My Dad says that all that young people think about nowadays is security."

"The sociologists might agree with him," Mr. Crews commented. "They say that college seniors, when they're looking for a job, ask first about the stability of the company and its promotion system and what kind of retirement plan it has. Then they get around to asking about salary."

Mr. Crews paused and smiled at Steve. It was curious, by now Steve had almost forgotten about Betty. She was now just a small part of the total social pattern, and so was he. "How about the new system?" he asked, almost as though he weren't a part of it. "Where do the stresses and strains come in there?"

"You ought to be telling me!" Mr. Crews laughed and slapped his knees. For an instant, Betty briefly surged to the front of Steve's memory, Betty infinitely desirable to have and to hold and as infinitely complex and hard to get along with. As Mr. Crews continued, however, she receded to her modest place in the Total Social Pattern.

"It's pretty obvious, isn't it?" Mr. Crews asked. "Take you and Betty. You've been going steady for about two years. Every relationship has a tempo, and the tempo has a way of speeding up. You want to go farther and farther; it's only natural. But it'll be how many years before you can think of marriage? If marriage is out, then what can you do except try to put the brakes on in time and slow down?"

"I guess that's what we've been trying to do," Steve said.

Mr. Crews looked at him intently, with friendly concern. "Was it after you put the brakes on that things began to get snarled up—the misunderstandings and so on?"

Steve thought. "I think it's been building up all fall, but after we put the brakes on, it got worse. I have the feeling we're both walking on eggs to keep things from blowing up."

Mr. Crews nodded. "I don't have a magic solution for your problem."

"What *can* we do?" Steve asked in sudden desperation.

"Some things help," Mr. Crews said thoughtfully. "Self-knowledge makes a problem easier to bear. Here's a book you might like to read. You can give it to Betty, too. It's based on personal interviews with over four thousand high school students, and it will help you to see that your problem isn't unique."

"Thanks," said Steve doubtfully as he put the copy of *The Time of the 'Teens* into his book bag.

"If you want to bring Betty in here with you some time, maybe the three of us could talk it all over together. Beyond that—what can you do? Well, you have to ask yourself, what builds up the pressure most? Isn't it when you're alone with her, when she's trying to be a good girl and you're trying to be a gentleman, and your basic drives are talking back in protest?"

Steve nodded. "I guess that's it, all right."

"I haven't anything unusual to suggest, but it might reduce the tension if you saw each other mostly when you were with other couples."

"We've been trying that lately," Steve said.

"Fine, fine," said Mr. Crews. "You have a lot of self-understanding. Of course, there's sublimation. Your football was all to the good, but the season's over. You ought to go out for something else, club activities, anything to drain off interest and energy. If you can encourage Betty to go into more things—"

"I'll try," Steve promised.

"Let's keep in touch about all this," Mr. Crews said with a resumption of his hearty and wholesome voice. "Here, stick some of these chocolates in your paw. They come out of my office expense account."

"Well, thanks a lot," Steve said. He took three final chocolates and left the room feeling vaguely comforted.

The comfort didn't last as long as the chocolates. Somebody—who was it?—that Greek, Socrates, had said *Know thyself,* and Steve at least partially knew himself. But what next? The confirmed alcoholic may know himself, may know that liquor is more perilous to him than a bottle of poison on the medicine shelf, but he still reaches for the liquor bottle. Self-knowledge is fine, Steve thought, but where do you go from there?

Something had to give, he was convinced. During a free period he began reading the book Mr. Crews had lent him, but there didn't seem to be anything new in it. Pages upon pages of statistics on the frequency of dating, what happened on dates, the causes of quarrels, etc., stared him in the face with all the prestige of science, but in a general way he knew this stuff already from firsthand experience. Besides, how could he read while the smiling and mocking face of Betty danced before his eyes?

When school let out, he started home with assorted textbooks and *The Time of the 'Teens* in his book bag. He would finish reading the book, he resolved, but he held no high hopes for practical wisdom to be gleaned from it. Halfway home his restlessness became so strong that the thought of home was painful. He didn't want to be where he'd have to act as if everything were normal. Why not drop by Betty's and take her to a quiet place where they could talk? But what would they say?

He'd drop by the Shack first. He wanted a thick, sugary doughnut, and maybe a cup of coffee, and time to think.

When he reached the Shack, it was sparsely populated. The approaching supper hour had thinned out the customers until only two giggling and painfully happy couples were there, sitting in the second booth. Steve headed for the last one.

Jerry immediately noticed and came over. "Betty on the way?" he asked.

"No, she isn't," Steve answered, and in the awkward silence he added, "Coffee and a big doughnut, I guess."

"Coming up," Jerry replied and went back to the counter. He returned almost immediately. "There you are, buddy."

"Thanks," said Steve. "Got a minute to talk?"

Jerry looked toward the booth and the two couples. They were laughing contentedly. There was no one else around. "O.K.," he said, and he sat down in the booth with Steve. "What's biting?"

"Biting me? Betty."

"Another guy?"

"Not that."

"Some other girl you got your eye on?"

"No!" said Steve.

"Then what gives?"

"Something always happens every time I date her. We get to talking. We say things. She's jumpy; I'm jumpy. It didn't used to be like this."

Jerry thought a long time. "Ever go out with any other girls?"

"Nothing except kid stuff once or twice."

"Betty ever go with another guy?"

"Back in Junior High—but nothing steady."

Jerry looked him full in the face. "How're you and Betty so damned sure you're made for each other?"

The question hit Steve like a blow across the face. His first impulse was anger; Jerry saw the mounting flush on Steve's face. Then it seemed to Steve that a hundred suppressed questions were suddenly released to dance like zombies in his brain. How *did* they know? Had they drifted into going steady and a pinning? Had they simply done the easiest thing? What did they really know of each other? Enough to be sure they wanted to share their lives together? Question after question. At the same time, cold desolation pulsed through his very veins. Life without Betty—the loneliness, the bleakness of it. It was as though he stood all alone in some far land of the utter north.

Jerry was watching him stolidly but said nothing further. Steve broke the silence and asked in a low voice, "How can we find out, find out for sure?"

Jerry thought. He wasn't given to snap judgments. He thought some more. "Seems to me the only way to find out is maybe chuck it a while. That'll show you whether you can get along without each other." Jerry's manner took on an added force and earnestness. "Believe me, brother, if a guy can get along without a woman, that's a sure-fire sign he oughter."

"You mean—" Steve began.

The two boys in the other booth were making signs of hunger. "Gotta take care of those guys," Jerry said, and he hastened toward them.

Steve drank his coffee and took the remainder of the doughnut in his hand. He walked to the counter and left the requisite coins. "Thanks, Jerry," he said as he walked into the gathering dusk.

Dinner was fortunately a quiet time at the Hadleys, except when Mrs. Hadley happened to be in a mood to give a news summary of all the neighborhood tidings. Tonight wasn't one of these times. After dinner had been quietly and efficiently consumed, Steve said he guessed he'd drop by Betty's and departed.

Betty opened the door when he rang and looked even more disturbingly pretty than he remembered her.

"Hi, Betty," Steve greeted her.

"Come in," said Betty.

Steve lingered at the door. "Any place we could go to talk?"

Betty looked puzzled. "I'm leaving in five minutes for a baby-sitting job up the street. Want to come along and help me keep the younger generation under control?"

"O.K.," said Steve.

"Come on in," Betty invited again. "I'll go clear it with Mama and phone the people to get their O.K."

Steve came in and stood in the living room. Betty returned in a few minutes, smiling. "Just a second till I get my coat."

The two of them walked up the street. When they reached the house and went in, Betty introduced Steve to the father and mother who said please excuse them if they dashed, for they had a dinner engagement, and be sure to remember to give the baby his ten o'clock bottle, and don't let the three-year-old get hold of crayons and mark up the wall again.

After the parents had gone, Betty—with some earnest assistance from Steve—bedded the baby and slowly persuaded the three-year-old to retire. At last, with a bedtime story as a reward, he was safely tucked in, minus any crayons. "Whew," said Betty, panting a little, as she and Steve hastily escaped to the living room. "Let's plop down here." They sat down on the sofa.

For a time they just sat there, and Steve's arm slowly advanced around her. It was almost as though they were married, Steve thought; the children they had just bedded might be their own. A warm glow of contentment pervaded him. It seemed that the problems with which he had wrestled all day were inventions of his own sick imagination.

But his warm glow was not to last long. Betty moved away from him by the smallest fraction of an inch and smiled up nervously. "You said you wanted to talk with me?"

"Yes—yes," he admitted.

"About us?" she asked in a tense little voice.

"I guess that's it," he said.

"Then let's go ahead and talk," she insisted.

At last the words came, came clumsily, each sounding harsher than he meant it to sound, came in little swirls and eddies of meaning, but came. He told Betty what was worrying him. He summarized his talk with Mr. Crews and the one with Jerry.

"So you even talked with Jerry!" Betty flared up. "I'm sorry," she said contritely. "Go on."

"I guess I've told you. So that's how it stands," Steve said abjectly, feeling as though he'd taken a kitten in his hands and slowly crushed it between his palms.

Betty was crying softly now. All at once she threw her arms around him and kissed him full on the mouth. He kissed back with a desperate strength. Memories of the deserted farmhouse flooded his mind. His breath came shorter; so did hers.

As Steve began to lean forward, Betty suddenly let go and sat bolt upright. Then she wearily leaned her head on his shoulder. "You dear, sweet Steve," she said at last. "You were right to talk with me, I guess."

She had never seemed more made for some man's love and protection than at that moment, quietly sobbing with her head on the shoulder of the one who had spoken such bruising words.

"Steve," Betty finally said in a low voice. "I guess I've been thinking the same things."

It was as though she had twisted a knife inside him. Now he knew the thing he had feared—Betty, too, was uncertain.

She continued sadly, "Maybe Jerry's right. We ought to have a cooling-off period and see what happens."

She sat up and smiled at him, almost tranquilly. Steve's wounded ego now cried for reassurance. It was all he could do to restrain himself. It would have been so easy to take her in his arms, his masterful arms, to abandon words and turn to action. Then he remembered the farmhouse.

"How long do you think it ought to be for?" he asked reluctantly.

"Long enough to hurt and hurt bad. Or to heal," she said, still with that peculiar serenity which plunged him into deepening gloom. "Christmas is over. How about making it until Easter Eve? Then we'll know how things stand."

"That's a long time," Steve said doubtfully. The sense of arctic desolation was closing in upon him again.

"Long for me, too."

"Then Easter Eve it is," Steve agreed wretchedly. "Have it your way."

"No dating each other during that time," Betty said in a businesslike voice.

"O.K.," said Steve. His heart sank.

Betty reached down inside her dress and with a quick motion extracted the Omega Alpha pin. It was as though she were twisting the knife again. Smiling, she kissed the pin and fastened it to the underside of Steve's lapel.

"You didn't need to give that back," Steve said in anguish.

"Wait and see," said Betty. "If you give it back to me, you can do it with a ring."

Weak and weary as though he had been in bed with a long illness, Steve said, "Is that all, I guess?"

"All I can think of."

Betty stood up as Steve rose. "This has got to last me a long time," she said, and she threw her arms around him and kissed him as though she could never let go. But let go she finally did.

"Good-bye, Steve," she said.

"Good—good-bye," he said. Since there was nothing left to say or do, he put on his coat and left.

13

ARRIVAL AND DEPARTURE

THE SECOND Saturday after Christmas, Tom remembered to phone Frank and remind him that YPF was meeting the next evening. "Thanks," Frank said. "If they can stand me, I can stand them."

Tom put down the phone and called to his father. "I'm going to pick Frank Buell up tomorrow. He's coming to YPF."

Dr. Bowman emerged from his study. "This is going to be interesting," he said. "How do you think he'll take to it?"

"Poorly," said Tom. "It'll seem more of the same to him. Like high school. People being busy and fussy about nothing much."

"Does it seem that way to you?" asked Dr. Bowman, a little distressed.

"Not all the time," Tom said. "Sometimes—well, God seems to be doing something with the YPF, using it. But a lot of the time—well, it's like everything else, people being busy and using up time and jockeying to see who's at the head of the pecking order. Like school, like business."

Dr. Bowman looked thoughtful for a time. "I wonder if this meeting wouldn't be a good one to bring this question of the North Side young people to some kind of decision."

"How d'you mean, Dad?"

"Frank's red hot on that issue. You know how he's reacted

against Oak Hill and all its sins as well as its virtues. I understand he has quite a lot of influence among the high school
crowd, if he'd only use it. If there's any really serious opposi-
tion to bringing the Stalwarts in, Frank ought to be able to
carry some weight. Besides, we've let the thing drag on long
enough."

Tom's eyes brightened. Though never a leader in school or
YPF politics, he loved to observe political activities and analyze
the structures of power and the practical manipulations needed
to get decisions made. His father, through the practical necessities of parish life, had become something of a practicing
politician, working with such power blocs as vestry, congrega-
tions, and potential donors. Thus it was that the two of them
were soon deep in a conversation—who would vote this way?
that way? who could influence whom? who was strong and
who was weak?—which to a stray passerby might have seemed
odd in tone, considering that it concerned a church organization. Its language and premises smacked more of the prover-
bial smoke-filled room.

Some realization of this finally dawned on Dr. Bowman. He
laughed and said, "We're a pair of holy conspirators. Let's let it
go now. We've planned our strategy enough; now we've got
to leave the Holy Ghost a little room to maneuver."

Dr. Bowman went back to labor in his study, until an emer-
gency phone call summoned him away. Tom, however, found
that his own mind did not easily give up its political musings.
It was fascinating to watch a small organization like the YPF.
It was human society in miniature. The same tactics would
get results. Political science, he knew, had made considerable
progress in analyzing all this and formulating it as a series of
"laws," laws of group behavior. Meanwhile, he had the chance,
in the YPF as well as in school, to watch the laws in action.

Late on Sunday afternoon, Tom drove to Oak Hill and
picked up Frank. When they came back to the parish house

and sat down at the supper, there was a subdued stirring and craning of necks. Everyone knew Frank and his general orientation toward life. His sudden appearance at YPF was close to a sensation. Frank himself seemed oblivious to the excitement.

After macaroni, watery salad, jello, and milk-or-coffee had been consumed, the YPF adjourned to the church where two of the students led Evening Prayer. The church was dimly lit. The candles shone with little spots of radiance. The words from the Bible and Prayer Book, though haltingly read, aroused feelings of majesty and mystery. The singing was an invitation to a kind of love and a kind of peace. Frank found himself happily and passively carried along by the gentle current of the service. He did not believe in what it expressed, not in any literal sense. The God it proclaimed was a highly theoretical and unprovable possibility to him. Nevertheless, he was able to respond to Evening Prayer with a temporary suspension of disbelief, respond to it as to poetry. He wondered, how would it feel to be a Christian and believe all this? Half seriously, he began to be an actor, pretending to himself that the service was something more than beautiful poetry, that it pointed toward Reality, rather than collective delusions.

The mood of pleasant make-believe faded quickly but didn't entirely vanish when he joined the others in the parish house after the service. "Have a seat?" Betty asked with a smile.

"Thanks," Frank said, and he sat beside her. "Where are Tom and Steve?"

"Tom? I think—oh, there he is, always breathless and last minute." Tom was coming through the door. He looked about, caught Betty's eye, and headed for the vacant seat by Frank.

Betty didn't get around to saying where Steve was. As a matter of fact, he was on the last row, trying not to study the back of Betty's head and trying still harder not to look and feel self-conscious at not being with her.

President Randall called the meeting to order. The first thirty minutes were devoted to a report (and following discussion) of work opportunities in summer church camps. The secretary, who gave the report, announced that all the pamphlets and announcements would be on file in the church library.

"Any more business?" Pete Randall asked. "Any more business?" He paused briefly. Before anyone could speak up, he pulled a four-by-six card out of his pocket and began: "We have an item of unfinished business. You remember, a while back our rector talked with us about the idea of broadening out the base of the parish by trying to get new members from the people who live nearby—the North Side and people like that. His idea is that we ought to start here with the YPF—invite any of the North Side kids that want to join and ask the Stalwarts if they'd like to have their meetings in the parish house. He says he thinks our age group is more willing to try something new, and then if it works, that'll make a big impression on the whole congregation, and they'll be game to go ahead and try to broaden out. We've been kicking this thing around. How about talking it over and nailing it down tonight?" Pete glanced over the audience. For the first time he noticed that Helen Greenwood was missing. Very unusual. She was one of the most faithful.

"I move that we go ahead and do it," a girl's voice called out from somewhere.

"You've heard the resolution," Pete said. "Any second?"

"Second!"

"Moved and seconded," Pete said. "Any discussion?" He paused for several seconds.

Steve stumbled to his feet and coughed. "I'm for it. The old families in this church are mostly moving to the suburbs. If we don't get in some new people, the church will gradually go to seed." He happened to glance over at Bill Pendleton, and caught Bill's glare of mingled amusement and contempt.

"I'm for it, too," a girl in the next to the back row said. 'We're so much one class in this church it seems more like a club. Maybe if we take in different kinds of people, this church will really become a church."

A tenth-grade boy from the third row stood up. "Those kids on the North Side have a rough time of it. If we can help them, we ought to do it."

Pete looked around. "Anyone else want to speak?" He paused. "Then all those in favor—"

Bill Pendleton stood up. "Mr. President," he interrupted. "We've hashed this thing over so much it's grown stale. I see Frank Buell here. Maybe he has a fresh viewpoint. I'd like to hear him speak."

Everybody turned to watch Frank. He stood up and turned toward the group. "Thanks for asking an agnostic to speak. I'm just a visitor here. I don't think I have the right to have an opinion. This is a church organization. You're the people who believe in God and Christ. I don't. When you make decisions, you can base them on your religious beliefs. I can't. I have to think things out as best I can without any supernatural aid and advice. I envy you," he added with a sudden smile. "It must be a lot easier for you than for me."

Frank sat down. Tom bent over and whispered to him. Frank shrugged. Bill spoke up again. "Agnostic or no agnostic, I'd like to know how Frank stands on all this."

Frank rose once more to his feet. "All right. I'm for it. I'm not sure how much the North Side needs us, but we need it. Oak Hill and Trinity Church are so small, have so few people. I want to join the human race. I don't know about God, whether there is any God to join. But we can ask the human race to take us in."

Once again, Frank sat down. Pete remarked, "I guess we've pretty well discussed this thing. We have a motion before us to go ahead with it. Are you ready for the question? All those in favor—"

"Mr. President!" Bill said, and stood up. For several seconds he said nothing. His eyes slowly traveled about the room, picking out one face after another. Tom watched him with fascination. There was a power, a brooding intensity in that gaze, in the very stance of his body, something violent and dangerous.

Bill started to speak. "If nobody else has the guts to cut through all this pious double talk, I'll have to. We've heard how good it's going to be for us, and good for them, to bring the slums in or go out and join the slums. We've been told that it's the will of God or our initiation into the inner circles of the human race. We've been exhorted to rally around the good old banner of God and mankind and prove what very saintly people we are."

Bill stopped for five or six full seconds. Once again, his eyes went around the room, seeming to light on faces that he had overlooked before. Finally he laughed as though with sudden, irrepressible contempt, and continued, "All of the saints seated in this room are also students at Blanton Senior High. Every day they have a chance to pal around with the Stalwarts and the other fair flowers of the slums. How many of us ever do more than say a 'Hello' to guys from the North Side? How many times do you ever see one of the saints from Trinity Church YPF sitting down with a North Side guy in the cafeteria? We're a bunch of big phonies. If we believed in joining the human race or the brotherhood of man under the Fatherhood of God, we wouldn't restrict it to church Sunday mornings and YPF Sunday evenings. We'd start in school where we're already thrown in with the human race five days a week."

Once again, that strange hypnotic glance began slowly circling the room. "I'm sick of phonies. Especially pious phonies. Moralistic phonies. I know you all—" his voice rose as he looked more wildly about the room—"I know why you want to do this thing. You'll invite the slums in. You'll feel virtuous. Your consciences will be pure and glistening. Of course, once you get the North Side guys here in YPF, you'll be polite to them but keep them off in one corner the way you do at school. You hypocrites!"

"What do you call yourself?" a voice from somewhere asked.

Bill's glance traveled to the general area of the voice. "A typical member of Trinity Episcopal Church," he said. "A young man of lower-upper social class, I believe it is. Somebody who likes to associate with people like himself. Someone who believes that if you start artificially mixing people together just in order to feel moral and smug, you'll end up with everybody unhappy and ill at ease—or else everybody doing the phony act and pretending they're one big happy family. I'm a bigoted, narrow-minded fellow, but I refuse to be a phony." He seemed at the point of sitting down. Then his eyes suddenly fixed on Frank. "I see Frank Buell here. An upper-upper if there ever was one. Lives in the two-acre section of Oak Hill. Frank Buell is the apostle of joining the human race. Do I see him joining it? Do I see him selling all that he owns and going forth to minister to the poor—"

"Let's not get too personal," Mr. Steinbrecher pleaded.

"Question! Question!" someone shouted.

"Are you ready for the question?" Pete asked. "All those in favor—"

A pale, slight girl stood up near the middle of the room. "I think we're all too upset. I move that the motion be tabled."

"I'm against that!" Frank leaped up. "How will you be any better prepared to vote next time?"

The slight girl spoke gently. "I think that a motion to table cannot be debated. Isn't that right, Mr. Steinbrecher?"

"That's right," he assured her.

"Second," Bill said.

"But look here—" Frank interrupted.

"We've waited long enough," Tom protested.

"Question on the motion to table!" Bill roared.

Steve sat uneasily, wishing he knew what to think and say.

"Quiet!" Pete Randall implored. "This is supposed to be a church organization, not a prize fight. There's a motion that we table—an undebatable motion. All those in favor, say Aye."

There was a chorus of Ayes.

"All those opposed?"

The chorus this time sounded about as loud.

"We'll have to have a show of hands," Pete said. He counted carefully as each side voted. "The Ayes have it by a majority of three," he announced. "The motion to table is carried. Now is there any other business?"

Frank rose. "Yes, Mr. President. Is there a telephone here?"

"Right out in the hall," Pete said. "Is anything wrong?"

"Thanks," said Frank. "I wanted to call a taxi."

"I can drive you," volunteered Tom.

"Don't bother," Frank said to Tom. Then he spoke louder. "I just wanted to drive out to Sid Pruitt's place and see if he'd let me join the human race."

No one spoke as he started for the door, and it was some seconds after his footsteps had died away before anyone did. Then it was to make a motion for the adjournment of the formal part of the meeting. The motion carried.

14

TWO FAMILY CONFERENCES

ABOUT A MONTH later John and Sarah Buell were sitting in their living room. They had just come back from a conference with Mr. Johnston and Mr. Crews.

"I'm afraid they know what they're talking about," Sarah Buell said. "Mr. Crews has the reputation of keeping in close touch with students."

John Buell picked up his empty glass and half rose. Then as though by an effort of the will he sat down again and put the glass aside. "That boy," he said. "If he gets drunk—well, don't we all? If he smashes up a car—lots of teenagers do, and other people, too. If he goes out slumming and dates a slum girl —I sowed my wild oats, too. If he'd run away to see that dream mother of his—I could understand that. It might be good for him to discover that dream and reality don't tally. But to join a bunch of dull, broken-English dead-end kids like the Stalwarts and to keep going to their meetings—a boy with a background like his—I've *got* to have another drink!" John Buell said desperately, looking defiantly at Sarah as he rose.

"Take mine, too," she said, handing him her empty glass. Soon he returned with the refills and took a big swallow. He continued bitterly, "That little fool. What do you think, Sarah? Shall we do it together, or do you want me to talk with him alone and get the truth out of him?"

Sarah Buell looked steadily through the large picture window, out to the dry grass of the lawn where only the clumps of evergreens showed any clear color. "You'd better, Jack. I can't get through to him."

"I'll get through to him or know the reason why," Mr. Buell promised and took another swallow. "There's a limit, and that boy has reached it."

"Go easy on him at first," Sarah advised. "If he closes up with you, nobody can reach him."

"Go easy, go easy, go easy," Mr. Buell repeated. "That's all we've done. Protecting his tender psyche. Trying not to give him complexes. Go easy. And look at him. Taking up with the scum of the city. Not even the best kind of kids on the North Side, like that Arrondo girl, but the very scum. Probably mixed up in holdups and those housebreaking cases. First thing we know he'll be in the paper—" In an agony of the imagination, Mr. Buell drained the remainder of his glass and then stood up.

Sarah sighed. "Do your best, Jack. I'm not good at it." She looked at her watch. "He ought to be in soon. I'll go upstairs so you can be alone with him." She gave her husband a sudden kiss and went swiftly up the stairs.

"The young *fool*," Mr. Buell muttered to himself as he looked out the picture window.

Four o'clock came soon, and then four-thirty, but no Frank. Five o'clock, five-thirty, six o'clock. By this time even Mr. Buell was willing to admit that he had drunk too much. He resolutely put the empty glass away, rinsed his face in cold water, combed his hair, and sat down to smoke and read. The words had blurred edges, however, and his mind was more of a blur. He found himself constantly rehearsing the speech he would make to Frank—a speech sternly commanding him to grow up —a speech that grew longer with each silent repetition. But where was the boy?

Six-thirty and no Frank. Dinner was to be at seven. At precisely five of seven Frank came through the front door looking cool and collected. "Hello, Dad," he said. He went back into the hall to hang up his coat.

Mr. Buell half rose to follow him, but he knew he must wait. Dinner was in five minutes. It was the one hallowed act which the whole family respected. So dinner progressed without episode and almost without conversation, except for an unsuccessful effort on Sarah's part to be lively and interesting and draw the men out.

After dessert, Frank excused himself and started up toward his room. His father hastily rose and called out to him, saying in a troubled voice, "Come along with me, son. I want to talk with you."

Mr. Buell was, for all practical purposes, completely sober by now. His face had an unfamiliar look of serious concern. "All right, Dad," said Frank, and he followed him into the study.

"Sit down, son," Mr. Buell said. He wearily sank down on the big sofa, and Frank sat beside him, bolt upright.

"I heard a crazy story at school today," Mr. Buell said at last. "Mr. Johnston and Mr. Crews phoned Sarah and me and asked us to come over. When we got there, they said they thought we ought to know that you had joined that North Side gang, the Stalwarts."

Frank said nothing. His face showed no change of expression. His father waited. "Have you?" he asked sharply.

"Yes." There was still no expression on Frank's face.

Mr. Buell studied his face a moment. Suddenly he flushed a fiery red. "You young fool!" he yelled and clenched his fists.

Frank looked him full in the face as though he were studying a stranger. "Is that what you called me here to say?" he asked, still in a flat, quiet voice. "You've said it, so I'll be going now."

"Sit *down*," his father said, and he pushed Frank down by

the shoulder. "I suppose," he said with heavier sarcasm than he had intended, "you spent the hours between school and dinner today with your precious juvenile delinquents?"

"Is that a question?" Frank asked. "If it is, and if you mean did I spend the time with the Stalwarts—yes. They were having a meeting."

"Where did they meet?" his father asked savagely. "I'll have the police—"

"I can't tell you," Frank said. "It's against the rules."

"Oh, so they have rules. And a constitution, too, I suppose," Mr. Buell continued. "And I suppose they recite the pledge to the flag before they go out for a bit of knifing or housebreaking." He stopped and struggled to get possession of himself. When he spoke again, his voice was tired and calmer. "Frank," he said, "I haven't been the best father in the world. I admit it. I wish to God I could do better, but I don't seem to be able to. But I do want to help you. You believe me, don't you? You believe me?"

He studied Frank's face for a long time. Frank was pale. The muscles of his face were drawn tight. He said nothing.

His father spoke again. "Let me just say one thing, son. I want to help you. This thing may seem like a harmless prank to you—seeing how the other half lives. It appeals to the idealism in you. I can understand, sympathize with that. Every young man ought to be a rebel. But let me tell you—you're playing with fire. One thing leads to another. First thing you know you'll be in trouble so deep that neither I nor anybody else can help you out. I'm telling you the truth."

He studied Frank's face yet again. The paleness, the tension of the muscles had increased. Frank still stared straight ahead.

"I do want to help you," his father pleaded. "Those boys aren't your kind. Frank, they're the leavings of society, the dregs, the misfits—"

"What do you know about them?" Frank screamed full in his face and stood up. "What does anybody in Oak Hill know about them? Oak Hill doesn't know anything except Oak Hill. Oak Hill can go to hell. The Stalwarts are my friends." He leaped up and headed for the study door.

"Frank, come back," his father called roughly and ran after him. "I won't have you—"

But Frank was out of the study and bounding up the stairs. His father followed him and reached Frank's door in time to hear a key turn.

Earlier that same day the first-semester grades were passed out. Steve and Tom ran into each other in the corridor between classes. "I got an F, ha, ha, ha," Tom sang out as loudly as possible, imitating the traditional response of Blanton High students when they received their report cards.

"You really mean it?" Steve asked earnestly. "You?"

"Even I. An F, and a D to keep it company. Behold." Tom held out his card and Steve carefully studied it:

> Advanced mathematics D
> English C
> American Problems B
> Physics F
> Chorus A
> Physical Education A

Comment: Not working up to capacity. Apparent lack of motivation.

"A brain like you," said Steve reproachfully.

"I should be ashamed," Tom said sternly. "A disgrace to my long-suffering parents. What about your fate, Steve? Did Dame Fortune smile on you more benevolently?"

"I pulled it up to an A, a B, and two C's, and of course they give you A in physical education and shop."

"Brain, I salute thee!" Tom said and bowed with more than a trace of seriousness.

The bell for the next class rang at this moment, and the two friends went their separate ways, Tom to the austerities of physics and Steve to commercial arithmetic.

The rest of the day was malignantly haunted by the report card Tom carried in his book bag. If he were an only child, it would be bad enough—the inevitable "heart-to-heart talk" in the evening, the attempt "to think this thing through constructively."

"Why can't they just blow up and let it go at that?" Tom thought wearily, and then with a ray of hope, "Maybe Mama will."

Betty, who had no discernible goal in life other than a husband, was certain to get all A's and B's. Sue for months had been proclaiming that she was going down hill, that she would be lucky if she managed a D average, that her family must prepare for a shock, for she had goofed on every test so far— Sue would get all A's, or at most one or two B's. Nancy, in the third grade, wouldn't get formal marks, but Tom could already see the comment written in the teacher's neat hand: "Cooperative and conscientious in all her work. Contributes well to class discussion. Unusually advanced in reading."

"Black sheep Tom," he said to himself as he walked home. Once, years ago, he had got good grades, too, but no more, and he hadn't the faintest idea of what he wanted to do next year. He had applied to half a dozen colleges, just in case, and one or two of them were second-rate enough so that they would probably admit even him. Maybe it would be better to go on into the army, he told himself, and shake down.

When he reached home, he left the report card on its traditional place—the top of the piano—and went upstairs to study physics. After fifteen minutes he turned to American Problems. Soon he put that down and stared out the window.

Downstairs, Dr. and Mrs. Bowman had garnered in the four report cards and were conferring together in privacy. "You handle it," Mrs. Bowman said pleadingly to her husband. "If I talk to him, I'll blow my top."

Dr. Bowman was studying the telltale report card as though it were a sermon outline. "An A in physical education," he said. "That means he plays basketball. A in chorus. He can carry a tune, and he attends the rehearsals. American Problems—B. They're graded there for handing back the official philosophy of Blanton Senior High. That leaves three subjects where it takes some work. He can talk, read, and even write, but he got only a C in English. And the math and physics . . ."

"You handle it," Mrs. Bowman said with finality.

"I will, after supper," Dr. Bowman promised. "Feed the culprit before he faces the firing squad."

"I'll feed him all right," Ellen Bowman said darkly. "But with those grades, is he ever going to be able to feed himself when we are dead and in our graves? I suppose there's always room for one more ditchdigger—as long as the bulldozers don't put them out of a job." With these parting words, Mrs. Bowman stormed into the kitchen.

Dr. Bowman continued staring at the report card. What could he say to Tom that he hadn't already said at intervals of six weeks the last year and a half, ever since Tom's work began slipping? He wondered if they ought to try a private school, a new environment, but the thought of the cost chilled him. Besides, would it really be a good idea to have Tom run away from his problems?

This is one counselling situation where I wish I weren't a priest, Dr. Bowman thought. It complicates things. If I were just his father, I could give him holy Hades and let it go at that. No, I couldn't, really.

Dinner was soon ready. It was consumed with a careful avoidance of talk about school. After dinner, Tom turned to his father. "O.K., Dad, let's get the post-mortem over with."

"O.K.," agreed Dr. Bowman. They retired to the study. "You do the talking," Dr. Bowman said after they had sat down.

"There's nothing to say," Tom replied. "I got what I deserved—maybe a little more. I bulled my way through American Problems."

Dr. Bowman was silent a long while. Finally he smiled pleadingly. "Are you interested in *anything?* Not just in school —but anything, anywhere?"

"Superficially in a lot of things, but enough to do any hard work—no."

"I wonder if we ought to put this session on a lofty, idealistic basis or talk bread-and-butter."

Tom was in no mood to help. He fidgeted and kept silent.

"Let's be idealistic first. It's usually more practical in the long run. Start with this: you aren't an idiot, imbecile, or even a moron. Your aptitude tests are in the upper twenty per cent. The principal says your I.Q. is well above average. So you have gifts."

"That I'm not using. The parable of the talents."

This session was going even worse than he had feared, Dr. Bowman realized. Tom was showing no fight.

"And I ought to be ashamed of myself," Tom added.

"But you aren't."

"*Ought* is one thing, *being* is another," Tom said. "How do you make yourself feel ashamed when you know you ought to feel ashamed, but you really just don't care?"

This question of practical psychology troubled Dr. Bowman, and he didn't try to answer it directly. He had come up against it so often in all its manifestations. Men who knew that cheating is wrong, but blandly cheated their way to success. Men and women in the midst of extramarital amours who in their hearts prayed in the words of the early Augustine, "Lord, make me chaste, but not yet." St. Paul had said something about all this, that knowing what is right is a far cry from doing the right thing. Tom knew all this. It would do no good to fling Paul in his teeth.

"Let's shift to the bread-and-butter level," Dr. Bowman suggested.

"I know," said Tom. "If my work doesn't improve, the colleges won't look at me. How will I ever support a wife and children in the style to which wives and children are accustomed?"

"What you've said sounds like a platitude," his father said, "but it isn't. It's unhappily the plain, sad truth, but let's skip it . . . One thing you said a moment ago—that you are superficially interested in a lot of things, but not enough to work hard at any of them. What kind of things?"

"Oh, you know pretty well, don't you, Dad? I still like the idea of science, but my picture of it seems to come more from comic books and science fiction magazines than from textbooks. I want the glamor without the drudgery. Another thing, I suppose I like to watch people, to see how they act, why they do the things they do. That's about it."

"You like words, too, don't you? You can use them."

"Words," Tom said impatiently. "Anybody can use words. It's like saying, 'You can walk, can't you?' "

"How about a career in public relations or advertising?"

"And high-pressure people into buying cars with an extra tail fin every year and TV sets that will bring more idiotic programs into their homes more hours per day? Or condition them into electing Mr. X or Mr. Y as the next president? No, thank you,

Dad. I've got an immortal soul—you said so yourself—and I don't want it to go to hell."

"I like the term 'resurrection of the body' better," Dr. Bowman mused, then laughed. "I mustn't let myself get off on a theological tangent. Yes, Tom, you really are in a mess, aren't you? You don't know why you're here on earth and what you'll be doing the next fifty or sixty years, so you don't have any good reason for hitting the books hard."

"I'm drifting and I know it. Oh, I could give you the theological answers, and I suppose they're true—you've taught me well—man's chief end is to glorify God and to enjoy Him forever—"

"That's a Presbyterian way of putting it," Dr. Bowman chuckled. "But I won't quarrel with them. They have a gift for phrasing things succinctly. A Scottish economy."

"I wish I knew how to glorify God," Tom said, suddenly more serious.

"Do you really mean it?" his father asked.

"I think I do," Tom said slowly.

"Then ask Him."

"Ask Him what?"

"How to glorify Him," Dr. Bowman explained.

"You mean pray?"

"Yes, really pray."

"I've tried to sometimes."

"Any answer from the other end?" Dr. Bowman asked.

"None I could hear."

Dr. Bowman thought a moment. "Tom," he suddenly asked with a broad smile, "do you think it's just possible you've really been praying, 'God, teach me to glorify You, but not yet, and certainly not by anything so unromantic as hitting the books and preparing to make a living'?"

Tom laughed. "I'm afraid that's it."

His father stood up. "Give it another try. It's up to you and God. The interview is over, and it'll be the only one of its kind for the next six weeks. Good luck."

"Thanks, Dad," Tom said, and he meant it. He started for the door. On an impulse he turned around. His father had looked away, and his face suddenly seemed haggard and tired. "I'm sorry, Dad," Tom said.

His father looked up and smiled. "I'm not drooping all over the place because of you," he said. "If you want to know, I'm still stewing over the way things went at YPF the night that Frank Buell walked out. I'm afraid we tried too hard to be clever politicians, and it kicked back."

Tom said nothing. His father went on, "I've been thinking about what you told me Frank said to you—that if you're right, you ought to go ahead and not worry about whether you have 51% of the public on your side. That has a biblical ring to it. I've been too careful, too sweetly reasonable, too cautious. I've been a coward. I should have taken the responsibility and gone ahead instead of expecting a bunch of teen-age kids to be the spearhead."

Tom hesitated a moment, wondering what to say. He discovered that he felt proud of his father, and he wished there were something he could do to make him feel better, to encourage him. Simple, naïve impulses assailed him. He almost slapped his father on the back, almost said, "I think you're a wonderful Dad." If he'd said it, he would have meant it, but shyness or self-consciousness or whatever it was held him back, and the moment passed.

"What do people expect?" he asked indignantly. "Do they expect you to do the whole thing? You do more than one man can do anyway, Dad. It's up to some of the other people to throw their weight in a bit."

"You're right, of course," his father said. "But it's still true that they hired me to be the spearhead and goad. In the future I've got to do more spearing and goading. That's my job."

Tom still wanted to say something that would help, but the words wouldn't come. He stammered something, he wasn't sure what, and left the study. The rest of the family, with the exception of his mother, were clustered around the TV. Their attention was so fully occupied that none of them bothered to look his way.

"Gaze on, proletarians of the spirit," he muttered and put on his coat. When he stepped outside he was buffeted by cold winds and eddies of snow.

"Give it another try," his father had said. Well, he would, but later in the evening. There was no hurry. God was always there when anyone took time to turn to Him. You didn't have to make an appointment. Meanwhile, it was some kind of comfort to be in the driving wind and feel the gusts of snow.

As he walked, one desire grew until it was imperious. He wanted a double chocolate malted. He felt in his pocket. A few small coins were still there. He speeded up, and he was soon at the Shack. A scattering of students were in the booths. He sat down at the counter. "Hello, Tom," Jerry said, looking up from the grill. "What'll it be?"

"Chocolate double malt," Tom answered.

Jerry expertly put the mixture together and set it under the electric beater. An impulse seized Tom, and he asked, "What would you do if you didn't know what you wanted to do?"

"What's that? A riddle?"

"A riddle I've got to solve. I'm just coasting and drifting along. Grades way down. Not specially interested in anything."

"Woman trouble?"

"Nothing simple like that."

"Hey, Jerry," a voice called from the back booth. "Two cheeseburgers."

"Right away," Jerry called back and turned to the grill. After the cheeseburgers began sizzling, he turned around and looked at Tom steadily. "You see me?" he asked.

"Sure."

"See me slinging cheeseburgers? See me making double malts? Here's yours—" Jerry shoved it across the counter. "If you come back ten, twenty years from now, what'll you see? Old Jerry slinging cheeseburgers and making double malts. You wanna do that, sling cheeseburgers and make malts all your life?"

"What's wrong with it?"

"Nothing. It's an honest living, keeps you out of jail and the poorhouse. I'm my own boss. But you wanna do it?"

Tom had to admit he didn't.

"You see?" Jerry said, and he swung around to turn the two cheeseburgers. He faced Tom again. "You got a dad who'll send you through college. My old man walked out on Mom when I was twelve, and she was always hitting the booze. You got some stuff up there." Jerry tapped his forehead. "I'm no quiz kid. I fit here. You don't."

"You mean—"

"Wake up, kid, count your blessings, and do something with 'em." Jerry swung around emphatically, scooped up the cheeseburgers, and went to the farthest booth.

Tom lingered over his double malted. If only it were as simple as that—"Wake up, kid, count your blessings, and do something with 'em." That was about the same thing his father had said. But how? how?

Jerry came back. "Thanks, Jerry," Tom said. He put some coins on the counter and disappeared once more into the night.

Back at the rectory, up in his room, he tried with unusual intensity to study physics and mathematics, and once or twice some sudden gleams of understanding seemed to pierce the fog, but they slipped away before he could commit them to memory. At last, wearier than he could remember being in a long time, he prepared for bed.

After he had brushed his teeth and put on his pajamas, memory stirred. He knelt by his bed and prayed as he had planned: "Give me something to do; tell me what I ought to do."

In a rush of agony he kept repeating the words, "Tell me what I ought to do." Weariness, even deeper, was his only answer. At last he grew so tired that he almost ceased to worry. His prayer dwindled into a mumble. He climbed into bed.

Just before he fell asleep—or perhaps he was already asleep and it was a dream—he seemed to hear something, not words, not anything he could describe, but he seemed to be hearing something, and he found himself saying, as though he were repeating what he had heard, "There is everything to do in My world. Do what you will." Next morning, when he woke up, the words echoed in his mind, and he arose in a darker emptiness and despair to another day of school.

15

DECISIONS TO MAKE

THERE WAS a tap at Helen's door. "Phone call for you," Mrs. Blumenthal said.

Helen hurried to the extension in the hall. It was Dr. Bowman. "I've got some church business to do in the city," he explained. "Could I fly up tomorrow afternoon and see you?"

She excitedly agreed. His visits were a welcome break in what had become a smooth routine. It seemed she had always lived with the Blumenthals. He was a retired shopkeeper. They had no children of their own, but took in girls in Helen's predicament, in co-operation with the local social agencies. At the moment, Helen was their only guest, and they showered upon her a great deal of unostentatious care and unabashed affection. She was their substitute daughter, and in a way they were her substitute parents, though her actual father and mother managed to come up a couple of weekends each month.

The stirrings of the baby inside her were stronger and more insistent now. She had not suffered from "morning sickness" or any of the other terrors and nuisances she had sometimes heard women discussing. In fact, she felt fine. About half of each day she spent working on the textbooks and assignments sent her by the extension division of the state university. She was trying to get ahead of schedule so that during the last two months of pregnancy she wouldn't have any schoolwork to do.

Her various teachers, none of whom she had ever met face to face, had been noncommittal about her work at first, but had progressively warmed up, so that penciled comments of "Good," "Improving," and even "Excellent" were now no novelty. Her grades were better than they had been in Blanton.

Soon after she had arrived in the city, Dr. Bowman had arranged for the rector of the nearest Episcopal church to see her, and he had come by every week since then. Sometimes he would bring along the social worker who was handling her case, and they would discuss the procedures for putting the baby out for adoption and the type of family they wanted for it. Most often the rector came alone, and Helen always looked forward to his visits. He was a man with a quick wit and spontaneous laugh, whose conversation easily ranged from baby care to God and the absurdities of parish life. Still, it was a special treat to have a visit from Dr. Bowman.

Her stay in the city had so far proved peculiarly serene. Ever since she had knelt at the Communion rail in Trinity Church and confessed the plain facts with no attempt to make excuses, she had viewed herself and her predicament in a double way. First of all, she saw the fix she was in. No state of inner serenity could wipe out the fact that she had voluntarily committed fornication, that she was pregnant, that she was in hiding to avoid public shame, that she would have to give away the little life now stirring in her. Her words of admission at the Communion rail and the sense of forgiveness had not changed any of that. She was still pregnant, and the baby would be illegitimate. At the same time, everything *had* changed. She found herself looking at her memories as though they were about events that had happened to another person. A transparent curtain had fallen between the girl of five months ago and the girl she was now. She could think of the boy with neither desire nor hatred. She had no feeling whatever about him. He was a name, a memory from someone else's life.

Her earlier mood of wishing to be punished had passed. She went to church regularly, not in an agony of self-reproach, but because the presence of Christ seemed most certain and intense there.

Next afternoon, when Dr. Bowman rang, Helen met him at the door and took him to the deserted parlor of the big old house. "All you need to do is play that dusty melodion in the corner, and I'll feel like a gay young blade of the nineties, come a-courting," Dr. Bowman said.

They sat down, and Dr. Bowman continued, "You've got to come back soon, Helen. The soprano section in the choir isn't what it used to be."

For almost an hour they talked, sometimes plunging deeply into some question of God and man, but mostly skimming from one light topic to another. As time went on, Helen had an odd feeling that Dr. Bowman's thoughts were wandering away. He seemed to be conversing with the top of his mind.

All at once his manner grew more serious. "I talked with the rector and the social worker before I came over here. They think they've got it worked out."

"About the adoption?"

"That's right. There's a teacher in this city. He and his wife have badly wanted children, but none have come. They're a fine couple, the rector tells me, active in the church, very fond of children. You understand that I can't tell you their name. In fact, I took care not to learn it myself, so I wouldn't be tempted to make a mistake and tell you. Anyway, I think they'll be as fine parents as a baby could ask for."

Helen sat quietly while a kind of drab misery flowed through her mind and heart. "I suppose so," she said. "I'm glad that's over with."

Dr. Bowman looked at her sharply with a glance of concern. Then he opened his brief case. "The social worker said that since I was coming on here, I might as well bring these papers along. You and your parents will need to sign them. There's no hurry, but he did say—and I think it's true—that the sooner you sign them, the better. It's a bridge you have to cross, a painful one, and putting it off doesn't help."

"I'll take care of them later," Helen said dully as she laid the papers on the coffee table.

"Enough business for today," Dr. Bowman said. "Let's kneel together for a bit and then explore the neighborhood." They knelt there on the floor in silence for some time. Then Dr. Bowman quietly offered a series of prayers: for strength, for guidance, for a blessing upon Helen, the baby, and all who were helping her. They ended by saying the Lord's Prayer together.

Dr. Bowman stood up and helped Helen to rise. "Now let's go exploring," he suggested briskly. The two of them wandered outside, down a street of big old Victorian houses and spacious yards.

"You aren't dieting?" Dr. Bowman asked anxiously.

"The doctor hasn't said anything about it yet."

"Good. I'm hungry. How about joining me in a snack at that little place down the street?" She panted a bit but kept up beside him as he strode toward the small short-order stand with the determination of a man who can smell food from afar.

It was later, back at the house after Dr. Bowman had left to catch his plane, that all the life and hope seemed to drain from her body. It happened all at once. She was up in her room. On the desk before her, beside her neatly stacked textbooks, were the papers Dr. Bowman had left—papers crisp and impersonally legal in their language, papers by which she would forever give up all claim to the life that was moving in her at that very moment, relinquish it into the hands of people whose names she would never know.

She stared again at the papers. The abrupt anger of desperation seethed in her. She knew for certain now. She would not, she could not sign them. Nobody could make her sign them. She would be damned and burn in hell forever before she would sign her baby away. It was hers! Before she would sign, she would take the baby back with her to Blanton and rear it herself, and public opinion be damned. She would ask her parents to pretend it was a belated child of their own. They were still young enough for this to be plausible.

Or she would run away to some distant city and pretend she was a widow or divorcee. People move around so much that few questions are asked. Or she would search and find someone, almost anyone, who would marry her and give a name to the baby. She would even beg the father of the baby to marry her. A shudder went through her body as she pictured this, but she did not repudiate the thought. She would do anything rather than give up the baby.

She burst into wild tears. She threw the crisp papers against the wall. "It's mine, it's mine," she screamed to the blank walls. "It's mine!"

Exhaustion overcame her at last. She lay down. Her heart was beating wildly. Perhaps she half dozed. She woke again, a little calmer now, and very weak. With a painful effort she got down to the floor and knelt there. "Not my will but Thine be done," she slowly said, and slowly rose.

She sat wearily on the side of the bed. "But it's still mine," she sobbed dully. She looked off into the distance. "Thy will— what is Thy will, God? Are You the kind of God who goes around snatching newborn babies from their mothers' arms? Are You a kidnaper?"

A strange pleasure coursed through her tired body. She hated God. She knew how she could outwit Him. He was biding His time, waiting to take her baby and give it into other arms. But what if the baby were never born? If she died before that, and the baby with her? Suppose she had the last laugh on God?

She imagined herself drowning or jumping from a high place. She laughed with triumph. She laughed again. She couldn't stop laughing. She fell over on the bed in paroxysms of laughter.

There was a knock at the door. Mrs. Blumenthal softly opened it. She walked quickly to the bed and sat Helen up. "Stop it!" she commanded sharply.

The insane laughter continued. Mrs. Blumenthal shook her by the shoulders. The laughter kept on. Deliberately she drew back her open palm and gave Helen a hard, stinging slap on the cheek. Helen gasped, as though she had momentarily stopped breathing. The crazy laughter ceased. Tears and sobs started. Mrs. Blumenthal sat down beside her on the bed and put Helen's head on her own shoulder. They sat there a while, Helen sobbing but less violently and Mrs. Blumenthal patting her head and occasionally kissing her as though she were a much younger child. Finally, Mrs. Blumenthal gently put her down on the bed, covered her with a sheet, and said, "Go to sleep now." She kissed her again and tiptoed out.

Helen slept for several hours. When she woke, the memory of everything came back to her. Wearily she reviewed the possibilities, the ways of keeping the baby. Each of them had something wrong with it—obvious deception or eventual shame for the baby or poverty and hardship. There was no magic way out, no solution that didn't cut and sear and burn someone. She or the baby—one or the other must pay the price.

Wearily she repeated, "But it's mine." Yes, it was hers. But was it hers alone? She clasped her face in her hands. The baby was hers. Her body, yes, made this new life possible. But what of the time when the baby was no longer in this temporary home of her body? To whom does a baby really belong? To the mother? To the father? To society? To someone else?

There was no way out. Once more she fell to her knees.

"My Lord and my God," she said in a voice that was more a groan than a prayer. "Thy will, not mine, be done. Into Thy hands."

She knelt a long time. When she rose, she knew that she would sign the legal papers. But there was no hurry. She could sign them whenever her parents came up to see her.

Meanwhile, Dr. Bowman had taken a taxi to the airport and was snug in the plane with his safety belt fastened. Soon the plane was high over the city, and wispy clouds veiled the earth below so that it was indistinct and unreal.

Poor Helen, Dr. Bowman thought. Caught in a situation with no easy way out, no way without pain and agony. He shut out the distracting noise of the plane, and centered his awareness upon the thought of God. Something seemed to slide into focus. Then he let the memory of Helen come into his mind. "She is Yours, God," he whispered. "Help her, be with her."

The vision of Helen and the Presence faded; he looked out the window at the clouds so many hundreds and thousands of feet below. Betwixt heaven and earth, he thought. Pulled every second toward the earth by gravity, yet sustained by air and wings and propeller.

"Thank God I've finished high school," Dr. Bowman said devoutly to himself and chuckled. Half the sorrow and pain of teen-age life came from a mistaken idea, promulgated by the popular arts, that the 'teens are or ought to be a happy time. When of course it's obvious, Dr. Bowman said to himself, that of all times of life, the 'teens are the most wretched. You're growing up, cutting your teeth on life and on each other; you're physically and psychologically and socially clumsy. In short, it's natural and proper to be wretched from the age of thirteen to nineteen, and if this important fact, now to be known as "Bowman's Law," were more widely disseminated, the occasional flashes of contentment or even happiness which momentarily lighten the Stygian gloom of adolescence would make the period of life reasonably tolerable. But if you *expect* happiness . . .

His thoughts turned to his own daughter. Poor Betty, he mused. She had told him about the cooling-off period, told him soon after the agreement was made, and now she was trying so hard to act normal, happy, and well-adjusted. Day before yesterday he'd heard her sobbing up in her room. When he went in and she was finally able to talk, it appeared that she had gone to the Shack with the editor of the high school paper and while there Steve had come in with a loquacious sophomore who kept looking up into his eyes with yearning and admiration, and Steve had appeared to be having a very good time. "But you were out with another boy," Dr. Bowman had said. "I *know* that." Betty had answered. "But I was having a *miserable* time, and Steve looked *happy.*" She had paused and then said in a less certain voice, "At least I had a miserable time after Steve came into the Shack."

It's hard to be young, Dr. Bowman thought. Not only did Betty get upset now at the slightest thing, but then she would go around for hours afterwards feeling embarrassed and ashamed because she had "acted like a ten-year-old." It's bad enough to be adolescent, but worse still if you feel guilty at acting like an adolescent. Hooray for middle age!

Middle age. Middle age. As he repeated the words to himself, they didn't have quite as jolly and contented a ring as the first time. He found his memory traveling back to his own 'teens when he had decided he was willing to live up to the age of thirty but not beyond. What had he feared about the stretch of life beyond thirty? As he remembered, he hadn't worried much about the decline in physical vigor. No, his fear was that in middle age you became an old fogey—that all the spirit of adventure and taking a chance faded out, and you played it safe and became complacent.

Well? A voice seemed to sound in Dr. Bowman's mind. Taking chances? Or do you play it safe? Have you become the middle-aged old fogey you once feared you would be?

This whole business of broadening out the base of the parish. How courageous, how Christian was it to operate like a ward politician, trying to manipulate other people into taking the initiative—like expecting the YPF to pave the way? Or this idea of a Spanish Eucharist. You don't have to get the approval of the vestry before you at least learn to read the service aloud in Spanish. The question of a curate can come later. And you don't have to win over the vestry before you do a bit of calling on the North Side and invite anyone who's interested to attend Trinity Church. In short, you've been trying to bring up the rear of the procession. It's time for you to put yourself in front —that's what the congregation hired you for and God chose you for—and march ahead. Maybe the people will follow or maybe they won't, but if you have Christ marching beside you, you belong to the majority.

Dr. Bowman was sitting up straight now. When he got back to Blanton, he would call on Carlos Arrondo. He would be a good man to talk with to get advice on how to reach other people on the North Side and interest them in the Church. Possibly Mr. Arrondo, who seemed to have no strong Church connections, might himself start coming to Trinity.

Dr. Bowman's mind raced on ahead. He should have the Spanish Eucharist under way in a few weeks. Once it was established—say a month or six weeks from now—he would get in touch with Sid Pruitt and with Frank Buell (if he had actually joined the Stalwarts) and see whether the Stalwarts would like to meet in the parish house. Dr. Bowman smiled. The YPF, when debating the thing in the abstract, might evade taking formal action to invite the North Siders in, but once the Stalwarts began meeting in the parish house, he was sure that the situation would take care of itself—particularly as some of the North Side boys were extraordinarily good athletes and would be a godsend to the YPF basketball team. Perhaps that was too cynical a way of putting it. Dr. Bowman was convinced that the YPF was really more ready than the older people in the church to welcome one and all. His mistake had been in not simply taking that readiness for granted. One should not make Christians hold plebiscites on whether or not they want to be Christians.

16

FLIGHT

FRANK'S initial impression of the Stalwarts was that their reputation had been much exaggerated. At close hand they seemed not so much sinister as pitiful, a group of little boys who happened to have big bodies and who met together with much show of secrecy in order to do nothing in particular. Weekly and sometimes oftener they assembled, usually in the back room of the Greasy Spoon. There was much talk about "planning," but nothing definite ever seemed to emerge. At times the discussion took on a darker tone as the talk turned to the presumed plans of *them*. It wasn't at first clear to Frank just who *they* were. Sometimes the term seemed to apply specifically to the Omegas; frequently it broadened out to embrace by implication the whole middle and upper levels of Blanton life. Nor was he ever certain what *they* were guilty of, except being what they were and occupying the positions into which they had been born.

After a succession of meetings in which little was talked about except *them* and what *we* are going to do to frustrate their plans, Frank admitted to himself that he was beginning to feel bored. He even wondered if there were some tactful way he could resign, but in his mind he could picture the bitterly hurt and cynical look Sid Pruitt would turn on him. It had taken some talking to get accepted as a member in the first place. He could imagine Sid's biting inquiry, "Had enough of slummin', huh?" He had also grown to know a number of the boys' families. He must have seemed a strange visitor in their homes, but they received him without question because he was a friend of their sons. Before Frank quite knew what was happening, he had developed a sense of belonging, of personal loyalty, which he had never experienced as he looked about at the large, well-landscaped lawns of Oak Hill.

A few days previously Rosa had stopped him in the school corridor and said hastily, "Frank, I hear you're with the Stalwarts. Are you doing it because you've turned against Oak Hill and want to identify with the North Side? I ought to tell you this—the North Side isn't proud of the Stalwarts. They're the wrong kind." He had wanted to ask her some questions, but before he could frame them, she had given him a troubled smile and fled like a frightened bird to her next class. Frank had felt a surge of resentment. If Rosa and her family represented the "right kind" on the North Side, and if her door were closed to him, who was she to lecture him if he ran with the "wrong kind"?

This latest meeting of the Stalwarts had a more electric tone from the beginning. It had been called on short notice for 10:30 in the evening. This time it was definite that *they* were the Omega Alphas. Just what had happened was not absolutely clear. All anyone could prove for certain was that Sid Pruitt had been out with his girl the night before, had driven her home, parked his car on a side street, and that as he returned to his car he had been set upon by five persons. Four of them had held him firmly while the fifth systematically worked him over from the chest to the head, leaving bruises and scratches on his face which were still livid when the Stalwarts met in conclave. The alley was very dark and by the faint light from an upstairs window no certain identification could be made. But Sid was

morally sure that he recognized one of the boys: his assailant.
It was Bill Pendleton. He had recognized his voice, also. When
Sid was finally released, he saw the five persons speeding away
in a car which was either Bill's or a duplicate of it. There
couldn't be any real doubt.

It was the kind of evidence that probably would not stand up
in a court of law, but a meeting of the Stalwarts was not the con-
vening of a court. Simpler rules of evidence prevailed.

As the discussion raged with mounting fury, Frank thought
for a brief moment of suggesting that they phone the police and
bring charges against Bill Pendleton; but he had been with the
Stalwarts long enough to know that this was an unthinkable
suggestion. The police and the school system belonged with
them and were part of a total system to keep *us* down. The
Stalwarts believed in justice, but it had to be homemade. Thus
their meeting took on the functions of police, prosecuting at-
torney, judge, jury, and executioner.

The meeting was rushing toward a speedy verdict of Guilty
when Frank interrupted, "What real proof do we have?"

Half a dozen Stalwarts turned on him savagely. In the loud
chaos of their shouts he could not make out separate sentences, but a general meaning came through. Was he with
them or not? If he was with them, O.K. If he wasn't, he could
go back to Oak Hill where he belonged. Inwardly, Frank
wavered. It still seemed to him that the Stalwarts were working themselves up into an orgy of emotion and hatred on in-
sufficient evidence. If he left, however, they would think, and
have a right to think, that he was just a playboy who had walked
out when the going got rough. These boys of the North Side,
some of whom could hardly speak English and whose faces
were a whole human spectrum of complexions, had accepted
him as he was, accepted him with his expensive clothes, his correct English, and a thousand more subtle differences. Was it

for him to set himself up as a standard and say, "Follow my advice or I'm pulling out"? Bill Pendleton was almost certainly guilty anyway. Frank decided he would stay with them. Maybe he could persuade them not to do anything too dangerous.

The meeting continued noisily to a unanimous verdict of Guilty. "O.K., guys," President Pruitt said through swollen lips. "What we gonna do to 'im?"

"Work 'im over!" somebody screamed, and there was a chorus of assent. The combined judge and jury had a simple system of law: tit for tat, an eye for an eye and a tooth for a tooth.

The boys settled down to make practical plans—how to lure Bill into a car; where to drive him; who should have the privilege of holding him while Sid worked him over; whether or not to add brass knucks for good measure.

Frank began to be alarmed at this point. "Can't we do anything better than just imitate them?" he asked.

"O.K., bright kid," Sid snarled. "What do *you* suggest?"

Frank did not flinch. "We're letting them call the turns. Can't we do something different?"

"Such as?" Sid asked, drawling the last word.

Frank was caught short. He thought frantically.

"The bright guy's *thinking*. Let the guy think," the president said solemnly and settled back to enjoy Frank's discomfiture.

"It seems to me," Frank said at last, "that if there's something that Bill is especially fond of—"

"That hi-fi set of his!" one of the members shouted.

"Let's smash it up!" another suggested.

"No, not that," Frank interrupted. "Let's take it."

"We could use it for dances," Sid agreed, and he looked pleased.

"He's sunk a thousand dollars of his old man's money in it," another Stalwart said.

Sid remarked, "I'd still like to work that guy over, but Frank's right. The hi-fi's better."

Frank's heart might have risen. He had made a successful suggestion, and he had saved Bill from possibly being marred for life, but he felt a sinking sensation in his stomach.

By now Frank was forgotten. The meeting was given over to energetic planning. Sid hastily disappeared into the main part of the Greasy Spoon and returned to say that he had phoned Bill's number, and nobody answered. Now was the time to strike.

"Five guys will do it. Four to carry the stuff, one to watch outside. I'm going. How about you and you and you?" He pointed to three of the numerous volunteers who were clamoring to go along. Very slowly he turned to Frank. "Wanna go?"

"Yes," said Frank. A fleeting silence fell over the meeting. Frank felt all eyes on him. Then the clamor resumed. In that brief moment he had experienced the most delicious of sensations—complete acceptance and approval. It was funny that his stomach felt more like a ball of lead than ever.

"Come on, guys," Sid said. "Meeting adjourned."

He strode from the room into an alley, followed by Frank and the three others. They chose a beat-up station wagon belonging to one of the five. He was a relatively new member and his vehicle was not well known to the police; it was also roomy enough.

Frank and Sid sat on the front seat as they drove toward one of the few good residential districts still left in the heart of Blanton. It was after midnight, and no other cars were in sight when they approached Bill's house. Sid parked half a block away. "You guys stay here. I'll go ring and hide in the bushes and make sure nobody's home."

They waited in silence. They could see Sid striding down the sidewalk, see him as he went to the door, see him give a quick push on the doorbell and duck behind a clump of evergreens. No lights came on. Sid dashed out and rang a second time, then disappeared once more into the bushes. There was still no response. Soon he was headed back. "Somebody said at school they were going off someplace for a wedding," he said. "Now's the chance."

Sid reached in his pocket and pulled out a flashlight and some small tool, then put them back. "I'll park in the driveway," he said.

After the station wagon was parked, Sid turned to the three other Stalwarts. "Come along with me," he said. He turned to Frank. "You wait behind them bushes. If you see anybody come up the walk, whistle loud and run like hell."

A mixed feeling went through Frank. Was he being treated as a second-class member? Nevertheless, he felt relief.

"Hold this flashlight," Sid said to one of his assistants while Frank stationed himself behind the evergreens. He could see Sid take the small tool from his pocket and work at the lock. In a moment the door was open. The four Stalwarts disappeared inside. The door closed again.

Nothing happened—for a long time, nothing. No sound came from inside the dark house. Then Frank noticed a very faint glow from the shiny evergreens. He looked up. A window on the second floor was faintly bright as though from the gleam of a flashlight. He waited and waited. The slight radiance danced now and then from the needles of the trees. The house was as still as death. Once he thought he heard the sound of men lifting some heavy object and setting it down again, but he couldn't be sure. If there had been a sound, it soon ceased. The street was utterly deserted; no lights burned in any of the neighboring houses.

All at once something snapped in Frank. For a split second he saw the Stalwarts as they were: boys who indeed had been handicapped from the start by poverty or sordidly broken homes or difficult racial or ethnic backgrounds but whose resentment had been turned in wholly destructive directions. His heart went out to them, but he would not be helping them if he became one more of their kind. He looked up and down the street. All was quiet and dark. He wasn't really needed as a sentry. "Good-bye," he said softly and started running for the street as fast as he had ever run in his life.

He had barely reached the street when it happened. A loud scream rang out from the house and then another. There was the sound of tramping feet and scuffling. Suddenly, another scream pierced the air and there was a noise as though some heavy object were tumbling down the stairs, several steps at a time.

Frank turned and ran into the house. "Run like hell," Sid said as he bore down upon him with the flashlight. "Run to the car." The three others were close on his heels. On the landing between the first and second floor lay a heavy-set man in pajamas. It was Bill's father. At that distance, Frank couldn't tell whether the man was breathing.

Panic took over. Frank followed the four others and tumbled into the station wagon. They backed out and roared down the street. All the way back to the Greasy Spoon he expected to hear the sound of police sirens, but the night remained quiet.

"What happened?" Frank asked on the way.

"Light me a smoke, will you?" Frank lit the cigarette and put it between Sid's lips.

"Thanks. What happened? We was disconnectin' Bill's hi-fi. Didn't seem to be nobody in the house. Started carryin' the stuff out in the hall. All at once, hall light come on. There was old man Pendleton a-standin'. One of the guys give it to 'im. He fell backward, the old guy did, rolled down the stairs."

There wasn't much more talk in the station wagon. When

they reached the alley by the Greasy Spoon, the Stalwarts piled out, fled to their separate cars, and departed. The Greasy Spoon, which catered to the swing and graveyard shifts, was still open. Frank's panic subsided for a moment, and he went inside to the telephone booth. He dialed the hospital. Disguising his voice to make it sound as old as possible, he hurriedly said, "Send an ambulance at once to the home of William Pendleton," and he gave the address. When the voice at the other end pressed him for details, he added, "The door's wide open, go right in," and repeated the address.

For the rest of that night, it seemed, he acted like a mechanical man, but a cunning one. He took a taxi home from the Greasy Spoon. Everyone was fast asleep. He tiptoed up to his room and packed a small suitcase. He searched a jacket of his father's, hanging in the hall, and found a substantial trove of banknotes. These he put into his own wallet. He telephoned for a taxi. When it arrived, he tiptoed outside with his suitcase and gave the address in a whisper. It was a small bar on the outer fringes of the North Side.

"Slumming?" the taxi driver asked. Frank laughed knowingly.

"If you're looking for it, you can get it there," the driver said with a touch of disapproval.

Frank said nothing. Soon they arrived at the bar. Frank paid and got out. Not far beyond was a filling station where trucks frequently stopped. It was on the four-lane highway which led to the big city. Luck again was with Frank. He caught a ride with a truck driver who wanted someone to talk with, or rather, talk to. During the long night he regaled Frank with his adventures among the female life of the countries in which he had been stationed during his military service. It was a distinguished record, but Frank only half heard.

Dawn had already broken when they arrived at the edge of

the great city. Frank thanked the truck driver, got out, paused long enough for a solid breakfast at a roadside restaurant, and took a taxi to the airport. He quickly walked to the counter and asked for a ticket, one-way, to Los Angeles.

"Very sorry, sir, but we're completely sold out for this flight," the clerk said. "If you could wait until afternoon—"

The sense of panic gripped Frank again. He *had* to leave. "Isn't there any chance, any way—?"

"If you wish to stay in the stand-by line, there's always the chance of last-minute cancellations. There are two persons ahead of you."

"Thanks," said Frank, "I'll gamble it." He walked over to the stand-by line. The minutes and seconds ticked slowly. The plane was called over the P.A. Passengers, who had been sitting around in the lobby, arose with tickets in their hands and disappeared. The clerk came and spoke to the two men in front of him. They also disappeared. Frank was left alone.

The P.A. was calling the flight again. Frank had a wild impulse. Suppose he tried to sneak onto the plane? Could he be a stowaway? While he was thinking about it, the clerk motioned him over. "Just in time," he said. "Another passenger failed to show up. Here's your ticket, sir, and you'd best hurry."

Frank paid his fare. In three minutes he was on a powerful jet plane, flying nonstop to Los Angeles.

17

QUIET CRISES

DURING the morning that Frank was flying to Los Angeles, it was reported over the radio and TV that Mr. William Pendleton, Sr., had been found unconscious and suffering from a heart attack in his home and that he had been taken to the hospital where his condition was regarded as critical. The account said that in young Bill Pendleton's room the parts of his hi-fi set were scattered about. The police were investigating certain undisclosed clues, but so far there had been no arrests. A major political scandal involving the mayor broke the same morning, and as a result the escapade at the Pendletons' got sketchy treatment.

At the breakfast table, Mr. and Mrs. Buell for once really discussed something. They admitted they were afraid. Frank hadn't slept in his bed; the money was missing from Mr. Buell's wallet; there was the episode at the Pendletons' which they had just heard over the radio.

"The boy's a fool," Mr. Buell said, more sadly than in anger. "In his reaction against Oak Hill and me he will go to almost any crazy lengths, but he's still decent underneath. I can't believe he'd really get mixed up in a housebreaking."

Sarah shook her head. "I wish I could be sure. When you get involved in a club, there's group pressure. He may have drifted into the situation until it was too late to turn back. More bacon? Here, I'll go get some more."

When Sarah Buell came back, her husband said slowly, "The one thing that's certain is that he's run away from home. We can't know for sure whether it's tied in with this Pendleton business. It *could* be plain coincidence."

"Do you suppose he's gone back to his mother?" Sarah asked.

"He hasn't seen her for years!" John Buell protested.

"I know. Yet he has a kind of dream picture of her."

"The flight back to the womb. Well, it could be. Anything could be." He thought a while. "We've got to handle this thing carefully and keep it out of the papers. I'll talk with the school and hush it up there."

"Where do you really think he is?"

"I don't know. Your guess is as good as mine. Anyway, maybe he's got to get this restlessness out of his system. One thing I will do. Your idea about his mother may be right. It's the crazy kind of thing he'd do if he were in a muddle. I know a lawyer in L.A. I'll have him check up quietly."

Thus life in Blanton went on almost as usual. The day had something strange in it only for a handful of people—the mayor, facing a besieging throng of newspaper reporters from the metropolitan newspapers and *Time* as well as near-by papers and the standard press services; Mr. Pendleton, in an oxygen tent for the first time in his life; his son, Bill, who had hastily returned from a wedding in another city.

Life in Blanton went on almost as usual except for a few people, another of whom was Tom Bowman. This morning he had a physics test coming up. He had spent much more time than usual studying for it. He knew now that the life of science was not for him, but he had signed up for physics, which he would never conceivably put to any use. He wasn't one of the spaceship boys any more except in imagination, yet by a grim act of the will he had studied for the test as though the safety of the nation and the health of his soul hinged on the results.

Now, in the classroom, while plaster busts of Newton and Einstein glared down at him in disappointment, he studied the test questions. Blind panic, different in cause but not in quality from Frank's of the night before, invaded his inner parts. The words, the symbols before him were as familiar as the letters of the alphabet, but their combinations meant nothing, absolutely nothing. It was as though he were looking at a set of physics problems for the first time. He might be little Nancy, for all he knew of physics, and he had spent so many weary hours at it. Hours he might have devoted to subjects in which he had a chance ... or to reading for pleasure ... or to praying ... or to helping with housework. At the moment, any of these alternatives seemed delightful.

Two or three of the problems, at most, he might do with ease; half a dozen were borderline possibilities, but the rest ...

It isn't fair, something inside of him protested. If I hadn't studied, O.K., but I studied and studied hard, harder than I ever do in the courses where I get a C or B. I wasted all that time ... for nothing.

The hectographed sheets in front of him blurred to a purple haze and his thoughts wandered. He had read enough in popular anthropology to know that the things which one society takes with great moral earnestness can seem trivial and ridiculous to people in another society. Each society has its own system of fetishes and tabus. There are things you've got to do and things you mustn't do or Mama will spank or the hangman will hang. Look at this school, thought Tom. Wouldn't it provide a field day for an anthropologist from the Fiji Islands? It would take an outsider to observe and analyze the whole network of tabus and fetishes that keeps Blanton Senior High functioning after a fashion. Take physics. Everybody makes an inward genuflection at the mention of physics. Even those (maybe especially those) who have never studied it assume without question that it's of absolute worth and you can't have enough of it. The hours I've spent studying physics—why, they're like the living sacrifices offered on the altar of a pagan god. The name of the god is physics, and holy is his name.

A sudden sense of liberation flowed through Tom. He laughed to himself and said in an almost audible whisper, "Ye mice of Blanton, I perceive that in all things ye are too superstitious. For as I passed by and beheld your devotions, I found an altar with this inscription, TO THE UNKNOWN GOD. Whom therefore ye ignorantly worship, him declare I unto you. His name is PHYSICS."

The test on the desk now seemed a comic thing, and the earnest students all around him were half-naked primitives, solemnly doing their duties by sacred stones, bits of colored cloth, and feathered tokens.

The exciting sense of liberation grew rapidly. It didn't matter whether he learned physics. No one really expected him to. The requirement was merely that he go through the motions, that he make the right marks on pieces of paper so as to satisfy the high priest, the shaman, his teacher. Then he could forget all about it.

The comic vision of the world lifted up his heart to unaccustomed joy. He looked to the front and slightly to the left where a student was devoutly at work on problem number 11. This was one of the true believers, a young man to whom physics was an entrée into ultimate mysteries. Twenty years from now he would be seen in the priestly white coat of a professor in some famous laboratory. Verily they have their reward.

No longer a naked savage bowing down to sticks and stones, but a liberated spirit who recognizes tabus and fetishes for what they are, Tom turned back to the test with peace of mind. The hectographed sheets looked almost friendly now, as though they were a child's jigsaw puzzle. Quickly, in a playful spirit, he did the three problems that were obvious. Two of the others took very little longer. He then worked four others which at first had seemed mere nonsense. Enough accomplished for a good solid F-plus or D-minus, he thought to himself. I'm making progress.

Ahead of him the true believer had finished all his problems and was systematically going through them again to check his work. Suppose, Tom asked himself and played with the idea, suppose I decided to profit from his labors? Who would really suffer loss? The true believer is certain of an A, no matter what the curve is. The general public? It won't be defrauded. I'll never list physics on any letters of application. What harm will it actually do? None that I can see. What difference will it make? Maybe the difference between the letter F or D and the letter C on a piece of cardboard. I won't be any more ignorant nor any wiser than now.

The physics teacher was one who made a point of leaving the room as often as possible during tests so as to emphasize his faith in the students. It was not that cheating was unknown in the school, but physics, with its special aura of the hallowed, seemed to have very little of it. The teacher was out of the room now. It was Tom's opportunity. Inwardly laughing with the intoxication of freedom, he leaned forward slightly and carefully studied the answers on the desk of the true believer. Then, when the latter some minutes later sighed with contentment and turned his test in a good ten minutes before the bell would ring, Tom swiftly reverted to his own work and completed as many of the problems as time permitted, handing the test in as the second bell rang. He would get a C at least, he was certain, possibly a C-plus or even a B-minus.

As he left with the other late-finishers, he was surprised to realize that some of the problems which he had completed with the help of the true believer were now lucid and simple in his own mind. This struck him as comic in a peculiarly delicious way. "The wages of sin," he said to himself. He had put himself above the whole system. It was a charming irony that in rejecting the system he had come a shade closer to fulfilling its requirements. He had actually learned a little physics.

This mood continued until after lunch. Then it collapsed. Another corner of his mind demanded a hearing. This new voice didn't try to argue about comparative anthropology, but quite simply said, "You cheated." When the amateur anthropologist within Tom tried to argue back, the new voice said, "You're getting credit for something you didn't do. You're a thief."

The two voices rose higher and higher in Tom's mind until his inward ear was deafened by their strident clamor. He was glad he had a study hall in midafternoon. Carefully placing his physics book, open, before him, and sitting in an attitude that suggested deep study, he tried to think it through. The two halves of his mind were engaged in a cold war. Could there be any reconciliation?

The inner clamor of competing voices continued, but at last, by an effort of the will, he stilled the voices sufficiently to do some thinking. It took him most of the period to reach a point where he thought he saw a possible meeting ground between the two voices. As he saw the meeting ground shaping up, a sense of dread deepened in him.

It was true, he decided. Everything the first voice said was true. The customs and values of Blanton High, as of Blanton the city, as of an Eskimo tribe or Tibetan village, were taken for granted, passed on from generation to generation with little change and less examination. These customs and values simply *were*. Many of them could not stand up under the microscope of logical analysis. Their survival depended on their being accepted as part of a total, unquestioned pattern of thought and behavior.

The thing was as comic as he had earlier thought it, but a new realization was forcing its way in. The sacred status of physics survived or fell with the sacred status of a number of other assumptions which were equally incapable of proof. In Blanton Senior High and Blanton the city it was generally assumed that kindness is better than cruelty, love is better than hate, honesty better than dishonesty, beauty better than ugliness, and a church more important than a race track. Many people in their daily lives might show by their actions that they really held to other beliefs, but at least they paid lip service to the values assumed by the community. Indeed, most people did not, at least in public behavior, do anything which grossly contradicted the norms of Blanton.

Now, none of these assumptions, these norms, could be proved. Suppose someone said, "I think cruelty is better than kindness." What answer could you make? You might invoke the authority of God, but the person could say, "I don't believe in God." You might use the "I'll scratch your back and you scratch mine" argument, but then all the person needed to say was that he didn't like to have his back scratched. Then he might say, "I enjoy cruelty." There was no answer to this. It was the same with honesty, beauty, with everything that made Blanton, even Blanton, something several notches higher in development than the jungle.

But where did this leave him? Should he secede from society? There must be some desert isles left. If he stayed in society, wasn't it up to him to recognize the comic and absurd elements in the tabu and fetish system, but still to say, "On balance, the good features of the whole pattern much outweigh the bad; on balance, I'll buy the whole system, since it hangs together as one piece."

If he did this, he couldn't be above the system and inside it at the same time. It was one thing or the other, the desert isle or playing the game according to the local rules.

This was as far as Tom had got when the bell rang. The next hour, American Problems, was so filled with class discussion in which the teacher frequently called on him, that he had no further time to think it out.

The bell rang for the end of school. With a sense of doom that grew at each step, Tom walked to the home room of his physics teacher. He knocked. A voice called, "Come in."

The teacher was putting a rubber band around the stack of tests. "Hello, Tom," he said. "Did you want to see me about the test? I'll have them ready by tomorrow."

"Could I see my test?" Tom asked.

"Here it is," the teacher said, fishing it from near the top of the pile. He handed it to Tom.

Tom took it, stared at it for a moment, and slowly tore it into little bits which he threw into the wastebasket. His teacher looked at him intently.

"I guess—I guess that's all," Tom said and turned to go.

"Wait a minute," the teacher said, and he stood up. "Don't you want to talk with me, Tom?"

Tom turned around, very pale. He swallowed and managed to say, "No, thank you, sir."

After Tom left, the teacher drummed nervously on his desk a moment, then took a sheet of paper, wrote "Bowman, F" on it, and inserted it where Tom's test had been. He wasn't sure he understood but was almost sure. It was strange that he often caught himself liking Tom more than the altogether admirable young physicist who sat in the front row.

That night, after supper, Tom went upstairs to study, but he found he was more shaken by the events of the day than he had realized. It was still a little early to consider the possibility of going to bed. To pass the time he walked down the hall to Betty's room and rapped. "It's Tom."

"Come in," she called.

Betty was sitting at a cluttered desk, and Tom's sure intuition told him that she was making about as much progress studying as he was.

"What's the latest on the chastity test?" he asked.

"Oh, the poor dear thing!" Betty said, giggling with a hint of sobs. "The silly angel! Look at this—he sent it to me in a sealed envelope by another boy today." She handed a sheet of paper to Tom.

"What's this?" he asked. Then he read aloud:

DEAR BETTY:

If you agree with this, sign it at the bottom and return it to me by the same messenger.

Love,
STEVE

Agreement

Steve promises not to be at the Shack with another girl between 3:30 and 4:45, and Betty promises not to be there with another boy between 4:45 and 6:00. Either may be there with anybody after that.

(Signed) ....

STEVE HADLEY

P.S. I think this would make it easier on us both, don't you?

"Whew!" exclaimed Tom. "It's true love or the green-eyed monster or a powerful combination of both."

"I know how he feels," Betty said ruefully. "When I saw him there with that sophomore, I could have scratched her eyes out!"

"How about Steve's eyes?"

"No, they're too nice."

Tom smiled and studied his sister's face. Undeniably pretty, he admitted to himself with a twinge of surprise. "I gather that the sun is about to break through the clouds and reveal love's young dream pure and unalloyed?"

"I wish I were sure!" Betty said petulantly. "Oh, Tom, he's the sweetest boy, but he is such a boy. Such a solemn, serious, earnest boy. And when I get to thinking about him—"

"Do you ever stop?"

"Hush!" She slapped him across the lips. "When on rare occasions I think about him, I'm just as much mixed up inside as ever. I want to disappear into his arms and all that. At the same time I keep thinking of irritating things he's certain to say and the irritating replies I'll make."

"As much up in the air as ever? Life is a mess, a bewildering, surrealistic mess. Good night, sweet lady. 'We are such stuff as dreams are made on, and our little life is rounded with a sleep.' I'm going to hit the sack."

"Toodle-oo," said Betty.

Five minutes after Tom fell into bed, he was asleep, but around five in the morning he woke up, feeling he had slept enough. Breakfast was a lifetime away. He quietly turned on his reading lamp and sat at his desk, flipping through the pages of his physics book. It was curious. He was more sure than ever that he would never make any use of physics, but he found it was as though a black mist were clearing away. He now understood without difficulty a great many things that no amount of hard effort had enabled him to master.

Despite his new penetration into the occult mysteries, his thoughts soon turned to more personal matters. He had learned something about himself yesterday, about his capacity to play the cold-blooded and detached cynic. What had seemed to him at the time a delicious sense of the comic and a glorious liberation was now terrifying to remember. It bore the face of hard and complacent pride, a feeling of superiority based on deception.

Was there any real alternative between being a beachcomber

on a desert isle or an uncritical member of the social herd? Was there any way you could be a co-operating member of society and still recognize the good and the bad in its value-system and work to strengthen the good and change the bad?

"I wish I knew why people act as they do, why *I* act as I do," he muttered to himself. Certainly, he saw now, before he could offer himself as a skilled remodeler of Blanton's inherited house of custom and tradition, he needed to learn much more about the workings of society and the individual psyche. Most of all, however, he wanted to understand that deep well of mystery, himself.

The lone man on the desert isle or the ant in the anthill . . . Is there any compromise or midway point? Must one be either an anarchist or a conformist? Dad would probably say I'd find light on it somewhere in the Bible. O.K., light from any source is welcome.

On the bottom shelf of his bookcase was the old Bible concordance his father had given him upon purchasing a newer one. Tom picked it up. Conformity, conform. Here it is. Romans 12. Where's my Bible? He found it under the American Problems text and turned to Romans 12:

I beseech you therefore, brethren, by the mercies of God, that ye present your bodies a living sacrifice, holy, acceptable unto God, which is your reasonable service.

And be not conformed to this world: but be ye transformed by the renewing of your mind, that ye may prove what is that good, and acceptable, and perfect, will of God.

Conformity . . . At school everybody was against it. Yet everyone was for "social adjustment," and what's the difference? "Be not conformed to this world." Not *to this world*. But was there something else to which one *should* conform? "Be ye transformed by the renewing of your mind, that ye may prove what is that good, and acceptable, and perfect, will of God." Could this be the key, the way to escape the two horns of the dilemma? Was it possible that man was meant to conform only to the mind of God, and that in conforming to this he would acquire simultaneously his own freedom and also the insight and patience to work within the fabric of society, never its prisoner, and never its enemy and total destroyer, either; working within to renew and transform it closer to the mind of God? Working with love and patience, and in perfect freedom?

But I've got to know an awful lot more about what makes people tick and about God and that A number 1 mystery, myself, if I'm going to do all this, Tom reflected soberly. Anyhow, he felt better. It was still an hour before breakfast time. He tumbled back into bed and sleep took over again.

18

REUNION

THE PLANE was the biggest and fastest available for non-stop flights to Los Angeles, but to Frank the trip seemed endless. The image of his mother danced constantly before his eyes. He could see her peculiarly blue, but warm blue, eyes; the soft waves of her light brown hair; her body perhaps a little on the plump side, maternal and soft; her expression of mingled playfulness and tenderness.

Once or twice the phrase "return to the womb" flashed through his mind. He didn't try to argue with it. What was wrong with a womb? This day of all days he didn't try to convince himself that he was the captain of his own fate. He wanted to be comforted and protected and to live without asking or answering questions.

The interminable flight continued. Then all at once the plane was turning on its side, and buildings were visible, leaning at wild angles. The plane came to a smooth landing and taxied to the terminal. Finally the FASTEN YOUR SEAT BELT sign went off. Frank stood up. He felt stiff and as though he had traveled to the moon.

The endless line of passengers straggled out the narrow door and down the stairway. At last he was outside. He walked into the terminal and waited another ten minutes for his suitcase. Free at last, he went to the information desk. A bus downtown would leave in five minutes, but that was too long for Frank. He ran into a phone booth. Roger Lindquist, that was the name of her present husband. Here it was in one of the suburbs. He rushed out to where a line of taxis was waiting, hailed one, and gave the address.

It was another interminable extent of time as the taxi purred its smooth way through a landscape constantly reminiscent of the film industry whose world headquarters were not many miles away; a landscape with no winter in it. There were palm trees instead of leafless maples, golden oranges instead of the dark needles and brown cones of pine trees. It was as though time had stopped. The slow progress of the seasons, the alternation of hot and cold and life and death, had been overthrown; man had returned to the paradisiacal garden that had been his first home. On every side his helpmeet, in shorts and halter, was happily lounging or puttering among the flower beds.

"Here it is," the driver said. Frank hurriedly paid him, stepped from the taxi, and saw that he was at the beginning of a long sidewalk leading across an ample lawn to an impressive reproduction of a Moorish courtyard. He might have been in Spain, for all the eye could testify.

"Where's the door?" he wondered, as he started up the sidewalk with his suitcase. To either side the flamboyant flowers were in full blossom.

The sidewalk led to an exquisitely carved archway. Inside the arch was a door, complete with a functional-looking doorbell. Frank put down his suitcase and reached for the bell. He stopped. A strange reluctance or fear made him pause. It had been years. How could he be sure? Would his mother be the person he remembered? Would she be glad to see him? It had been so long. Would he find that he had come all this way only to discover that this, also, was not home?

If he had obeyed his impulse, he would have picked up his

suitcase and fled down the street, but with an effort he stilled his questions and rang the bell. He must find out, one way or the other.

He waited. There was no sound. He stood there with growing nervousness. At last a woman opened the door and stood framed in it. She was wearing a richly embroidered dressing gown, but what he most noticed was the bright gold of her hair. She was slender, almost girlish in figure. Her face had the complexion of a girl, except that a network of barely perceptible wrinkles could be seen under her eyes.

"May I speak with Mrs. Lindquist?" Frank asked.

The woman looked at him intently. She studied his face. "Frank, my Frank!" she suddenly gasped. She opened the door wide and flung her arms tight around him. They stood there a long time, it seemed. He was home at last. Finally she let go of him and took his face in her hands. "I didn't recognize my little boy's face, but I knew his voice, even if it is a man's voice now. Come in, darling Frank!"

"Do come in," she repeated, and she rushed ahead into the living room. Frank followed with his suitcase. "Sit down, my dear," she urged.

"How sweet of you to come and visit me," she said. "I really must count it among the blessings of my new life." She gazed far away and upward, then turned back to Frank. "You must be starved."

Frank was at that moment aware that indeed he was starved, despite the excellent meal he had eaten on the plane. Sudden visions of the kind of lunch or dinner which only his mother could prepare on short notice danced deliciously in his brain.

"Do help yourself," said his mother, pointing to a bowl of mixed nuts and another bowl with three chocolates in it. "I don't eat them, but I keep them here for anyone who cares for them."

The vision of the quickly prepared dinner faded reluctantly as Frank, feeling guilty as a glutton, ate all of the nuts and chocolates with the exception of one of each, which some vestige of good manners impelled him to leave.

"You must tell me all about yourself," his mother said brightly, but to his relief she didn't press for an answer. "I'm so sorry that Roger is away on business. He will be disappointed to have missed you. But perhaps you can stay till he returns."

When would Roger—that is, Mr. Lindquist—return? Frank wanted to ask. Conversation was proving more sluggish than he had expected. Was this really his mother? She looked younger than he remembered her. Of course, he was older now, and that made a difference. Her hair was certainly blonder. Well, that was easy enough to explain. She was slenderer. Oh, there was no question about it, this was his mother.

The physical changes were nothing, really. It was the other changes that he most noticed. Or were they really changes? Had he created an imaginary mother out of his childhood memories? Had he returned home looking for a mother who never existed, except as a character in a novel exists?

His mother—it was undeniably his mother—had hugged him once when she first recognized him. She hadn't touched him again. Here she sat, across the little coffee table from him, talking graciously and yet somehow impersonally, as though she were entertaining a respected stranger.

"How dear, how very thoughtful of you to come," she was saying. "You must tell me sometime about your spiritual life. I am sure we could help each other by sharing our insights."

If Frank had a spiritual life, and he wasn't sure he did, it was the last thing he wished to share with any living soul. He was preparing to change the subject by making some remark about the beauty of the house when his mother continued,

"How fortunate you are to be as young as you are so you can begin early the way of purgation and come soon to the way of illumination and the way of unity that leads to release from the wheel of endless death and rebirth and reveals at last that blessed nothingness where the divine spirit returns to its source and is blissful forever. How fortunate you are to be young so that you can learn this lesson early and throw off the heavy cloak of the senses and learn to live for the spirit, free of egotism and the sense of individuality . . ." His mother's eyes closed as though in a quiet ecstasy, and Frank gazed in astonishment at her.

"It's very important to breathe properly," she said in a hushed tone, her eyes still closed. "It brings the spirit to a focus." Frank watched her uneasily. Was she about to demonstrate? At this moment, however, there was a sound at the front door, and someone came into the room.

Mrs. Lindquist opened her eyes, and a sudden animation came into them. "How fortunate!" she exclaimed. "Dr. Sindh, this is my son, Frank."

Dr. Sindh, strikingly handsome in a full black beard and white turban, advanced gravely upon Frank. "How do you do?" he said in a slow, deep voice. Each word had a hint of blessing in it. He carefully shook Frank's hand.

"How do you do?" Frank managed to reply.

"Do sit down, both of you," Mrs. Lindquist said eagerly. "And now, I really must make some sandwiches. I'm sure that both of you are starved." She flitted from the room, and the two men sat down.

Dr. Sindh studied Frank's face as though it were a map of his soul. "Have you entered upon the way of illumination?" he asked at last.

"I'm afraid that's something new to me," Frank admitted. "My education is very spotty."

"It is so sad," Dr. Sindh remarked. "In this land of material abundance, there is such poverty of the soul. I will teach you the first steps."

Frank waited uneasily. Would it be breathing exercises? The sound of his mother clattering around briskly in the kitchen came to their ears, and Dr. Sindh's line of thought shifted.

"Your mother is a potential saint," he said in his slow and intimate voice. "Never have I known anyone under my spiritual direction to progress faster in the way of illumination."

It sounded like a compliment. "I'm glad to hear it," Frank said.

"She has subdued the senses," Dr. Sindh stated proudly.

This must be good also. At this moment Mrs. Lindquist came back, smiling broadly and carrying a trayful of sandwiches, cups and saucers, and a pot of tea.

For one devoted to the life of the spirit, Dr. Sindh did all right with the sandwiches. It was a draw between him and Frank. Mrs. Lindquist nibbled slowly on one sandwich and drank large quantities of tea. Frank remembered her as a hearty eater. In a flash of earthly illumination, he understood the secret of her girlish slenderness.

"And now," said Mrs. Lindquist gaily, "shall we have a swim?" Evidently the one-hour rule was not necessary for those who had subdued the senses.

"I didn't bring along a suit," Frank said.

"I'm sure one of Roger's would fit you if you pinned it up a little." She disappeared to another part of the house and came back in a gold-colored swimming suit which, though in perfect good taste, emphatically dramatized the amazingly firm and youthful lines of her body. In her hand were a pair of gray trunks and a safety pin. "Just run into the kitchen and put it on," she said. Frank retreated. With the safety pin, there seemed reasonable hope of keeping the suit on. When he came back, he saw Dr. Sindh standing there in a pure white pair of trunks. The hair on his chest was as abundant and impressively black as that of his beard.

Back of the house they came to the tiled swimming pool. Mrs. Lindquist raced to the diving board and disappeared, a perfect arrow, under the water. She came up laughing. Dr. Sindh, also in good diving form, followed gravely. Not to be outdone, Frank dived, but he lost his footing at the end of the plank and landed with a humiliating noise as of a gigantic smack.

"I must teach you the secret of co-ordination," Dr. Sindh called out to him, almost jokingly. "It lies in the way of illumination and the subduing of the senses."

Frank was about to make some reply when it became clear that Dr. Sindh had shifted to other interests. He and Mrs. Lindquist were engaged in a water battle, splashing water in each other's faces. His deep laughter and her high giggle sounded remarkably like the merriment at a high school swimming party.

Frank swam toward them and started to join in the game by splashing water impartially on them both, but a brief frown passed over his mother's face. He gave one more splash and swam to the opposite end of the pool where he practiced treading water, floating, and underwater swimming.

At long last his mother called, "Up and out, everybody!" He clambered up the ladder and stood on the edge of the pool.

Mrs. Lindquist, closely followed by Dr. Sindh, walked over to him. "And now, if you will excuse me, dear Frank, it is time for my spiritual instruction. Regularity is very important. Dr. Sindh will first show you to your room. Dinner is at eight."

Dr. Sindh and Frank walked to the kitchen where Frank reclaimed his clothes, and the two of them wound next through a maze of courtyards to the room that was ordinarily inhabited by Mr. Lindquist. Isn't he coming back soon? Frank wondered.

"A potential saint," Dr. Sindh said as though no time had elapsed since he said it last. "I shall begin your lessons soon."

Alone at last, Frank looked about the room. On the wall was a splendid collection of hunting rifles and several elk heads. On one table reposed a pipe rack with expensive pipes. The rich aftersmell of good tobacco was in the room, but it was very faint. Certainly the room did not belong to anyone who had progressed too far on the way of illumination. It had a hearty, down-to-earth, exceedingly masculine quality about it.

For that matter, Dr. Sindh, who had now disappeared, was sufficiently masculine, almost blatantly so. Frank had always thought of mystics and saints (he was vague about which was what) as being frail and pale. Dr. Sindh could outswim him, and when Frank recalled the water fight between Dr. Sindh and his mother—but he shut off that line of thought with haste.

Promptly at eight he went to the dining room where the three of them sat at one end of a large table and were served by a maid with the air of a vestal virgin in her early forties. Mrs. Lindquist was now back in her state of detachment and remote peace; she seemed scarcely to see the food before her and barely did more than nibble at it.

Dr. Sindh ate heartily. Frank was prepared to do so until Dr. Sindh mentioned that the meat dish was actually a wholesome and spiritually pure substitute made of various algae, cereal products, and nut concentrates. No wonder she can keep that figure, Frank thought—no meat, and, it soon became clear, no eggs and no milk. Frank glanced at Dr. Sindh, and an unworthy thought crossed his mind. Did the teacher fudge?

Was meat his secret vice? He had to admit it to himself—he cordially loathed Dr. Sindh and all his works. He loathed him most vehemently when the teacher's eyes and Mrs. Lindquist's happened to hover in mid-air and meet.

The time after dinner was devoted to the *Bhagavad-Gita* which Dr. Sindh read aloud with a running commentary. Frank listened curiously. The book was not too difficult to understand. It was, of course, as far removed from being literally true as the Bible, but since it was completely new to him, its words came with a certain freshness and innocent appeal.

At ten o'clock, Dr. Sindh said firmly, "It is time now for bed."

His mother turned to Frank. "Breakfast is at eight o'clock. Do have a good night's sleep. And thank you *so* much for your kindness in coming here."

This seemed to be good night. Frank rose and waited for Dr. Sindh to rise, but the latter was in no hurry. Where did he live? Right here, perhaps? In this house? Frank's loathing deepened.

When he crawled, dead tired, into Mr. Lindquist's single bed, Frank's mind was a whirlpool of memories and impressions. It was no good trying to sort them out now. As sleep finally overtook him, he found himself thinking of his stepmother, Sarah. He saw her troubled face, the hurt look when he offered nothing more than hard, cold courtesy to his "father's new wife." Her arms seemed to be reaching out to him, in pleading and proffer. He fell asleep.

Breakfast next morning was served by the vestal virgin to the three of them. It was strong on tea and devoid of coffee, which was apparently considered inimical to the spiritual life. Orange juice abounded, and there was sufficient toast, carefully spread with the highest-grade oleo.

Dr. Sindh had promised to begin Frank's spiritual instruc

tion that day, but Mrs. Lindquist found she had to go into
town for some essential shopping, and her spiritual director
volunteered to go along and help. They departed soon
after breakfast.

The vestal virgin prepared lunch for Frank, and when he
had eaten it, she whispered like a conspirator, "Would you
like some meat?"

"Yes!" he said with a surge of gratitude. The maid disappeared and a few minutes later came back with an authentic,
all-beef hamburger. "Don't tell," she said in a hollow voice.

"Cross my heart," Frank said, making the sign of the cross.
"Dear lady, you have saved my life."

The hamburger brightened a day that needed some
brightening, and in the days following he found great comfort
in the vestal virgin, or Maggie Beth, as he had now learned
to call her. Every day Mrs. Lindquist and Dr. Sindh were
obliged, for one necessity or another, to go into town. There
never seemed a good time to begin Frank's spiritual instruction.
Maggie Beth and Frank developed a routine of their own.
As soon as his mother and Dr. Sindh left after breakfast,
and the sound of the car had died away, Maggie Beth would
produce her secret cache of meat and fry two hamburgers.
These, with plenty of coffee, they would consume sitting at
the kitchen table. At odd moments throughout the day, when
there was nothing to do, they would have another snack of
hamburger or other meat and coffee. Once she baked a small
chocolate cake. As they became better acquainted, Maggie Beth
proved talkative. Much of her conversation was of daily trivia,
but (and this brightened that particular day) he found that
she shared his dark doubts about the spirituality of Dr. Sindh.
"I don't trust that man, never did," Maggie Beth said firmly.
As for Mr. Lindquist, "A fine man, a real man," was about
all she would say. When he pressed her and asked when Mr.

Lindquist would be back, she would only shake her head and say, "We'll see, we'll see."

Only once did Frank's resentment and misgivings flare up in words to his mother. It was one of the rare times when the two of them happened to be alone in the living room. The subject, as usual, was the spiritual life and how wonderful it would be for Frank after Dr. Sindh found a convenient time to begin his instruction.

Something snapped in Frank, and he blurted out, "Why does that man have to *live* in this house?"

The echo of the words appalled him, but they had been spoken.

The expression of spiritual sweetness abruptly faded from his mother's face. "Frank," she said in a biting voice, "you have a very vulgar and common mind, just like your father." Then, as though it had been turned on again, the spiritual quality returned to her countenance, and she added in a tone of loving patience, "After Dr. Sindh has instructed you in the spiritual life, you will avoid these crude misunderstandings."

She had to excuse herself then for her own spiritual instruction. When he next saw her, it was as though the little tiff had never occurred.

Soon he had been at the house a week, and there seemed no good reason why he shouldn't stay indefinitely. Nothing ever changed. Nothing seemed capable of change in this lovely world of Moorish courtyards and trees that did not drop their leaves.

Then he happened to pick up a newspaper from the coffee table. He was alone at the time. It was late afternoon, and his mother and Dr. Sindh were still out on some expedition.

He had almost finished the paper when a headline on page 14 caught his eye, "Gang Marauders Arrested." It was most likely Los Angeles, but he read it anyway. It was Blanton. The brief news story told how one of the Stalwarts had blabbed to his girl friend who had blabbed to the police, and four Stalwarts had confessed and were scheduled for trial in juvenile court. The story added that the mystery of the entry into William Pendleton's home was now considered completely solved. In a last sentence, it mentioned that Mr. Pendleton was still in the hospital, and his condition was critical.

"Thieves' honor," Frank said to himself. The Stalwarts were being true to their code, the code of a jungle, the code of the North Side, but a code with its own kind of honor. They hadn't told on him. They were prepared to face the juvenile court and shield him. He was saved by the honor of the boys who would pay the penalty for an escapade which he had suggested. If he stayed on in California till the case was tried and disposed of, he could probably return to Blanton eventually, make up some plausible story for his absence, and never get involved in the case. Or he could stay in California indefinitely. If his mother couldn't keep him—but for all he knew she could—he could get a job somewhere, perhaps finish high school in two years by going part time. And there were so many ways he could get help through college.

He had all sorts of avenues for escape, but the four Stalwarts had no exit. They were like rats in a trap, but they were honorable rats.

After dinner Frank excused himself, saying he had a headache. His mother smiled brightly and added as a good-night wish, "When Dr. Sindh teaches you to think positively, you will have no more headaches."

Long that evening he sat in his room, thinking. He was a fool—but better be a fool than hate yourself. The next morning he told his mother he had to go back to Blanton. He made no explanation. She asked for none. "It was so sweet of you to come," she said and kissed him lightly on the cheek. "You really must come again."

He made vague promising sounds. Dr. Sindh gravely pressed

his hand and said "Godspeed" in a tone of blessing. The taxi
soon came and took him to the airport, and by midmorning
he was on his way back to Blanton.

Across the aisle in the plane was a rather pretty girl with
a gray smudge on her forehead. "Ash Wednesday," he suddenly thought, as he saw that the smudge was shaped like
a crude cross. It was the beginning of Lent. His weary mind
dropped the subject, and he found himself dozing off and on,
now watching his mother in a water fight with Dr. Sindh, and
now coming upon the unconscious Mr. Pendleton stretched
out on the stair landing.

19

BACK TO BLANTON

FRANK hadn't written in his diary since he left Blanton. When he discovered that none of the available magazines held his interest, he fished out the old diary and passed the time writing in it. He began:

On the way home. I feel stagey and unreal, like a character in a soap opera or class B movie. Such a manly, moral criminal, going home to confess it all for the sake of honor. This brunette stewardess has been friendly, sitting on the arm of my seat and asking me questions about myself. Everything is a temptation. Not the stewardess, but her questions. I had to bite my tongue. I wanted to say, in a very quiet voice, "I'm a juvenile delinquent, and I'm returning home to confess that I took part in robbing a house." I'm beginning to understand one reason why people take to crime. It gives them self-respect. Attention is paid to them. Better to arouse fear or horror or even loathing than to be regarded as perfectly harmless.

The plane continued its fixed course. Gradually Frank's eyes closed, and his ballpoint pen dropped onto his lap. He slept most of the way. It seemed almost no time before he heard the stewardess' voice, "Check your safety belts, please, and observe the no smoking sign." The plane was gliding toward the vast, impersonal airport. Soon they landed, and he filed out with the rest. He looked around. There was no one he recognized. He was relieved. The two-engine plane that would take him to Blanton would leave in forty-five minutes. He bought a paper, had a sundae, and by then the plane was ready for boarding. He was one of the first on.

The front page of the paper had the usual headlines. Frank read it listlessly. "Fasten your seat belts, please," the stewardess on the little plane was saying. He fastened his belt and put the newspaper on the empty seat at his side. Wide awake now, he took up his diary and wrote some more:

On a much smaller plane now. Flies lower and is fond of sudden heaves and bumps. Soon we'll land at Blanton. Homecoming. Yes, I think I can say that now. Blanton is home, even the house on Oak Hill is home. This sounds like a phonograph record when the needle is stuck. I'm going to read the paper some more . . . (Later) The news that matters is always on an inside page. On page 10 was a little item from Blanton, "Victim of J. D.'s Suffers Second Attack." Mr. Pendleton had another coronary in the hospital yesterday. Condition extremely grave. Even if recovers, may be an invalid the rest of his life. Story went on to repeat that the mystery had been solved. The four Stalwarts had confessed. They are coming up for trial in juvenile court on Friday.

Some things are easy, some things are hard. Doesn't this sound like the occult wisdom of the Orient? What I'm about to do is easy, at least fairly easy. I'm going to confess, turn myself over to the police, stand trial with the Stalwarts. I'll have a nice, clean feeling. The Stalwarts will admire me. Even decent, respectable people will admire me. Probably I'll get off with a suspended sentence. Oh, damn it! Why do I have to take such a cheap, cynical tone, even in my diary? Can't I give myself credit for a little more integrity? I don't know why I'm going back to confess except that I'd hate myself forever if I didn't. That's all there is to it. Some actions are crazy, and so is this one, but there are worse things than being crazy.

What I've got to do in Blanton is simple enough. But how did I get myself in this mess in the first place? Let me trace it back.

Mr. Pendleton has just had a second heart attack because he had been weakened by his first one. He had the first one because the Stalwarts broke into his house. The Stalwarts did that because I suggested it. I suggested it to save the face of Mr. Pendleton's son, president of the Omegas. Bill's visage was in danger because *somebody*, possibly named Bill, had worked over Sid Pruitt. If the name was Bill, the motive was doubtless the episode at the Shack. And that episode went back to earlier episodes. How far back can you carry the line of causation? Maybe to the Garden of Eden.

But what good does this cosmic way of looking at it do? I was part of a line of causation, but that doesn't mean I had to be merely that. I could always have said No to destiny. I know the stock answers Dad would give. He'd say I turned to the Stalwarts because I was revolting against him and Sarah and Oak Hill in general, that the poor waifs and strays of the North Side appealed to me because, by associating with them, I was thumbing my nose at Oak Hill.

A good deal of truth in that. True as far as it goes, but it doesn't go far enough. I'm more than a psychological mechanism, more than a rat in a laboratory maze. I think I found in the Stalwarts something good in its own right. They accepted me just as I was. Their acceptance bridged the very great chasm fixed between Oak Hill and the North Side. When they accepted me, I felt that I had become a naturalized member of the human race. They taught me what decency and honor can be. When the test came, they didn't squeal on me. I can't say that I regret my experience with the Stalwarts. Out of evil came some good. I've got to be careful how far I push that argument. Mr. Pendleton might not be impressed. For him, no good came out of it.

Strange that I'm writing about Blanton and that already Los Angeles seems a bizarre episode from a novel. You can't go home again, or if you do, you discover it isn't home any more. I'm glad I went; it was necessary. But Blanton is my home now.

"Fasten your seat belts, please," the stewardess called out as she paced up and down the short aisle of the plane. So soon? Frank put away his diary and mechanically checked his seat belt. It was still fastened. Below he could see the little one-story building. Soon he felt the wheels touching the runway, and the plane taxied a short distance and came to a stop near the building.

This time Frank was one of the first off. He quickly reclaimed his suitcase, raced through the building, and took one of the cabs waiting outside.

The driver showed no personal interest, and this was a relief. In twenty minutes at most he should be at his home. Then he could decide how best to break the news about his part in the Pendleton affair. At least it would be a relief to have it out in the open. A relief? All sorts of questions assailed him from nowhere. Was he planning to confess merely for psychological reasons? Was he confessing out of a secret and suppressed desire for public attention and admiration? What real good would it do for anybody if he confessed? Would it help the Stalwarts in any way? It wouldn't restore Mr. Pendleton's health. It certainly wouldn't help his father and Sarah. Was it possible that his unconscious motive for confessing the crime was to make them suffer, to humiliate them and all of Oak Hill? Wasn't his determination to confess a kind of psychological luxury? Wouldn't it take more courage and manhood *not* to confess?

He thought about all this the remainder of the way to Oak Hill. If he confessed, it would humiliate his family, complicate his own life, give him a false kind of glamor; it would not restore Mr. Pendleton's health; it would not save the Stalwarts; it wouldn't help anybody. He must think this through, and not go off the deep end.

The cab now pulled up in front of the familiar house on Oak Hill. Frank quickly paid the driver and walked to the door. He was almost ready to ring. Then he laughed. It was his home, and it would be open. In the late afternoon his father and Sarah were almost always there, anyway.

He walked quietly into the hall, hung up his coat, and put his suitcase down. Then he stood a moment in the doorway lead- ing to the living room. Nothing had changed. At the far end of the room, on a sofa, sat his father and Sarah. In front of them was the coffee table with two glasses. His father's glass was almost empty. Sarah's was half full.

Their eyes were cast down; they seemed to be silently study- ing the coffee table. Something made Frank hesitate about speaking. It was not fear. It was more a feeling that he wanted to photograph this scene on his mind; he might need to carry it with him in days ahead.

At last Sarah looked up. "Frank!" she called, and she rose so quickly that her knees hit the coffee table, and the two glasses went crashing to the carpet.

"Frank," she said again and rushed to him. She hugged him, and he found himself hugging her for all he was worth. He was home again.

Mr. Buell came forward more slowly and stood watching Frank and Sarah. Finally they let go of each other, panting and laughing with joy. Clumsily he put his arm around Frank's shoulders and said, "Thank God you're back. The questions can wait. Thank *God* you're back."

"You must be starved," said Sarah, trying to collect herself. "How about a ham sandwich?"

"I *am* starved," said Frank.

"I'll fix it right away." Sarah disappeared into the kitchen.

"Sit down, son," Mr. Buell said. They sat together on the sofa. "Drink?"

"No, thanks, Dad," said Frank.

"I don't think I want one either," said Mr. Buell in a tone of awe. He paused. "Tell me everything."

"You know the beginning of it," Frank said, but at that moment Sarah's voice came from the kitchen. "Hold everything. I want to be in on it."

Mr. Buell laughed. "We'll wait." He patted Frank on the back. "Frank, Frank, you do these middle-aged eyes good. We've missed you, boy."

I must ask his advice, Frank thought, his advice and Sarah's. What's best to do. I'm so mixed up. I must ask their advice and follow it. It's their responsibility. There's the rub. Whose responsibility is this thing? Can responsibility be shifted? I'm a mess, thinking in circles. What's best?

"Be there in a minute," Sarah called gaily.

If it were a clear-cut question of right and wrong. But it isn't. If I confess, it won't restore Mr. Pendleton's health. It won't even help Sid Pruitt and the others. It will half kill Dad and Sarah.

"Be there in a minute," Sarah repeated. "Hold everything."

Frank suddenly laughed at himself—silently. The clamorous debaters inside him quieted down. He seemed to see something clearly now, perhaps not in a way he could talk about, but he saw it.

"May I make a phone call? It'll just take a minute."

"A girl?" his father asked, and smiled. "Go ahead."

Frank disappeared into the hall. Soon Mr. Buell could hear him speaking in a low voice, too low to catch the words. If it were a girl he was calling, provided she was the right kind, maybe that was what the boy needed. He had always been so solitary.

Frank soon returned and sat down on the sofa.

"Good call?" his father asked.

"One I had to make."

Sarah came in bearing a tray with three sandwiches and a coffee pot and cups and saucers. "I didn't have any fatted calf in the icebox," she said, "so this'll have to do." She turned to her husband. "If you're as hungry as I am, you'll join Frank and me in a sandwich."

The three of them began eating as though they had invented appetite. "Now tell your story," Sarah said. "From beginning to end. I'm dying to hear it."

Mr. Buell interrupted. "We know this much—you were with your mother—a lawyer friend of mine checked up on that. I thought I ought to tell you."

"We decided it was best to leave you alone and let you work out things for yourself," Sarah hastily explained.

"You've been—you've been better to me than I deserve," Frank said. "A stinker like me."

"It wasn't easy," Sarah said. "It wasn't easy to leave you on your own. We worried so much about you." Suddenly she was sobbing as though she could never stop. Frank put his arms around her, and then, the first thing he knew, he was keeping pace with her sobs. At last Sarah calmed down and gently withdrew from his embrace. "Do you have a handkerchief?" she asked Frank. "You use it first."

So his handkerchief did double duty, and Sarah was able to smile once more. "I feel better," she said, "don't you? Now, tell us your adventures."

"You know the beginning," said Frank again. "The Stalwarts."

"Yes, yes," his father interrupted. "I knew you were still attending their meetings. Those poor devils, they've gotten themselves in really serious trouble. I'm glad you pulled out in time."

"I'll have to tell you more about the Stalwarts if I'm going to tell my story," Frank said. A worried look passed between his father and Sarah. "My story really begins with the last meeting of the Stalwarts which I attended before I lit out for L.A. It was the meeting just before Mr. Pendleton's house was broken into."

Frank stopped. Sarah's face was drained of color. "Frank—you weren't—?"

"Yes," he replied. "I was one of the five that went to Mr. Pendleton's house."

"Oh, my God," his father said. "You little fool. You really did it."

"Yes," said Frank. "I was in on it as much as any of the others. So I suppose I'll be put on trial at the same time."

Mr. Buell's manner became less chaotic. He seemed to be thinking rapidly. "Frank," he said urgently, "we've got to talk this thing through. The first thing I must make clear is this—I don't want you to do anything dramatic and noble like confessing all this. Not yet. We've got to think it through. It may be best to arrange for you to live in another city for a time, but that can be handled. Or if it seems best for you to admit your part, we'll want to work this out very carefully with the lawyer before you do anything."

"But suppose—" Frank interrupted.

His father's face flushed angrily. "No suppose! Your reputation is at stake in this, and if that doesn't interest you, I have a reputation that does interest me. I'm not particularly happy at the thought of the Buell name being dragged into juvenile court and keeping company with the young gangsters of the North Side."

Sarah spoke up gently. "But if Frank feels that he ought to own up to this—"

"Feelings be damned!" Mr. Buell turned on her furiously. "It's feelings that got him into trouble in the first place. I'll go call up my lawyer and ask him to come right over. We can't go off half-cocked on this." He rose and started for the hall.

"Just a minute," Sarah said. She jumped up and raced past him. "Heard the doorbell."

"I didn't hear anybody ring," John Buell said, but he sat down and nervously lit a cigarette.

They could hear Sarah talking in a low voice with someone at the door. "Salesman or solicitor for a charity?" Mr. Buell asked. "They can go to the devil."

Sarah returned with a slender, rather pale man who might be in his late thirties though his hair was almost completely silver.

"Good afternoon," Mr. Buell said, rising. "Mr. Wembley, may I introduce my son, Frank?"

The two shook hands.

"Please have a seat," said Mr. Buell, drawing up a chair for the visitor.

"Would you care for a cup of coffee?" Mrs. Buell asked.

"That would be very kind of you," Mr. Wembley replied.

Sarah disappeared and quickly returned with cup and saucer. After Mr. Wembley had sipped the coffee, Sarah said, "Mr. Wembley has some questions he wants to ask us."

Mr. Wembley coughed. "I'm afraid I seemed very mysterious. The whole thing is awkward and quite preposterous, but just as a matter of routine—to make it brief, as you know I'm a social worker attached to the juvenile court."

"Yes, yes," Mr. Buell said.

"Well, just a few minutes ago the chief of police called me and said he had received a very peculiar phone call. Someone who insisted he was your son had just phoned in, confessing that he had a part in breaking into William Pendleton's house. Mind you," Mr. Wembley added hastily, "the chief was sure it was some practical joker, but just as a matter of form, he phoned me—"

"Mr. Wembley," said Frank, "I made the call. I was the one who suggested breaking into Mr. Pendleton's home."

"So you did call the police," his father said slowly after a stunned pause. "That was your phone call." The muscles of his face worked and twisted. "You damned little fool!" he said, pausing with each word.

Sarah burst into tears. All at once a smile broke through her tears. She threw her arms around Frank.

"Frank!" she said. "My Frank!"

20

DIES MIRABILIS

FRANK wanted to face the juvenile judge as soon as possible, but his father insisted that adequate time was needed to confer with the lawyer and study the situation from all possible angles. Judge Strood was willing to co-operate, and the trial was postponed for another week.

The four Stalwarts, who had been held in jail, were now released on bail, thanks to Mr. Buell. They returned to their homes, such as the homes were. Frank also was on bail, committed to the supervision of his parents.

Curiously enough, this time of waiting was one of the happiest periods of Frank's life. He went to school, and everyone knew he was about to stand trial so there was nothing to hide there. At home he had nothing to hide, either. The crisis that had come upon the Buell family had engulfed the normal pettinesses of daily life. Recriminations and even idle self-reproach seemed to have vanished. The three of them were brought together in a new harmony by a brisk determination to meet a situation which threatened them all and to handle it as best they could, which in any case would not be ideal. But it was more than that. It was the dropping of all pretense and polite fictions and the discovery that each of the three needed and loved the others. It was as simple as that.

They listened to the radio and TV and searched the *Blanton*

Daily Times every evening to see whether there were any new reports on Mr. Pendleton's condition. He was still in the hospital. Much would depend on how he was when the case came to trial. Already the newspaper was adopting an increasingly ominous tone about the coddling of juvenile delinquents, and in two editorials it had made pointed references to delinquents born with silver spoons in their mouths who thought they were above the law.

It was one day during this period of waiting for the trial that several surprising events occurred in Blanton.

Steve Hadley had been unusually restless and after school had walked several miles. Even that hadn't done much good. All the time that he was walking, his mind went its same weary paces. Did he love Betty? He missed her. He felt at loose ends without her. The thought of her could set his very flesh tingling with quick desire. But did he love her? He felt a twinge of irritation. If Betty hadn't been so cranky in the first place, during their dates back in the fall, this cooling-off, testing period wouldn't be necessary. She was the hardest person to get along with, always leaping to conclusions . . . If she were in his arms . . . His imagination brightened into the memory of the deserted farmhouse. But something always went wrong. His mind continued on the weary treadmill. Finally he walked to the Shack and found it almost empty. He had a booth by himself. "Coffee, black," he ordered.

"Coming up," Jerry responded.

He sipped the strong black coffee, and it tasted good. The door opened. He looked up. There was Bill Pendleton. Come on over, Steve motioned. Bill came and sat across the table from him. They shook hands, using the special handclasp known only to Omega Alphas.

"I want to talk with you," Bill said. "Came by on the chance you'd be here." He paused and looked searchingly at Steve. "How do you feel about the Omegas?"

Steve fidgeted. There were ready-made answers quick to the tongue: brothers till death do us part, the joys of fraternity, all the rest. Yet how did he really feel? Bill was the president; he seemed the spirit of the Omegas.

"Pretty much of a bore, isn't it?" Bill asked.

Was this a joke? No, Bill obviously meant it. "I got a lot out of it at first," Steve said. "At least, I guess I did."

"But you wish you could gracefully pull out now? So do I."

"What?" Steve was literally openmouthed.

"I've been feeling more and more that the Omegas are pretty juvenile. You see what happens when you have a group like the Omegas and another like the Stalwarts. One thing leads to another, and the upshot is that Dad's in the hospital and may be an invalid the rest of his life. I don't think the dear old Omegas are worth that kind of thing."

"I guess not," Steve said. "How is your Dad today?"

"Thanks. About the same. It may be weeks before they really know. O.K., you agree with me about the Omegas. How about coming to my house, and we'll do some phoning and call a meeting for tonight?"

They paid at the counter and drove to Bill's home. By dint of intensive phoning, they arranged for well over half of the Omegas to come for a special meeting at nine that evening. When the brotherhood convened, Bill stated his proposal briefly, pretty much as he had in his conversation with Steve. Surprisingly, only four or five Omegas seemed to have any life-and-death devotion to the organization. Many more agreed with almost indecent readiness that the brotherhood had really served its purpose and outlived its usefulness. When a motion was offered from the floor that the Omegas herewith cease to exist and that their constitution and minutes be burned, it carried on a voice vote with only a scattering of Nays. Thus the Omegas stepped quietly out of existence.

"Neat going," Steve said afterwards in sincere compliment at the parliamentary skill that Bill had displayed.

"Thanks," said Bill in rather a distraught tone.

"Well, I'll be running along," Steve said.

"See you tomorrow." Bill's voice trailed off.

Steve looked around uncertainly, then left.

After his friend was gone, Bill threw himself down on his bed and pressed his hands against his head. "God have mercy on me!" he implored. "God help me." He groaned and lay there in misery.

"It's no good," he said at last. "I've got to face it." He picked up the phone book and quickly located a number. He dialed it on his extension phone. A man answered.

"Mr. Greenwood?"

"Speaking."

"This—this is Bill Pendleton."

Something like a gasp sounded from the other end. "Yes?" the voice asked sharply.

"Can you give me Helen's address? I've got to see her."

There was a pause of a second or two. "No!" the receiver barked. There was the click of a phone being hung up.

Blocked. Bill sat down on the side of the bed. If he could find Helen's address—he was sure she must be holed up in some city, waiting for the baby to be born—what good would it really do? Could he pretend that he loved her? No. What good would it do to marry her if their marriage had very little chance of success from the start? To "give the child a name"? But what good is a "name" in an unhappy home? Wouldn't it be better for the baby, better even for Helen if he stayed out of this? Undoubtedly an adoption was being arranged. That was how these things were handled. Anyway, it had been such a fly-by-night thing. A date, a drive in the country, the realization that Helen was as hungry for acceptance and admiration as he himself secretly was—two weak people, each hoping to find strength in the other's eyes and body. People do this sort of thing all the time, and nothing happens, but this one time, something did happen.

The phone rang. Bill picked it up. "Hello."

"This is Mr. Greenwood again," the voice at the other end said.

"Yes—yes, Mr. Greenwood?"

"I decided I had no right to make Helen's decisions for her. I phoned her and asked whether she wanted me to give you her address. I must be candid and say that she did not seem enthusiastic, but if you want to see her, she feels she shouldn't refuse you the opportunity. You will forgive me if I cut this conversation short. Do you wish her address?"

"Yes, I do," Bill said with a heavy feeling in his stomach.

"Very well." Mr. Greenwood slowly dictated the city, street, and number. "One word more," he added. "I think you may find Helen a very changed girl. Good night!" The final words had something of an imprecation in their tone.

Bill sat down dully on his bed. Next day was Saturday. He would get up early and drive there. He should be able to make it by early afternoon.

He undressed and fell into bed. The walls were closing in; he could feel them closing in, and it was hard to breathe, but the thing had to be done.

The same evening it happened that Dr. Bowman called on the Arrondos to ask their advice on several matters having to do with the North Side and Trinity Church. So far, things were going rather well. Attendance at the nine o'clock Spanish Eucharist was running ten to fifteen. An increasing sprinkling of North Siders—about a third of them Puerto Ricans, the rest a general mixture—were coming to the late service. The old-time members of the church were rising to the occasion better than Dr. Bowman had counted on. Some, of course, retreated to the 7:30 Communion and avoided close contact with anyone, new or old. Some were overeager and overeffusive in their welcome of the "new people." Most of them, however, seemed natural enough, and it was hard to realize that two months ago Trinity Church had consisted almost wholly of "old families" who for the most part lived several miles away.

As he drew up in front of the house where the Arrondos lived, Dr. Bowman realized how much he had grown to depend on Carlos Arrondo. Mr. Arrondo had taken his time; he hadn't come to the first Spanish service. He was still enough of a Romanist to be troubled at the thought of the *Protestant* Episcopal Church. On the other hand, of the four Roman Catholic churches in Blanton, one had sermons in Polish, one in French, and the two English-speaking churches were so dominated by the Irish that the Arrondos felt conspicuous and out of place in them. So the Arrondos had made the plunge, had started going to Trinity Church, and had liked it.

One by-product of their coming was that Rosa, a general favorite in high school, was immediately urged by half a dozen friends to join the YPF. Once she was there, people thought of other teenagers from the North Side, and the vast debates on bringing in North Side kids were resolved by casual action rather than parliamentary maneuvers.

Almost resolved, but not quite yet, Dr. Bowman reminded himself. One of the reasons he wanted to see Mr. Arrondo had to do with this. After he had reached the apartment, exchanged greetings, and sat down to a glass of wine with the three Arrondos clustering about him, Dr. Bowman brought up the matter. "I'd been planning to invite the Stalwarts to meet in the parish house," he said, "but after this Pendleton business, public opinion is so strongly against them I suppose I'd better wait a while."

"The Stalwarts are no good!" Mr. Arrondo said.

"I imagine there are a lot of extenuating circumstances in their backgrounds," Dr. Bowman said. "Many of them come from broken homes or very poor homes."

"Bah!" Mr. Arrondo exploded. "Everybody can find an excuse for himself. One man has broken home. Another no money. Third got mean wife. Everybody got excuse. Look at that young Frank Buell. Silver spoon in his mouth. But he almost kill my Rosa. And he break into house, old man Pendleton's house. He got excuse? Sure, rich man's son. That's his excuse. Phooey!"

It was evident, Dr. Bowman could see, that Mr. Arrondo would not urge him to outrage public opinion and take the Stalwarts immediately under the roof of the church. He felt a twinge of disappointment. Unconsciously he had been hoping that Mr. Arrondo would strongly urge the cause of the Stalwarts, would put pressure on him to go ahead.

Dr. Bowman now turned the conversation to undramatic matters of parish life and, as always, found Mr. Arrondo an invaluable source of common sense and insight. I'll have to see to it that he's nominated for the vestry next time, Dr. Bowman mentally noted. He would be ideal to represent the new people.

On the drive home he felt better, as he always did after talking with the Arrondos. He found himself wondering about Rosa. She was a very pretty girl, had a certain *joie de vivre* and natural goodness about her. Was there still any feeling between her and Frank? After all, their one date was the night of the smashup, and her father had stopped her from seeing Frank again. Probably there had not been anything serious in the first place, but he wasn't quite sure. He remembered the sudden alertness that Rosa showed the few times that Frank's name came up. If Frank ever came to church or YPF—but he didn't . . .

Hardly was Dr. Bowman home when the phone rang. "Hello," he said. "Dr. Bowman speaking."

"This is Dick Jenkins," the gruff voice at the other end said. Old Mr. Jenkins had stalked out of the church five years ago and stayed away over a year because he didn't want to kneel at the same Communion rail with the McIntire boy who'd been in the State Institution for Delinquent Boys. Dick Jenkins was now the senior warden . . .

"Dick Jenkins," the voice repeated.

"Yes, how are you, Dick?" Dr. Bowman asked.

"Fine. Look here, Henry, we've got to do something about those boys."

"What boys?"

"Those boys on the North Side. The Stalwarts and their kind. Nobody in Blanton is doing anything to help them. It's up to the church."

Dr. Bowman gasped.

"It's up to the church, I say, and we better get moving."

Dr. Bowman had finally caught his breath. "I thought at one time of inviting the Stalwarts to meet at the parish house—"

"That's right!" Mr. Jenkins said.

"But look here, Dick," Dr. Bowman said. "With this trial coming on—we can't do it now—"

"Trial or no trial," Mr. Jenkins interrupted emphatically, "somebody's got to help. It's up to the church. Think it over, Henry." The phone went dead.

Dr. Bowman didn't think it over long. "I'll probably be out late," he shouted and ran to his car. He knew the general section of the North Side where Sid Pruitt lived. He drove there and parked. "Glory be to God," he half sang as he got out of the car, "glory be to God who has the queerest and most devious ways of getting things done. Glory be to God for all His servants, including our senior warden, Dick Jenkins." People were beginning to stare at him. He realized that his inward song had become an outer one. Better be careful, he told himself, or you'll be called the Whiskey Priest. "My soul doth magnify the Lord," he sang aloud as an acceptable set of words upon the lips of a priest.

He found the Pruitts' flat at last and introduced himself. Suspicion flickered in Sid's eyes. To him a priest belonged in the same category with parents, police, teachers, and parole officers—people commissioned by society to do the things for your own good that you didn't want done.

Sid's younger brother scampered about the appalling room on noisy missions of his own and paused every once in a while to stare with cold curiosity at Dr. Bowman. Sid himself now and then condescended to utter a monosyllable, but otherwise left the conversation to his unexpected guest.

Dr. Bowman hadn't worked out in his mind what approach he would take; he had no sales talk on his lips. He simply said it briefly. He said that his church wanted to reach the people who actually lived in the neighborhood; that he'd be glad to let the Stalwarts meet in the parish house, where there were facilities for preparing refreshments and dancing, as well as a basketball court and some other sports facilities; that they were welcome to use the parish house, regardless of whether they joined the Church, but that he hoped some of them would get interested in the church and in YPF.

His exposition wasn't much for eloquence, Dr. Bowman realized as he finished. Sid's expression betrayed no hint of his thoughts. He sat puffing on a cigarette and blowing smoke rings. He gave a shrug at last and said that since the judge was sure to send him off, the future of the Stalwarts wasn't in his hands anyway. It wasn't for him to decide.

Could he call the Stalwarts together so the proposition could be put up to them? With another shrug and after a pause to blow three rings, Sid said he guessed so.

Dr. Bowman waited. He pulled out his pipe and matched smoke against smoke. He waited some more. Two could play at this game of laconic speech. Sid eventually spoke out of the side of his mouth which held no cigarette and said he'd see what he could do about rounding up the guys.

Within an hour, operating by phone (and, Dr. Bowman was convinced, by carrier pigeon and tribal drum), Sid had notified most of the Stalwarts. From their various directions they came by ones and twos to the Greasy Spoon and occupied the back room. It was almost full by the time Dr. Bowman and Sid arrived there, and Stalwarts were still coming.

If the police raid this place, they'll be sure I'm the power back of the Stalwarts, Dr. Bowman told himself as he sat down beside Sid. He saw an interesting variety of newspaper headings: Whiskey Priest Nabbed in Criminal Lair; The Man Behind the Switch Blade Wears Round Collar; Singing Parson Masterminds Juvenile Punks. He could have laughed for joy. "Crackpots for the glory and love of God," he told himself. "Let's all be God's crackpots and be happy, and the *Blanton Daily Times* be damned."

He looked about from one Stalwart to another. What a pitiful and forlorn bunch they were, to the eye of the impartial observer or the objective camera. He saw their veneer of hardness (and by now it was more than a veneer for some of them), their obvious sense of inadequacy down underneath, their clumsiness of manner as though they didn't belong anywhere in particular, not even in the Greasy Spoon. Some faces already had deep scars, probably from knives or broken bottles or jagged stones. How pitiful they were, and how glorious a throng. All at once something changed. He saw them differently. Their

medley of complexions, from Sid Pruitt's pale cheeks to the
deep olive and dark brown of others, seemed a foretaste of the
assembly of the saved in the presence of God. It was like a kind
of flower garden, and each face took on character. He saw not
so much the cynically curling lips and the hard, staring eyes as
what each face might become . . . by the grace of God. He saw
each Stalwart not as he was but as he could be.

The Stalwarts were watching him intently, with only an
occasional nudge in each other's ribs. Sid lit another cigarette,
ordered one of his henchmen to close the door, and banged on
the table. In less time than it took to finish the cigarette, he outlined the purpose of the meeting. He explained that he wasn't
going to be around for a while. The judge was certain to throw
the book at him. He added that anyway he was done with kid
stuff. When he came back, it was either the big time for him or
go clean, none of this kid stuff. In brief, as he made it clear in
words of his own choosing, he didn't give a damn any more
about the Stalwarts. They could do what they wanted to, and
here was Dr. Bowman who had a deal he wanted to put up
to them.

Sid paused and blew some smoke rings. Dr. Bowman gathered that the introduction was finished. He spoke as briefly as
Sid had and repeated the offer he had made to Sid.

When he was done, there was a faint moment of silence.
Then discussion and argument broke out all over the room.
Some were certain that he had an angle, a percentage, that
there was a catch. Others insisted, as one thin boy did, that you
can't have any fun in a *church*. One boy loudly suggested that
Dr. Bowman had been put up to it by the police who wanted to
be able to check up on the Stalwarts more easily. Indeed, for almost an hour it seemed that hardly anyone had anything good
to say for Dr. Bowman's proposition. The general trend of the

discussion was that *they* were back of this, it was a plot, it was for sissies, it was for the birds.

Once or twice someone spoke up briefly for the idea. The main argument seemed to be the basketball court and ping-pong tables, plus a larger dance floor than the Greasy Spoon afforded. No one mentioned the spiritual advantages of meeting in a parish house or the good effects on character from associating with young churchgoers.

Dr. Bowman occasionally spoke up to answer particular questions. Otherwise, he left the debate to the Stalwarts. Sid interrupted once in a while to reinforce or refute a point made by some member, but mostly his thoughts seemed to be wandering in some blue out-yonder, blue as cigarette smoke.

When, after almost two hours of discussion, Sid prepared to put the question to a vote, Dr. Bowman was sure of one thing: if by any miracle his proposition were accepted, it wouldn't be for edifying and idealistic reasons. The greatest obstacle his plan faced was that it involved a church and the suggestion of religion. The assets all seemed to be the secular appurtenances.

Sid was putting it to a vote. There was the show of hands for the affirmative. Now for the Nays. By a majority of almost three to one, the Stalwarts accepted his proposal. For whatever motives, they had voted Yes.

"Glory be to Thee, O Lord," Dr. Bowman sang as he drove home, and, drawing near to the rectory, he chanted at the top of his lungs:

> Heaven and earth are full of the Majesty of thy glory.
> The glorious company of the Apostles praise thee.
> The goodly fellowship of the Prophets praise thee.
> The noble army of Martyrs praise thee.
> The happy crackpots of God praise thee.

"What *on* earth?" asked Mrs. Bowman in horror as he came bounding and singing into the living room.

"Only light wine at the home of the Arrondos, eons ago," he stated, and he tickled her under the chin. "I am drunk on the Spirit."

She sniffed. "The Spirit doesn't smell too alcoholic. Sit down, Henry. I never see you! I'll get the coffee, and you can tell me everything that happened."

"Righto," he agreed heartily, and he sang while waiting—

The noble army of crackpots for the love and glory of God doth praise thee . . .

21

PROPOSALS OF MATRIMONY

THE NEXT morning, just as the Bowmans were sitting down
to breakfast, little Nancy whispered in a voice that would have
carried to all the bedrooms upstairs, "Betty, Betty, I've got a
secret for you!"

Mrs. Bowman laughed, and Dr. Bowman guffawed. Betty
flushed. "If it's a secret, keep it secret for me," she pleaded.
"Here, we'll go upstairs and you can tell me—"

"After breakfast," Mrs. Bowman said firmly. "The secret
will keep."

"He said to give it to you right away," Nancy explained
eagerly.

"So it was a he?" Dr. Bowman asked innocently.

"Do you want me to have secrets with girls?" Betty asked
sharply.

"Aw, pipe down, and let's eat," Tom said. His knife and fork
hovered over his pancakes.

"And who set you in authority over me?" Betty inquired.
"Who are you to tell me to pipe down?"

"The subject is dropped," Dr. Bowman said. "Let's have
grace."

"Who started it?" muttered Betty sullenly. Her mother
watched her obliquely as Dr. Bowman said grace. Her practiced

ear seemed to detect tears and tantrums in her daughter's voice, but breakfast proceeded without overt disorder.

When the meal was over, Betty turned to Nancy. "Let's go upstairs."

"The secret, the secret," Nancy chanted.

"O.K.," said Mrs. Bowman. "Have your secret, taste it, and eat it. But then come back down here. I've got your new skirt almost ready to try on."

"Make it tight enough," Betty pleaded. "You can make 'em so nice, but the last one was like a sack, it was so loose."

"Up with you," her mother said ominously. "Then back down for the trying on."

"Betty's got a secret," Nancy chanted. "Come on, come on." Betty, her hand firmly gripped by Nancy's, was propelled upstairs. They went into Betty's room.

"It's from *Steve*," Nancy said, handing a sealed envelope to her sister. Her eyes seemed twice their normal size. "He saw me out in the back yard and he put his finger on his mouth, and he gave it to me, and he said—"

"You're a sweet sister," Betty said absent-mindedly. She picked Nancy up in her arms and walked into the hall. "A sweet sister," she repeated and put Nancy down by her door. "You've been such a good helper. Thank you so much." Betty started back to her own room.

"Can't I read the secret, too?" Nancy asked with a long face.

"No!"

"Why not?"

"What do you think a secret is, stupid?"

"You called me stupid," Nancy wailed, ran into her room, and slammed the door.

"Can you beat it, can you beat it?" Betty asked in exasperation. But the sobs from the next room were gradually diminishing, and Betty dismissed them from her thoughts.

Back in her room, she feverishly tore open the envelope. It looked like a real letter. She read it rapidly, then again more slowly:

DEAR BETTY:

Easter is coming near, and I've been doing a lot of thinking. When we started our cooling-off period, I guess both of us thought that when it was over we would either call things quits, or we'd get pinned again and maybe officially engaged. But I've been thinking about it a lot. I guess Mr. Crews is right when he says that a long time of going together or engagement is hard on both people. You get frustrated and jumpy and hard to get along with. (I don't mean just you; I mean both people do.) So I want to make you an offer, and you can think about it. If we decide to come back together, I don't see that there is anything to keep us from getting married right after we graduate this June.

Look at it this way. I'll be eighteen by then. Mom and Dad may think I am a little young, but I know them. They'll end up by saying it's my decision, and I have to take the responsibility. I don't really care whether I go on to college. I know Dad can get me a job in his store, and since it's part of a chain, I'll have a good chance to work my way up and become manager of another store somewhere in a few years.

So it's perfectly practical for us to get married. We don't have to spend years and years waiting. The thing we've got to decide is whether we want to break the whole thing off or come back together. If we come back together, I want you to be thinking about all this. We could be married less than three months from now.

Love,
STEVE

An overpowering sense of sweetness and happiness swept through Betty's whole being. On the instant, she designed the wedding dress that her mother would make. She could see herself and Steve standing at the altar rail in Trinity Church.

Whom should she ask for bridesmaids? Was Nancy too old for the flower girl? A honeymoon in June—so many beautiful, quiet places they could go. Back in their home—she saw them in it, sitting by the picture window, their own home with a bedroom that either or both had the right to enter at any time. She saw the rhythm of the days and nights—Steve going to work after breakfast, home for lunch, she hoped, home for dinner, the evening and the lingering night together. Her mind leaped on ahead. Their first baby—she hoped it would be a boy . . .

The mood collapsed. There would be no college for Steve or herself. The serious business of breadwinning and starting a family would be only a matter of months away. Why did she have to be hurried and pushed? Why shouldn't she have her years of college, of gradually expanding independence and liberty, like any other girl? Was it fair of Steve to be putting this kind of pressure on her?

The vision of their little home with Steve coming home to the tasty dinner she had prepared returned briefly and with enough vividness to evoke a desperate groan from her. "I *am* mixed up," she moaned.

"Betty!" her mother called from downstairs. "Ready for the fitting."

"Com—coming," Betty called back. She dabbed her eyes, carefully put the letter away, and walked down to the den where her mother was standing with a mouthful of pins. The new skirt was on her arm.

"It's beautiful," Betty said in sincere admiration.

"Come here and I'll slip it on," her mother said in a muffled voice.

"Mama, for Lord's sake can't you take those pins out of your mouth?" Tom inquired. He was fiddling idly with the TV. "You'll swallow one of them."

The two women paid no attention to him. Betty was standing there in her slip. Her mother dropped the new skirt down over her. Then she began measuring and putting in pins.

"You aren't going to leave it like this?" Betty asked in an unbelieving wail.

"And what's wrong with it?"

"It sags, it droops, it's like an old bag," Betty exploded.

"And where does it sag and droop?"

"Here! Can't you see?" She slapped herself resoundingly on her hips. "This is the way it ought to be." She grabbed the skirt and pulled it tight. "Like this," she said, "so it won't droop and look dowdy. See how much better it looks, Mama?" Betty added pleadingly.

Her mother replied in a noncommittal voice. "Walk around the room."

Betty, clutching the skirt to hold it tight at the waist and hips, began a slow parade of the room.

"Tom," said Mrs. Bowman. "Tom—how do you like the way Betty's skirt is fitted? Keep on walking, Betty."

Tom looked up. Betty's back was to him at the moment as she slowly made the circuit of the room.

"Mama," he protested, "you aren't going to leave it like that, are you?"

Betty turned around with fire in her eyes. "And what's wrong with it?"

"Let me see it again," Tom said judiciously. "Resume the fashion march." Betty obeyed with an irritated jerk of the shoulders. Tom studied her retreating form with an expression of detached, scientific interest. "I was right," he volunteered at last. "When she waddles along in that tight skirt, it does look like the hind-end of a baboon—"

"Tom!" Betty swung around and, letting go of her skirt, leaped toward her brother. He caught her two hands and held them tight. Then with a push he sent her flying across the floor.

"Stop it!" Mrs. Bowman shouted, stepping between the two combatants. "I've spent hours on that skirt."

Betty had disentangled herself from the controversial garment. She hurled it upon the sofa. "This whole family stinks," she said with slow emphasis. Still in her slip, she stormed up the stairs. "Especially Tom Bowman!" she yelled from the head of the stairs. They could hear her door opening and slamming shut.

"Whew!" said Mrs. Bowman. She laughed. "Tom," she said in a low voice, "you were right."

"Anybody could see why she wanted it tight," Tom said. "To go wiggling around so all the boys—"

"Yes, yes," said his mother. "She's seventeen. Well, I'll make it the way I'd planned—maybe just a little bit tighter—but not as tight as she wants it. I wouldn't think of making it that tight."

Before dawn that same morning, Bill Pendleton heard the alarm go off. It was dark outside. He arose with the feeling of a man awaiting the procession of priest and executioner. After hurriedly fixing his own breakfast, he was soon outside and on his way. Around noon he stopped at a roadside stand and had a nondescript lunch. He was still at least an hour's drive away from the big city where Helen was living.

He felt numbed. He was like someone in a nightmare time of catastrophe, mechanically going around among the ruins, preserving the outward appearance of normal activity. He knew what he had to do. His desire to feel important had strewn ruin everywhere. It had provoked the Stalwarts into the raid that led to his father's heart attack. There was no way to undo that. It had also led to Helen's pregnancy. There he could do something. He would do it if it killed him.

After he had finished his second cup of coffee, he got up and resumed his trip. Driving was an automatic thing. He felt more numbed than ever. Dark doom was closing down upon him. He hardly noticed as the outlying suburbs gave way to the edges of the great city. He continued toward downtown. At a filling station he stopped and got a street map. He studied it. Luck, if you wanted to call it luck, was with him. He was only a few blocks away from the house where Helen was staying. He started the car again, and soon he was parked in front of the house.

Nothing was final yet. He was still free to start the engine and drive back to Blanton. He had made no promises. "Damn it!" he said, so loudly that a passer-by looked over his way in startled disapproval. He took a handkerchief from his pocket and wiped the sweat from his face. He studied his countenance in the rear-view mirror. There were sleepless hollows under his eyes. He took out his comb and parted his hair neatly. At least he didn't have to look sloppy.

He got out of the car, walked to the front door, and rang the bell. Mrs. Blumenthal opened it. She was a sweet-faced, white-haired lady who had shrewd and probing eyes. "I'm Bill Pendleton," he said. "Would you please tell Helen Greenwood that I'm here?"

Mrs. Blumenthal smiled and said briskly, "I'll tell her right away. Won't you have a seat in the parlor?" She led him to the room. "There are a few old magazines scattered around," she said, and she left him to himself. There was something about her eyes. She knew everything, he was convinced. Maybe Helen had told her, or probably the old gal was used to these situations and had learned how to spot the Men in Their Lives.

He picked up a copy of *The Reporter*. The sofa was big and thickly stuffed, but he didn't seem able to make himself comfortable on it. He tried to read. Then he heard footsteps in the hall. He rose. There was Helen. She walked into the room and smiled slightly. "Hello, Bill," she said.

"Hello, well hello," he said. He wondered whether he should kiss her, but it seemed funny. The unmistakable roundness where the baby was—it seemed to draw a line, set up a wall between them. This was silly. It was *his* baby as much as hers, but still the line seemed to be there. He hesitated, and the moment passed.

"Sit down, Bill," she said. He awkwardly settled down on the sofa, and she sat in a chair across from the little coffee table. She looked at him steadily. "Why did you want to see me . . . after all this time?"

He was prepared for this. He had rehearsed this conversation in his mind all the way to the city. "To ask you to marry me," he said.

Her expression didn't alter. "Why do you want to marry me?"

He hadn't quite expected this. The Helen he had known back in the fall was not one to question any sign of interest and affection.

"You haven't told me why you want to marry me," Helen continued in her almost casual voice.

"Well, I guess, you might say it's for the baby's sake," he blurted out. "I do have a conscience."

Perhaps he only imagined it, but Helen's eyebrows seemed to arch a tiny distance. Her remote smile took on a touch of wry amusement. She looked toward the other side of the room. The silence began to eat at him like an acid.

"A conscience late is better than a conscience never," he stammered.

Helen's eyes briefly met his. There was amusement in them and something else. Contempt? Pity? He wasn't sure. It made him uneasy inside. She looked away again.

"It's this way," Bill stumbled on. He could feel the sweat

breaking out on his face, and it annoyed him. "Let's see. We could get married right away, then announce it. We could say we were married last summer. People are having secret marriages all the time. A few people might suspect something, but what the hell? It wouldn't matter."

"No, I'm sure it wouldn't," Helen said. "If we decide to get married, we can work out the practical details."

"Then how about it?" Bill asked with a heaviness growing in his heart. "I could see Dr. Bowman tonight, or would you rather have somebody from up here?"

Helen was looking down at her lap now. In the growing silence, he noticed the lines of her face, her complexion. He'd never thought of her as very pretty, but there seemed a quiet loveliness about her. He wondered if it had been there all along.

"Well, how about it?" he asked. This thing was dragging along.

Helen looked up and smiled. "One other question. Do you love me? You haven't given me a kiss."

He leaned forward awkwardly. She pushed him away with her hands. "I didn't ask for a kiss! I want to know, do you love me?"

Bill fumbled for words. It hadn't occurred to him that this question would be asked. He was beginning to feel mistreated. After all, he had voluntarily offered to do the decent thing. What right did a girl in Helen's situation have to be so particular?

"I guess with the baby coming and all that, it isn't love. It doesn't matter, it's what's right for you and the baby—"

"No, thanks," she said coldly. She stood up. "I'm not going to have you marrying me out of pity or as a duty. What good would that do any of us? A marriage without love—think of a baby growing up in that kind of a family! He'll be better off with the people who plan to adopt him."

"But—but—I—" Bill tried to interrupt.

A flush of anger was spreading over Helen's face. Her eyes flashed with sudden fury, and her voice rose. "I made love once with a man I didn't love. I'm never going to do it again!"

She stood there leaning across the table, quivering with the intensity of her feeling. Slowly she drew back her open hand and with a sudden motion hit him hard and full across the mouth.

"Damn you!" he yelled and reached to grab her. The little coffee table tottered uncertainly. He stumbled. She skipped smoothly past him and was running up the stairs. He dashed into the hall and headed for the stairs. If he could get his hands on her . . .

Mrs. Blumenthal came in through the front door at this moment and looked at him sharply. He stopped in his tracks. She smiled and asked, "How did you find Helen, Mr. Pendleton?"

"Oh—oh, she was all right, she was fine," Bill replied lamely.

"I'm glad you think so," Mrs. Blumenthal said. "We are very fond of Helen here, and she has changed so much since she came. Much more self-confidence and maturity. I'm sure you noticed that."

"Yes, yes, I did." When could he escape into the open air?

"You must come back and see Helen again," Mrs. Blumenthal said in a tone of dismissal. She smiled shrewdly. Was there a touch of mockery? "I'm sure she appreciates it."

"Thank you," Bill said. "Well, thank you, good-bye."

He escaped through the door. He jumped into his car and stepped on the gas. There were some tentative grinds and sputters. "Start, damn you!" he growled and tried again. At last the engine started. He pulled away abruptly and was on the long road back to Blanton.

During the trip back, he had plenty of time to think, and to imagine. Who did Helen think she was to be so high and mighty? That night in the car, when they'd done it together, she'd been just as willing as he was. He wasn't out to rape her. She was out to be taken. Well, he'd taken her. So what? Sure, when the baby started, he had a responsibility. He'd ducked that responsibility, but he wasn't ducking it any more. What gripe did she have? He was trying to do the right thing. It was a hell of a way to be treated, to get smacked on the mouth. And not a love pat. The inside of his upper lip still smarted where it had grazed against a tooth. If he could get his hands on her! Ladies don't go around smacking you. All right, he wouldn't treat her like a lady. If he could get his hands on her . . . It was strange. In his anger he played with a number of pictures— slapping her hard, shaking her, spanking her till it hurt—but soon his resentment began to subside, and he no longer wanted to pay her back. With a slight shift of the imagination, another set of pictures danced before him. Making love with Helen. He found himself imagining it as though there hadn't been that night in the car. Somehow that Helen didn't seem to have much connection with this new Helen, this Helen who didn't need him. His imagination raced on. Damn her. Who did she think she was? If she thought she could get rid of him so easily . . .

22

TIME OF TRIAL

TOM BOWMAN didn't know Frank really well, but all the same he found that the trial was on his mind, and he couldn't shake it off. He wondered, what fatality leads people like Frank to go out on such a very long limb? Why does any city inevitably generate such opposites as the Omegas and the Stalwarts? But are they really opposites? Are they two editions of the same book?

Most of all, Tom still mused about himself. He remembered with a slight shiver the little graveyard where he had stood, so long ago, reading the tombstones. "It is later than you think." He often heard his parents talking of events from twenty years ago as though it were only yesterday—twenty years ago he had not been born, not even begotten. Take three twenties and add his own seventeen years, and he would be an old man, if he were still alive. The heritage of time that was his birthright was of strictly limited duration. Time was rationed. Each day eroded his portion of time as the warm water of the ocean erodes an iceberg drifting south. He would not live forever, not here on this earth. The life to come? He believed in it, yes, but abstractly. When he thought about planning his life, it included only the years on this green planet. One life at a time. There was so much he wanted to understand about himself, about others, about this strangely bittersweet fact called life, so quickly gone.

Meanwhile, almost without his noticing it, his schoolwork was going a little better. There were no spectacular gains, but a fair hope that his work was now good enough so that his teachers and Mr. Johnston could plead his case more convincingly and get him into at least a good second-rate college. "Do what you will . . . there is everything to do in My world," the unheard Voice had once told him. He wasn't sure, but he was beginning to think that for him "the proper study of mankind is man." What this meant in terms of college majors and jobs, he wasn't sure. It could conceivably lead to a major in any of the social sciences, or literature, philosophy, or religion, for that matter. Occupations? Teaching, counselling, politics, writing, the ministry? Time would tell. His thoughts returned to Frank. Were the psychologists right in their neat answers? Could a broken home explain it all? Was Frank merely reacting against the symbols of his unhappy environment? Or was there in Frank something of the holy madman, a desire to plunge into the direst depths out of love of God and one's brother? He wished he knew.

As Frank's trial drew near, Mr. Arrondo's conscience was deeply troubled. The decision to join Trinity Church—which he made for the whole family—had not been an easy one. The word "Protestant" still stirred up ancestral memories of heresy, wrecked monasteries, persecution of the faithful. But once he had made the decision and had led his family to Trinity Church, it was as though the springs of life could flow again. Each Sunday they knelt at the altar rail and received the Body and Blood of Christ. They belonged to Him and to the other worshippers. The serenity and joy of Sunday morning began to color the weekdays. As this happened, Mr. Arrondo found that he could not banish the thought of Frank. The boy was capable of mad and outrageous deeds, but he never whined, never lied. Whatever he did, he took the consequences.

Mr. Arrondo asked himself, had he been selfish in forbidding Rosa to see Frank again? Was he trying to protect her too much? How far is anyone, even a parent, justified in shielding another against all the dangers of life? He still wasn't sure he had made a mistake, but he kept thinking. Rosa hadn't said anything in a long time about Frank. But who can tell what a young girl is thinking?

For Rosa, the days before the trial were a time of constant prayer, but not much self-examination. The big decisions were for men and God to make. She did not believe that she was the cause of Frank's downfall nor that she could have prevented it. Day by day she said her rosary and knelt before her little crucifix and prayed, not that Frank would escape the penalty of his act, but that God would somehow break through his wall of loneliness, would break through and flood him with the supernatural virtues of faith, hope, and love, so that whatever came, he would bear it with God's Grace.

Sue and Nancy Bowman could think of nothing but Frank and his four companions as the time of the trial drew near. For days now, Sue had been praying for Mr. Pendleton's recovery and for the five Stalwarts. Since she wasn't quite sure just what kind of prayer she ought to say for them, she made the prayer a general one, asking God to take them over and do with them as He thought best. Whatever Sue prayed for, Nancy was likely to pray for, too. Sue had long been Nancy's spiritual director. Each night they knelt side by side to say their prayers, and then Sue would tell her a story about seddaglonks that fly in the night and suck your blood; promptly thereafter Sue would kiss her a firm good night.

The evening before the trial they had a special project. They planted themselves in the kitchen after the dishes were done, and measured out cocoa, three pounds of sugar, and milk, and added a pinch of salt. When the fudge was at the soft ball stage, they took it off the stove, added oleo and vanilla, beat it, and poured it into two large pans. After it hardened, they cut it and divided it into five piles, each of which they wrapped in waxed paper and tied with a blue ribbon. "You can scrape the pan," Sue said to Nancy whose lower lip was beginning to hang down. She put the five bundles into a large sack.

The next morning, the day of the trial—it was to be at two o'clock—a somewhat bewildered Tom stood at the main entrance of Blanton Senior High and intercepted Frank. Hastily he thrust the big sack into his hands, explained that parties unknown had asked him to pass it along and would Frank please give one of the packages to each of the four other Stalwarts. "Thank you," Frank said with no apparent surprise, and he added, "Tell the parties unknown that this will sweeten the bitterness of adversity." With a laugh, he disappeared inside the school.

Ever since he had come back to Blanton, Frank had of course run into various of the Stalwarts at school from time to time. Usually Sid and the three others were together, surrounded by an admiring knot of additional Stalwarts. He had found himself a hero in their eyes. He was a real guy who wouldn't let his pals take the rap alone. Their effusive admiration embarrassed him, for in his own eyes he was guilty of contributing to their downfall. He didn't quite know what to say in answer to their praise or in comment on the plans they were always discussing. The plans changed from day to day, without advance notice, depending on Sid's mood. He set the tone for the others. Occasionally he seemed to see things clearly and would emphatically state that once he got out of this tangle, he was going straight. More often, though, he spoke in the past tense of "kid stuff" and talked grandly of "big-time operations" in the future. Sometimes he simply pooh-poohed the whole thing and assured his accomplices that Judge Strood was chicken-hearted, and the most they'd get was a stern lecture and maybe a suspended sentence.

Every time Frank ran into the Stalwarts, he came away confused and depressed. Thus it was with a bit of moral effort that he braced himself to take the gifts of fudge to them. He found them quickly enough, laughing and smoking in a defiant little cluster in a cluttered corner of the basement. He gave them the presents with the explanation that somebody had asked that he pass them along. The Stalwarts gazed at the gifts in astonishment and began eating the squares of fudge. Frank stood there awkwardly, wondering what more there was to say. The bell rang and rescued him. "See you this afternoon," he said.

At noon he went home. He found Sarah sitting in the living room, with a stricken look. "The lawyer just phoned," she said. "Mr. Pendleton was sent home today, and the doctor's report is definite. He'll have to live the life of an invalid from now on."

What could Frank say?

Sarah continued. "Your father's gone to talk with the lawyer. He thinks we should ask for a deferment of the trial until public opinion dies down."

"I hope Judge Strood refuses," Frank said.

Sarah looked at him, started to say something, and burst into tears. Frank sat beside her and put his arm around her. At times she seemed more like an older sister—or even a younger sister—than a stepmother.

There was the sound of footsteps in the hall. "He'll try," Mr. Buell said as he came in. "He'll ask the judge for a month's deferment, but he isn't very hopeful."

Sarah sat up. "Come along, everybody, lunch time!" she said firmly.

During lunch they bravely talked of everything except

the trial. At 1:45 the three of them started driving to the juvenile court.

The Buells had no way of knowing it, but that morning had also been a difficult one for Raymond Strood, the juvenile judge. He had heard the news about Mr. Pendleton over the radio. He knew the state of public opinion in Blanton. To a large extent he shared it, as he admitted to himself. *Something* had to be done to check juvenile delinquency before it got completely out of hand. There was especially little excuse for a boy like Frank Buell, born with every advantage. If gentle measures had failed, and they seemed to have failed, perhaps it was time for the law and the courts to show their teeth. The defense would almost certainly ask for a delay. On the basis of many legal precedents, it was a plausible request. Should he postpone the case, let it drag on and on? There had already been one deferment. With young people in particular, speed was of the essence. If there were too much delay between crime and penalty, it would be like spanking a baby for something he had done two weeks ago. When Judge Strood walked into the courtroom, he still hadn't made up his mind.

Promptly at two the court opened. The four other defendants were there with as many of their parents as chose to come. Mr. Wembley sat to one side of Judge Strood's desk, the clerk at the other. The lawyer was in the front row. The general public was excluded since this was a juvenile case. Later Judge Strood, at his discretion, would issue whatever report on the outcome he thought best.

The clerk of the court read the charges, framed in the awesome language of the law, "that the aforementioned persons did assemble in a restaurant, to wit, the Greasy Spoon, and did unlawfully confer and conspire to break and enter the domicile or residence of one William Pendleton, Sr. . . ." On and on it went. Sid and his companions almost visibly drooped. They were being assailed by the winged weapons of language against which they had no defense.

When the clerk finished, the lawyer rose and moved that the trial be deferred for one month, "in view of the abnormal and prejudicial state of public opinion, as a consequence of the condition of Mr. William Pendleton, Sr." The North Side boys sat up a little straighter and listened hopefully.

Judge Strood sat in silence, obviously reluctant to make a decision. Slowly his gaze passed across the faces of the five boys. "Do all of you wish this deferment?" he asked at last.

Frank glanced at the others. They were saying nothing. Then he turned to the judge. "Your Honor," he said, "I can speak only for myself. I'd rather get it over with."

"Frank!" his father said sharply. Sarah looked at Frank and smiled.

"How about the rest of you boys?" Judge Strood asked.

Sid Pruitt looked at the others and they exchanged glances. "Guess we'll stick with Frank," he said. "No use waiting."

The judge turned to the lawyer. "Do you still wish to press your motion?"

The lawyer conferred in whispers with Mr. Buell. "Motion withdrawn," he said.

"The clerk will proceed," Judge Strood said with obvious relief.

The clerk turned to the lawyer. "How do these boys intend to plead?"

"They will all plead guilty, Your Honor," the lawyer said, "but we wish to present certain extenuating circumstances."

"Very well," said Judge Strood. "First let us all retire to my chambers where there is less of this courtroom formality, and we shall come back for the actual entering of pleas and disposition of the case."

The entire group slowly followed Judge Strood into his

office and were soon seated. He sat in his armchair and looked around the room. "Let me see whether I can tell you what the extenuating circumstances are," he said. "First, in the case of these four boys from the North Side, there is not one who does not have something in his home background to produce instability. Mr. Wembley has thoroughly investigated them. In the case of Frank, there seems less excuse—"

"If I may interrupt," said Mr. Buell, "a boy from Oak Hill can have as unstable a family background as one from the North Side. I'd like to take a large share of responsibility for Frank. He comes from a broken home, and I had a hand in the breakup."

"Very well," said Judge Strood. "I'll take your word, Mr. Buell, though it remains true, I'm sure you will agree, that Frank has had many advantages of background denied to these other boys. But may I ask you, sir"—he turned to the lawyer— "whether I have correctly summarized the extenuating circumstances?"

"Very correctly," the lawyer agreed. "Family circumstances for all of them, and, in the case of the North Side boys, an environment that makes crime seem natural and almost right."

"Thank you," said Judge Strood. He paused a while, then turned to the boys and spoke in a serious, low voice. "There are three reasons for punishment. The first is one I'm not sure I believe in—to make the person suffer because of the thing he's done. If that kind of punishment is needed, I'd just as soon leave it to God. The second purpose of punishment is to help straighten the person out so that he can make a new start. It wouldn't help you to straighten out if I let you off scot-free or too easily. The third purpose of punishment is the social one— to make it clear to others that society will not disregard it if they break society's rules. This third function of punishment becomes especially important in a time like the present when there seems to be a growing wave of juvenile delinquency in Blanton. In its own defense, society has to call a sharp halt at some point."

He paused. The four North Side boys had drooped again and seemed hardly to understand the judge's words.

"Does anyone here have any questions to ask unofficially or any explanations to make? There is plenty of time."

No one replied. The judge looked at the five boys again. "Let me just say this. I believe in you. I'm going to keep in touch with you. I want to do everything I can to help you. If you take this the right way, it'll be a new beginning, not an end. Well, let's go back to the courtroom."

Back in the courtroom the five boys, one after another, entered their pleas of guilty. Judge Strood, now looking impersonal and remote, pronounced sentence. Three of the Stalwarts were given suspended sentences and placed under the supervision of Mr. Wembley. The two others already had court records. Frank had been involved in drunken driving and a serious accident. Sid had been in Judge Strood's court several times. Both of them now received indeterminate sentences in the State Institution for Delinquent Boys. Judge Strood added a brief explanation. Under state law, this imprisonment could last as long as the twenty-first birthday of each boy, but the special parole board which handled juvenile cases always reviewed them each December and August. It was possible that Frank or Sid, or both of them, might be released in time to return to Blanton in the fall. It depended entirely on the two boys themselves.

23

CUPID IN A ROUND COLLAR

WHEN the Stalwarts, including the three who were under the supervision of Mr. Wembley, first began to meet in the parish house, it was without fanfare and publicity. Dr. Bowman was now confident enough of his congregation not to fear any major upheaval; on the other hand, if there were too much discussion in the community about the new role of Trinity Church, it might kick up some anxiety and criticism among the more paleolithic parishioners.

A few days after Frank and Sid had left Blanton for their indeterminate stay in the State Institution for Delinquent Boys, Dr. Bowman picked up the *Blanton Daily Times,* a paper he always read with foreboding, and felt his heart sink as he came to the editorial page: "Young Delinquents under the Church Roof."

Trust them, trust the *Blanton Daily Times,* to put the most sinister interpretation on everything. He must call up the editor or write a letter of protest. He read on. Say— Could it be that the *Daily Times* took a hopeful and approving view of something for once? In spite of the sensational title of the editorial, the text began: "Others have talked about it. Trinity Church (Episcopal) has done something about it."

It was not often that Dr. Bowman found himself lavishly and publicly praised by name. The editorial made him sound

like the new St. Francis and Trinity Church the Kingdom of
God come down to earth. Dr. Bowman read the editorial and
reread it. He ate it up. He ate it up three times. Then he
laughed and remembered that a Christian was supposed to be
humble. "Thine is the glory," he said to God, "but thank You,
God, for letting me give You a helping hand."

He read the editorial yet again. I mustn't fall into a facile
mood of optimism, Dr. Bowman warned himself. It isn't as
though the whole world were beating a path to the doors of
Trinity Church. If it did, the whole world, old members and
new members alike, would still be partially and imperfectly
Christian, not an army of glistening saints. Trinity is moving
in the right direction. It is becoming genuinely catholic, a
church for all men everywhere, including all men who live in
its parish. We are learning to dig deeper and discover by experience what the Church actually is, but the deeper we dig, the
deeper the problems and challenges and the agonies will be.

Superficial joys and superficial cares, good-bye. The stakes
are doubled and redoubled at Trinity now. Dr. Bowman was
definitely encouraged. The congregation, for the most part, was
co-operative. The young people were increasingly enthusiastic.
Only two or three had dropped out of YPF when the North
Siders began joining. The great majority stayed, and the organization now seemed to have more excitement and fire than it
used to have.

That evening the phone rang. It was Bill Pendleton. "Can I
see you right away?" he asked. He sounded under some sort of
strain. Dr. Bowman told him to come on over.

When Bill arrived, they went into the study. Dr. Bowman,
all day long in a general state of euphoria, felt particularly well-
disposed toward Bill, who, in a flipflop of attitude, had become
one of the YPF'ers who made the greatest effort to welcome
newcomers to the group.

"Mind if I smoke?" Bill asked, and he reached for a cigarette.

"I'll join you." Dr. Bowman took out his pipe and lovingly filled it. He struck a match and lit the pipe. "What can I do for you, Bill?"

Bill's face twitched. "All right," he finally said. "Helen Greenwood is pregnant—I'm the father."

"I knew she was pregnant," Dr. Bowman said calmly. "She came to me, but she didn't say who the man was."

"I'm not shouting it around," Bill said hastily. "But—oh, I'll have to go way back to explain why I'm here now."

"We've got the evening. Take your time."

Bill's face was working. "Lately, since Dad got hospitalized and all that, I've been thinking. I had to face up to it. I'm one of the main reasons that Dad's an invalid. I was the leader of the Omegas, and I egged them on to pick fights with the Stalwarts. One thing led to another. They tried to get me, but they got Dad instead. It makes you think.

"I've begun to see things in myself, things I didn't know were there. You know why I went after Helen? Love? No, it wasn't that. Passion? Don't make me laugh. I went after her because down underneath I didn't have any confidence in myself."

Dr. Bowman interrupted. "At YPF you seemed to have plenty of confidence."

Bill laughed sourly. "Sure, I put on a big act because down underneath I didn't have any confidence. I couldn't imagine anybody giving a damn about me. That's the way I see it now. Sure, I was a big shot at YPF—confidence, leadership, toughness, all that. Bet Napoleon was doing the same act, and Hitler and Stalin. Making love with Helen—that was part of the same act, I see now. I had to feel like a big shot. Maybe it was the same with Helen. I don't know. Maybe we were both a couple of confused kids trying to use each other to prove we were important."

Dr. Bowman sat listening intently and nodding sympathetically from time to time. Bill continued. "I was a real louse. Not just with Helen, but with everybody. I was all out for the dear old Omega Alphas because it gave me a chance to push people around. I was the fanatical one at YPF because I didn't feel secure where I was unless I was keeping other people out. I guess it was when this business happened to Dad that I began to look back and see what led up to it. Then I saw what sort of guy I'd been."

Bill paused and seemed at a loss for words.

"And Helen?" Dr. Bowman gently asked.

"I was coming to that," said Bill, the pain in his face deepening. "Once I began to see myself halfway, I started thinking about Helen. I'd done a pretty stinking thing, leaving her like that. I said to myself, I ought to take the consequences. It's not fair to leave Helen to go it alone. Least thing I could do was offer to marry her, make an honest woman of her and keep the baby from being a bastard. Only decent thing to do. Well, I went up and saw her, and she gave me holy hell and smacked me in the teeth and flounced upstairs."

"Pretty rough treatment to apply to a man who's in love," Dr. Bowman remarked.

"In love? I didn't pretend that. I laid it on the line. If she wanted me to marry her, I was ready and willing. I'd do the honest thing by her."

"And she smacked you?"

"Smacked me and flounced upstairs. Well, that's not all. I don't know how to say the rest. I'm all mixed up. To make it short, I still want to marry her. It's a strange thing for me to ask —but would you be willing to go up to the city and talk with her and explain some things?"

Dr. Bowman puffed on his pipe. "Are you in love with her?"
Bill fumbled for words. "The reason I'm asking," continued Dr.

Bowman, "is that if you really want to marry Helen, you've got to think it through. Marriage is for keeps. It might be a compassionate and noble thing if you married her just to make an honest woman of her and for the baby's sake, but it could be quixotic, too. Don't think about marrying her unless you really think it will be 'till death do us part.' That's why I asked if you were in love with her. It helps."

"I wasn't in love with her when I slept with her or when I went up to see her the other day," Bill said slowly. Then a look of wonder came into his eyes. "Damned if I don't think I am now. It's crazy, but all I can think about is Helen, with that pregnant bulge and all. The thought that maybe she'll up and marry some other guy—I can't take it. And that baby—it's as much mine as hers. But mostly it's Helen I want."

Dr. Bowman laughed. "You said a while back that you had come to see yourself in a new light and had changed. Maybe Helen has changed too."

"She has. She used to seem such a clinging, wistful little thing. Now she's got something. I don't know what it is, but she doesn't have to cling and beg."

"I know," Dr. Bowman said. He thought a while. "Don't worry. I'll help all I can. I'll take the plane up tomorrow and talk with the lady. It won't be the first time in history that Cupid has worn a round collar."

Dr. Bowman called in the morning to make sure that Helen could see him, and then took the next plane, arriving just around lunch time. They went to a Chinese restaurant, and there, over the chop suey and chicken chow mein, he undertook his role as Cupid.

"How do you feel about Bill?" he asked.

Helen frowned in concentration. "I demonstrated my first reaction to him the other day. If a fellow comes around and begins talking about his Christian duty or words to that effect and offers to marry you for the sake of your unborn child . . . what does he think I am? If he'd talked about love, I might have hated him, but I'd have listened. But he didn't talk about love." She smiled. "Dr. Bowman," she added earnestly, "I've made very little progress in the Christian life. I smacked him, and when I heard his teeth rattling, it gave me great joy."

Dr. Bowman laughed boisterously. "You confirm my theory —woman is the more savage sex. Notice how three-fourths of all women order beef rare. But that's off the subject. I'm the go-between, Helen. Bill came to me in a state last night. Poor fellow, his troubles are piling up. He isn't just trying to do his duty any more. He couldn't sleep last night because he kept thinking of you. He's fallen in love."

"In love? Are you sure?"

"Who's ever sure? But I really think so. You know how life is. You don't need him any more, and he promptly needs you."

"That doesn't mean he can have me," Helen interjected sharply.

"Not at all," Dr. Bowman agreed. "It isn't your *duty* to marry him just because he needs you. But I do want to say one thing. Bill's changed a lot in these past few months. He isn't the same boy you knew five months ago. And you've changed. The new Bill has fallen in love with the new Helen, so I don't see how you can decide anything as long as you remember only the old Bill."

Helen's thoughts seemed to be wandering. They both concentrated on eating for a time. Then she looked up. "Have some more?" she asked. "The doctor has finally cracked down on me about weight." She loaded Dr. Bowman's plate, and he didn't protest. "I honestly don't know," she said at last. "What do you think?"

Dr. Bowman spoke earnestly. "If you fall in love with Bill,

marry him. If you don't, it's much better to carry through the original plans for the baby."

"But the time's so short—"

"Yes. If there's to be a courtship, it'll have to be relatively brief. Seriously, here's what I think. You can't force yourself to fall in love, and you shouldn't try, but you shouldn't slam the door to the possibility of falling in love. You hardly know the new Bill. Why don't you give him permission to come up and date you as often as he can? I think he'll drive up every week-end. Let him court you. You can regard him just as you would any other man who became interested in you. If no answering spark develops in you, that's that. But who knows? Life has a way of taking funny turns. You might find yourself falling in love with him. You can't find out unless you open the door enough to let him see you."

Helen smiled as though she'd made up her mind. "It seems pretty farfetched," she said. "It would be a kind of miracle if it worked out that we both fell in love. I think I ought to give it a chance. Tell Bill this—if he wants to come courting, he can. Tell him to come ahead. But no promises."

"I'll tell him, and he'll do handsprings of joy," Dr. Bowman said. Then he added seriously, "Regardless of how it comes out, I think you've made the right decision. You may not fall in love with him, but I think you'll come to respect him as he is now. And he certainly respects you. Who knows?" He smiled broadly. "Respect isn't a bad steppingstone to love. Well, enough of this pastoral counselling. Cupid will fly back to Blanton and faithfully deliver your message."

24

EASTER EVE

MARCH is a peculiarly dreary month in Blanton. The heavy snowstorms, with an occasional exception, are over, but snow lingers on the ground until it takes on a dark, blotched gray from factory smoke. In March it seems a fable, a fairy tale, that the gaunt leafless trees could ever be clothed again in green, that whole flights of song birds will come to inhabit them, and that girls will soon be seen everywhere in bright spring dresses.

April is better. The trees are still gaunt and the grass colorless, but the last of the compacted snow melts away, the temperature rises by timid degrees, and there are occasional days when the smell and feel of new life are in the air.

As Easter drew near, the sensation at the YPF and indeed at Blanton Senior High was the return of a radiant Helen Greenwood, now Mrs. William Pendleton, Jr., with two rings on her ring finger. She and Bill set up housekeeping in his father's house. It was an arrangement that had advantages on both sides. It gave the young couple a good place to live, and Helen could help look after Mr. Pendleton, Sr. The two of them from the beginning seemed drawn toward each other with the understanding that the rather old and the rather young often have for one another. Each looked helpless in the other's eyes.

Blanton, of course, had its share of calendar turners and gossips. When Helen left town right after Christmas, her family had said it was for reasons of health. This was the explanation still given. Beyond that, Bill and Helen simply said they'd kept the marriage secret, as many high-school students did, until it became obvious that the secret wouldn't keep much more. Neither of them seemed worried about the curiosity and censorious conjectures of an occasional neighbor or school friend. They were married, that was what counted, married and "obviously and blatantly in love," as Helen's parents were obliged to admit.

The young Pendletons still had plenty of practical problems, Betty realized even in her moments of envy. Bill would have to earn a living, and would he be able to go on to college? But with *that* kind of problem—people can help you. Both families have plenty of money. Probably they'll work it out to send Bill through college and help on family expenses till he can get launched in a career. Practical problems can be worked out by practical people. But *this* kind of problem—like deciding whether you're really in love—how do you work *it* out? Who can help you?

All through Lent, Steve and Betty had gone on remarkably parallel paths. Their paths touched only on Sunday morning when, by an unspoken agreement, they worshipped together at Trinity, and he walked her to and from the rectory. About the middle of Lent they had agreed that each of them would pray every night for guidance. At no time did either of them hear any mysterious voice or see visions; no omens in the sky spelled out Yes or No. At most, they sensed sometimes, each at his separate prayers, that an infinitely patient, loving, and perhaps slightly amused Listener was at the other end.

Each pursued the experiment of the cooling-off period with a dogged thoroughness. Each dutifully dated a couple of other people at various times, enjoyed it, and was miserable afterward.

Blanton Senior High was fully cognizant of the Noble Experiment, as one of the teachers nicknamed it. The same teacher, during a rowdy moment in the faculty lounge, organized a sweepstakes on the question of whether they would drop the Noble Experiment prematurely, carry through to a Yes, or decide on No.

On Good Friday Steve and Betty had gone to church together. As they left, they agreed that Steve would come for her early next morning. They would attend Holy Communion together, then go downtown for breakfast—and decide. "Whatever the decision," Betty said as they parted, "let's have a kiss on it then. I'm undernourished." Steve almost kissed her then and there. She had never looked more desirable.

That evening Betty knelt and pleaded with the unseen and silent Listener, "Tell me what to do." There was no answer. "Tell me, tell me!" No answer.

She got up from her knees, sat down on her bed, and let her mind wander at will. Countless memories of Steve and herself passed before her eyes. Pictures of their first times together, pictures from the more recent and troubled months, pictures inevitably of the time together in the deserted farmhouse. If they had gone ahead then, they might be like Bill and Helen now, safely married, their only problems the practical ones.

New pictures of herself and Steve kept forming and fading in her memory. If only one picture would focus clearly and stay fixed, as a hint, a clue. Her feelings were as changeable as a kaleidoscope. They were a mixture of tenderness and longing and irritation and pity and admiration and boredom and other emotions she didn't know what to call.

She went to bed. As sleep began at last to claim her, she was thinking of Helen and Bill. How lucky they were. Their lives were mapped out now. They had undoubtedly had their misunderstandings and tensions in the past, their dark hours, but now they were past that. Their lives were happily merged from this time on. Well? O.K. Why envy Bill and Helen? Steve had made the same offer. Two months from now Steve and I could be married and in a house of our own, Betty told herself, as sleep finally closed in.

The next morning Steve came by for her, and they walked to church together. In one of the back pews they knelt as the first quiet words of the Eucharist were spoken. Betty was gradually aware of something that surprised her. She wasn't really think-ing of her problems. She hadn't decided anything, but she was unworried. She felt peaceful and serene. She glanced at Steve's face beside her. How strong and lovely (yes, she would use that word) it was. The same serenity had made its home there. She laid her hand on his and gave it a slight squeeze, then gently removed it.

They went to the altar rail and returned. The Eucharist came quickly to its end. They left the church and walked to a little restaurant not far away. There they sat at a corner table and or-dered breakfast. The waitress brought orange juice as the first installment. Betty picked up her glass and smiled at Steve as she took a sip.

"Well?" said Steve. "Do you know now?"

"I didn't last night," Betty said. "Maybe I do now. Don't you?"

"What is it?"

"It's no good. I don't mean it that way—"

Steve interrupted. "I know what you mean. Guess we found out in time."

Betty thought a moment. "I suppose we drifted into it, living so close together, seeing each other at church. It was the natural thing."

"I'm not sorry," Steve said. "It was wonderful. The two years, even the times we got in each other's hair."

"Yes," Betty said, "it was wonderful."

The rest of their breakfast appeared, and they both began eating heartily. Betty smiled up at Steve. The spell was broken. Steve found himself looking at her as though he had never seen her before. She was still more beautiful than he remembered her. Her beauty had in it a purity, a radiance, a plain goodness. For a few quick glimpses he saw her as perhaps the first man and woman saw each other in that long-distant garden or as the blessed spirits, to whom all the turmoils and psychological agonies of earthly life are over, are permitted to behold one another. He saw her as she was. He saw her with a long moment of that love which asks nothing and by asking nothing is able to liberate both the giver and the receiver.

Betty smiled back. She also was seeing Steve with the eyes of this new love.

They finished their breakfast and had extra coffee. Tastes and smells seemed richer and better than they could remember. At last they got up and walked back to the rectory. Steve said, "So long," and he started to go.

"How about that kiss?" she demanded, and she pursed her lips. He came back and hugged her soundly and gave her the kiss in the presence of three startled ladies walking down to change the altar hangings at the church.

Betty adroitly broke away and dashed for the front door of the rectory. She waved gaily at him, then she disappeared inside. Steve went on home. On the way a sudden thought crossed his mind. If their paths parted—say, if they went to colleges far apart and worked at different places in the summer—and if they happened to meet two or three years in the future, with that much more experience of life, that much more maturity, who could tell? But he put the thought aside. One day at a time. He returned home with a light step though there was an emptiness, too.

About the middle of that Saturday morning, Dr. Bowman was sitting in the living room, chatting desultorily with Tom. Both were in expansive spirits. The day before, Tom had received a letter from one of the fairly good colleges, definitely admitting him. Today he had heard from a better school, offering to put him on their waiting list; the letter added that no promises could be made, but the probability was that a vacancy would develop and he could be accepted. Obviously his teachers and the principal had worked hard in his behalf, but then his work was definitely on the upgrade now. On the last round of tests, his marks had ranged from C-plus to A.

Dr. Bowman was in fine spirits, first of all because of Tom's good fortune. Then there was the happy ending to Helen Greenwood's story. It wasn't often that such a tangled beginning straightened out as hopefully as this one had. "How do Bill and Helen strike you?" he asked.

"Head over heels in love and acting their age," Tom replied.

His father chuckled. "That means acting like seventeen and sixteen. You're right. I was over at their place yesterday, and they seemed like two children playing in a doll house, but playing very seriously. Then they had a brief spat about something—nothing serious—and I half expected one or the other to stick out his tongue."

"Do you think they'll make a go of it?"

"By the grace of God, probably. They've both done a lot of growing up, and they are madly in love. But they're still seventeen and sixteen, so there are special problems. I tell you, Tom, how about waiting till you are through college before you marry that girl, what's her name? It simplifies life."

"Yes, what's her name?" Tom asked.

"Miss X, the mystery girl," Dr. Bowman replied. "Invisible, inaudible—"

"Untouchable and unthinkable," Tom added. "That means she isn't."

Dr. Bowman's thoughts drifted to his greatest good fortune of all, the blessing that would set this Easter apart from any he had known before. It still seemed a miracle (perhaps it literally was a miracle) that he had been able to broaden out the church with so little protest from the congregation. The most common criticism he ran into was "Why did you wait so long?" rather than "Why are you rushing ahead?" The Lord had manipulated the pieces of the chessboard very neatly. He had turned Dick Jenkins into an advocate of the new policy. He had inspired the editor of the *Blanton Daily Times* to praise Trinity Church at a crucial time. Perhaps it was also the Lord who had worked on Sid Pruitt and persuaded him at least to call the Stalwarts together that memorable night so they could hear Dr. Bowman's proposal.

Tomorrow would be Easter, the first Easter in many decades that Trinity Church could honestly claim to be representative of all sorts and conditions of men living in its neighborhood. As Dr. Bowman chatted with Tom, he was haunted by an unformulated hope that some new Pentecost was close at hand. Certainly Trinity parish was experiencing a kind of resurrection. Who could tell what this Easter would mean in the life of the parish? "Praise be to thee, O Christ," he said silently, as he had so many times recently.

The doorbell rang. "I'll take it," Tom said. He went to the front door and came back with Steve Hadley's father.

Dr. Bowman stood up. "Hello, Jim," he said. They shook hands. "Join me, sit down."

The junior warden hesitated. "Got time to talk some church business?"

"Nothing I'd rather talk," Dr. Bowman said buoyantly. "And all the time in the world."

"I'll clear out," Tom said.

"Don't bother," said Mr. Hadley. "Tom may be useful. It's

partly about YPF." He sat down, and the others followed suit. Dr. Bowman felt a twinge of apprehension.

"What about the YPF?" Dr. Bowman asked.

Mr. Hadley did not answer the question directly. "Henry," he said, "I wish you'd talked with me about all this business of broadening out the church before you went ahead."

"We'd talked it to death at vestry meetings," Dr. Bowman replied a little sharply. "Then Dick Jenkins called me—"

"I know, I know. And I know it's your responsibility. The vestry just advises you on things like this. And mind you, I'm not against it. I'm not saying I'm for it, but I'm not saying I'm against it. I'm just thinking of the congregation. I don't think they've been sufficiently prepared. Everything is going too fast. A lot of them don't understand what you're trying to do."

"What do you think I've been doing in my sermons all these years? And in talks to all the clubs? And the outside speakers we've brought in?"

"I know, you've done a good job educating them," Mr. Hadley continued. "But it takes time. People are set in their ways. You can't move them fast. Same way in my business. Take furniture. Most people want to buy something that looks stylish, but not too new-fangled. People are slow to change in their ways. You're pushing them too fast, Henry."

Dr. Bowman was silent for a moment. He looked over at Tom, whose expression was one of concern, plus something that looked like admiration and loyalty. At least that was how Dr. Bowman interpreted it. His mood of expansiveness had ended. He needed comfort.

"Has anything happened?" Dr. Bowman asked.

"Nothing serious, not too serious, if we all handle it right," Jim Hadley said. "A little group of people from the church, old members—six of them in all—came to see me yesterday—"

"Who were they?"

"Let's skip that. They'll probably be seeing you. I'll tell you if you need to know, but let's just talk now about what they said."

"They came to complain about the new policy at Trinity?"

"I wouldn't say complain. Not exactly. To talk it over. They'd been to see Dick Jenkins first—"

"I'll bet Dick brushed them off."

"He did. Six months ago he was dead set against broadening out the church. Then he changed his mind. With Dick his last opinion is always the right one. He talks now as though he's been pushing you to take in the new people for the last four or five years."

"Let him think it." Dr. Bowman laughed. "Well, the committee came to you—"

"Wouldn't call it anything so formal as a committee. They hadn't been elected by anybody. They were just an informal group that wanted to talk things over. I told them to see you."

"Thanks," said Dr. Bowman. "But what did they say specifically?"

Mr. Hadley seemed to be collecting his thoughts. "They said they thought you were trying to do too much all at once. It would have been best if you'd concentrated for a year or two on bringing in the more respectable adults from the North Side, people like the Arrondos. They aren't against that, as long as you're careful whom you invite. They felt the second step might come in a couple of years when you could begin to make a systematic effort to get the nicer kind of young people from the North Side into YPF. Of course, they wouldn't say you ought to slam the door if some nice young person from the North Side wanted to come into YPF before that time, but they were thinking about your going out and trying to bring them in."

"How about the Stalwarts?"

"There's the real problem. These people are convinced you're asking for trouble in having them meet in the parish house.

I'll admit they made an impression on me there. They'll be seeing you and giving you all the details, but you'll have to grant we've had a lot more wallet-lifting around the parish house since the Stalwarts came, and there was that boy, one of those mixed up in the Pendleton case, who was seen taking a swig of whiskey off in a corner, and there was a case one man told me about—his daughter had been propositioned by one of the North Side boys, and he wouldn't take No for an answer— followed her all the way home. And you know yourself you never heard such filthy language as those boys—"

"Don't the boys on Oak Hill ever proposition a girl or use four-letter words?" Tom interjected.

His father frowned. Mr. Hadley turned to Tom. "Of course, but it sets better with folks when it comes from their own kind." He turned back to Dr. Bowman, "Well, that's how these people see it. A church has problems enough under the best of circumstances. They don't say they're against what you're doing, but they do say you've gone too fast, and it's time to slow down now and take a deep breath. If you ask me, there's lots of folks in the church who feel like that."

"How do you feel?" Dr. Bowman asked.

"If you'd asked me before you started all this—"

"I did ask you!"

"I mean if you'd really asked me—if you'd asked me after you talked with Dick Jenkins—I'd've said, 'Let's wait a while.' But that's water over the dam. When you start something, you can't turn around and go backward."

Dr. Bowman's face lit up with delight. "Then you're in favor of going ahead—bringing in more new people, wherever we can get them—"

"I didn't say that. I only said you can't go back. I didn't say you had to charge ahead."

"The one thing a church can't do," Dr. Bowman said meditatively, "is stand still. It's always going either backward or forward."

"I've told you all I had on my mind," Mr. Hadley said, as though he had not heard Dr. Bowman's last remark. He stood up. "Just thought I ought to tip you off, in case they come to see you."

"Thanks very much," Dr. Bowman said, rising. "Well, see you tomorrow."

As soon as Mr. Hadley was outside, Tom leaned forward in a state of excitement rare for him. "You aren't going to backtrack or slow down, are you? The new policy has made all the difference with YPF. It's—it's got some life now; it means something. It's solidly back of you."

His father countered, "If you were in my place, what would you do about these people who want us to call a halt?"

Tom grinned. "Frank Buell once said he'd excommunicate them from the high altar. I'd save that for a last resort. Short of that, I guess I'd try to love 'em, pray for 'em, and give 'em hell for their souls' sakes."

"Exactly!" Dr. Bowman said, and he slapped his knees. "Exactly! Excuse me, Tom, I've just thought of some changes I want to make in my Easter sermon." He started for his study. As he reached the door, he turned back and added, "We have just begun to fight."

"Amen," Tom replied as his father disappeared into the study.

At about this same moment, Frank Buell was going for his mail. He had been several weeks now in the State Institution for Delinquent Boys. On Saturdays there were no classes, and the morning was left free of planned activities.

Frank had an additional motive for going to the post office. He was less likely to run into Sid Pruitt there. Whenever there was free time, Sid had a way of coming to the little cottage that

Frank shared with a number of other boys. Sid had developed into a confirmed Frank-admirer.

The ex-president of the Stalwarts was constantly in Frank's thoughts. The occasional moods Sid had in Blanton, when he vowed to go straight, seemed to be less common now. At the State Institution, he lived more and more in a dreamland of anticipation. The ingredients of his imaginary world came mostly from movies, TV programs, and cheap novels. He was convinced that he was done with small-time stuff. When he and Frank got out, they'd both muscle into the big-time, into one of the really good rackets. As he spun his plans, they became more and more grandiose. He and Frank were destined to be the masterminds of organized crime first in Blanton and eventually in all the great cities of the nation.

Delusions of grandeur, obviously, delusions that might not lead Sid very far toward being the czar of crime, but would very surely get him back in jail again. Sometimes Frank tried to put it on the line with Sid. He tried to make him see that going straight was the only way to avoid wrecking his life, but usually Sid seemed literally not to hear Frank's words, or else he took them as an uproarious form of humor and responded by slapping Frank noisily on the back and laughing so loudly that any persons near by would begin staring.

Frank wished he knew what he could do to help Sid. It wasn't that Sid was absolutely doomed and fated to become a lifelong criminal but simply that the odds leaned strongly in that direction. If only there were some way of slowing down his course and changing it. About all Frank could do was be Sid's friend, be available, listen endlessly, and put in a word edgewise when he could—not that it helped much.

When Frank reached the little office where mail was distributed, he received a small package and two letters, all postmarked Blanton. Mail always gave him a desire for privacy.

He decided to go back to the cottage and gamble on Sid's not being there.

His luck held. Sid wasn't there. Neither were the two boys who shared the room with Frank. He could take his time. Boxes are likely to be less interesting than letters, so he opened the box first. Carefully packed in tissue paper was a small crucifix on a chain. He held it in his hand. The silver chain with the crucifix at the end looked theatrical to him. He laid it down on his bed and wondered who had sent it. Probably some organization, like the outfit that supplied free Bibles for the boys in the Institution.

Next he opened one of the letters—he recognized his father's writing on the envelope. It was a long letter, but the main point was that his father and Sarah would be driving up on Easter to see him. They would arrive in the early afternoon and stay till five o'clock. "One of your friends may come up with us," the letter added. Frank frowned as he read this. What friend? The letter seemed to assume he would know.

He opened the remaining letter. The very regular, careful writing was not familiar to him. "Dear Frank," it began:

Father has given me permission to come up and see you. I hope this is all right with you. Your father and mother say I can come with them in their car.

Sincerely,
ROSA

P.S. I hope you like the little gift I sent you.

Frank looked at the crucifix again. He picked it up and hung it on the arm of a chair. It dangled there, suspended between the ceiling and the floor.

Rosa was coming to see him. Here, of all places. Her visit was nothing he had deserved. The one time they had really been together it was God's mercy he hadn't killed her. Rosa was under no obligation to see him. The favor he would never have dared ask for was being given him without asking.

He sat down in the chair, holding the letter from Rosa. At his side the silver figure on the cross dangled between heaven and earth. He took the crucifix in his hands and looked long at it. In his thoughts he could not altogether separate Rosa from the silver figure at the end of the chain. He must ask her more about it, and about so many things.